THE CAMELOT CONSPIRACY

ALSO BY E. DUKE VINCENT

Mafia Summer
Black Widow
The Strip

THE CAMELOT CONSPIRACY

THE KENNEDYS, CASTRO AND THE CIA

A NOVEL

E. DUKE VINCENT

Overlook/Derby
New York, New York

THE CAMELOT CONSPIRACY

This edition first published in The United States of America in 2011 by
Derby Publishing
in association with The Overlook Press
141 Wooster Street
New York, NY 10012
www.overlookpress.com

for special and bulk sales contact sales@overlookny.com

Copyright © 2011 E. Duke Vincent

Library of Congress Cataloging-in-Publication Data
Vincent, E. Duke.
The Camelot conspiracy : the Kennedys, Castro and the CIA : a novel / E. Duke Vincent. -- 1st ed.
p. cm.
ISBN 978-1-59020-639-3
1. Kennedy, John F. (John Fitzgerald), 1917-1963--Assassination--Fiction. 2. United States. Central
Intelligence Agency--Fiction. 3. Organized crime--Fiction. 4. United States--Foreign relations--Cuba--Fiction.
I. Title.
PS3622.I527C36 2011
813'.6--dc22   201100742

Printed in the United States of America
FIRST EDITION

1 3 5 7 9 8 6 4 2

As before and for the fourth time: for *The Boyus*

A small body of determined spirits fired by unquenchable faith in their mission can alter the course of history.

MOHANDAS GANDHI

The only new thing in this world is the history you don't know.

HARRY TRUMAN

AUTHOR'S NOTE

IN 1981 G. ROBERT BLAKEY, chief counsel and staff director to the House Select Committee on Assassinations, published *The Plot to Kill the President*. In his book, he argues that there was a conspiracy to kill John F. Kennedy.

He agrees that Lee Harvey Oswald was involved but also believes that there was at least one gunman firing from the Grassy Knoll. Blakey came to the conclusion that Carlos Marcello, along with Sam Giancana and Santo Trafficante, Jr., were complicit in planning the assassination. He fails to identify the identity of the gunman on the knoll, but after reading numerous books as well as the confessions of two of the assassins I believe I have.

This novel is a work of fiction and the characters I've created bear no resemblance to anyone living or dead. However, the historical characters I've introduced accurately reflect their attitudes and actions. The events recounted are also accurate as to time and place with only slight variations to suit the telling of the story.

E. DUKE VINCENT

HISTORICAL CHARACTERS IN THE ORDER THEY APPEAR

Dwight D. Eisenhower, President, USA
Richard M. Nixon, Vice President, USA
Allen Dulles, Director, CIA
Richard Bissell, Deputy Director Plans, CIA
Richard Helms, Bissell's assistant, CIA
Johnny Roselli, Chicago Mob
Sam "Momo" Giancana, capo, Chicago Mob
Robert Maheu, Former FBI; CIA Facilitator
E. Howard Hunt, CIA
Tony "Big Tuna" Accardo, capo, Chicago Mob
Marita Lorenz, Castro lover and failed assassin
Santo Trafficante, capo, Tampa Mob
Rolando Masferrer, anti-Castro resistance leader
Fidel Castro, Cuban Premier
Raúl Castro, Cuban hierarchy
Che Guevara, Cuban hierarchy
Camilo Cienfuegos, Cuban hierarchy
Huber Matos, Cuban hierarchy
Phyllis McGuire, singer and Giancana girlfriend
Dan Rowan, comedian
J. Edgar Hoover, Director, FBI
William King Harvey, CIA
Rolando Cubela, Cuban hierarchy
Anastas Mikoyan, Vice P.M. Soviet Union
James Jesus Angleton, CIA
Kim Philby, CIA mole
Manuel Artime, anti-Castro resistance leader
John F. Kennedy, President
Bobby Kennedy, Attorney General
Dean Rusk, Secretary of State
Chester Bowles, Undersecretary of State
McGeorge Bundy, National Security Advisor
Arthur Schlesinger, assistant Latin American affairs
Dr. Miró Cardona, anti-Castro resistance leader
Harry Cohn, President, Columbia Studios
Frank Capra, multiple Academy Award director
Floyd Patterson, heavyweight champion
Ingemar Johansson, heavyweight champion
Anastasio Somoza, Nicaragua dictator
General Paul Adams, Strike Force Command
Jean Daniel, French journalist
Yuri Gagarin, Soviet cosmonaut
Jesus Carreras, Castro defector

Captain Mario Zuniga, anti-Castro pilot
General C.P. Cabell, Deputy Director, CIA
Nikita Khrushchev, Premier, USSR
Jimmy Hoffa, President, Teamsters
Carlos Marcello, capo, New Orleans Mob
John McCone, Director, CIA
Brig. Gen. Edward Lansdale, DOD, CIA
Joseph Kennedy, father of JFK
Frank Sinatra, star
James Donovan, New York lawyer
Maxwell Taylor, Chairman, Joint Chiefs
George Ball, Undersecretary of State
Anatoly Dobrynin, Soviet Ambassador
David Sanchez Morales, CIA
Jackie Kennedy, First Lady
Erneido Oliva, Bay of Pigs hero
Guy Bannister, former FBI and P.I.
David Ferrie, P.I. & Marcello's pilot
Lee Harvey Oswald, accused assassin
George de Mohrenschildt, Russian ex-pat
Lisa Howard, ABC journalist
Ted Shackley, CIA
Edwin Walker, retired general
"Harry" Ruiz-Williams, exiled hero
Juan Almeida, Leader, Cuban Army
Jack Ruby, Marcello soldier, club owner
Carlos Bringuier, anti-Castro leader
John Quigley, FBI
Dutz' Murret, Carlos Marcello bookie
James A. Brussel, NYC profiler
George Metesky, NYC bomber
William Morgan, Castro defector
Juan Orta, Castro private secretary
Pierre Salinger, JFK press secretary
Ngo Dinh Diem, President, Vietnam
Jim O'Connell, CIA
Michel Victor Mertz, hit man
Charles "Typewriter" Nicoletti, hit man
Charlie Holt, hit man

FICTIONAL CHARACTERS IN THE ORDER THEY APPEAR

Dante Amato, Chicago Mob
Monique and Kelly, aspiring actresses
Paul, maître d', Brown Derby
Marissa del Valle, Cuban exile

Elvira Amato, Dante's niece
Pat Amato, Dante's sister-in-law
Aldo Amato, Dante's brother, CIA
Dan Cantrell, CIA
Rafael Sanchez, CIA
Martine Adega, Masferrer bodyguard
Pepe Arroyo, Masferrer bodyguard
Luis Quevado, Masferrer follower
Miguel Olivera, Masferrer follower
Man in jump suit, Masferrer traitor
Lenny Mills, FBI
Leonora Harrison, D.C. socialite
Larry DiGiorno, Amato cousin
Adelaida, Marissa del Valle maid
Diego Lopez y Cubela, Dante pseudonym
Maria Lopez y Cubela, Marissa pseudonym
Hernando Flores, executed sugar baron
Tomaso Rodriguez, Flores major domo
Captain and mate, commandeered boat
Abril Soto, Masferrer mistress
Yolanda Tomaso, Masferrer niece
Elowese Margolin, aspiring actress
Captain Velasquez, Isle of Pines, warden
Dr. Zabaleta, Isle of Pines, prisoner
Jason Manly, Washington FBI SAC
Dwight Davies, Washington FBI SAC
Lorenzo Amato, Dante nephew
Tyler Dann, make-up man
Fred Naspo, actor
Aunt Philomena, Naspo disguise
Tawny, Carousel stripper
The Farley Harringtons, Aldo in-laws
Anthony, Harringtons' butler
Blossom, Marcello call girl
Paco, La Cabaña guard
Captain Delgado, La Cabaña warden
Ynilo Ramos, Lalo brother
Lalo Ramos, Trafficante spy
Bartolo Melendez, Trafficante spy
Carmen Orenstein, Trafficante spy
Lola, waitress
Laline, waitress, Cruz girlfriend
Uncle Emilio, gunsmith
Bearded sergeant, Cuban Army
Teofilo Cruz, CIA and Trafficante spy
Batman & Robin, undercover FBI
Dee Thullin, Vegas call girl
Eni Quintero, Key Largo marina owner

THE CAMELOT CONSPIRACY

CHAPTER 1

SHRILL, HIGH-PITCHED BELLS jolted me awake, and I pinched the bridge of my nose. My watch read eight o'clock. I'd been in bed an hour, asleep only half that time.

On the telephone's third ring, two young starlets nuzzled on either side of me stirred. We'd met at a William Morris cocktail party at five that afternoon—left at six—and were in bed by seven.

I reached over Monique, and she let out a low groan. She was a dark-haired ballet student under contract to MGM. They were touting her as the next Cyd Charisse.

Kelly was Monique's polar opposite—a buxom blonde with a four-star body, heart-shaped face, and pouting lips. Columbia was touting her as the next Kim Novak.

Everybody in Hollywood was somebody else.

I picked up. "Yeah…"

"I just got back. Meet me at the Derby in half an hour."

I recognized the voice, cleared my throat and murmured, "What's wrong?"

"When you get there."

The phone went dead. *Not on the phone.* He'd been in Vegas for a happy mixture of business and pleasure, and was expected to stay through weekend. It would have taken something significant to tear him away.

I levered myself over Kelly, caught a whiff of Chanel, and got out of bed.

Kelly sat up. Her pouting lips, poutier, "Dante? Where are you going?"

Monique rose up on an elbow, watched me pick up a pack of Marlboros, shake one out, and snap open a gold lighter.

"Are you coming back?" Her voice sounded sleepy—disappointed.

"Not sure." I lit the cigarette and glanced at Monique's perfectly formed tits. They looked like the baby sisters of Kelly's voluptuous rack.

I smiled. I was looking at the reason *variety is the spice of life* was a cliché.

Heading for the bathroom I said, "If I'm not back in an hour, head back to the party. Call a couple of cabs. There'll be cash on the foyer table."

The girls looked at each other, shrugged, and resettled under the covers. I got under a steaming shower, lathered my face, and shaved in a mirror opposite the spout. Spinning off the hot faucet, I steeled myself against a final deluge of cold water, and dried off. I chose a three-piece navy blue suit and pale blue shirt. Before putting on the jacket I removed a snub-nosed .38 from its shoulder holster, spun-checked the loaded cylinder, and strapped it on. A snap-brim fedora completed the outfit, and I checked the full-length mirror. The .38 wasn't causing a bulge in the jacket. It never did, but old habits die hard.

After leaving a pair of hundreds on the foyer table, I got into my tail-finned Cadillac and drove north on Roxbury. Turning east on Sunset, I passed the Beverly Hills Hotel and headed for Hollywood.

CHAPTER 2

THREE THOUSAND MILES away, Dwight D. Eisenhower snap shut a leather folder and slammed it on his desk. The scarlet TOP SECRET letters glared back at him, and he punched the intercom. "Send them in."

Seconds later the door to the Oval Office swung open, and four men entered. Vice President Richard Nixon, Allen Dulles, Director of the CIA, Richard Bissell, Deputy Director of Plans, and his assistant, Richard Helms. All were immaculately dressed in dark business suits for the hastily called, 11:00 p.m. meeting, and nodded deferentially.

Nixon was the first to speak. "Good evening, Mr. President."

Eisenhower rose and angrily waved them to opposing couches that flanked the fireplace. Dropping into an armchair at the mouth of the seating arrangement, he tapped the folder against his thigh.

"I've just finished reading this monument to under-achievement."

Nixon glanced at Dulles. Dulles, brother of former Secretary of State John Foster Dulles, took the cue. He leaned forward and winced slightly as he shifted his slipper-clad feet into a more comfortable position. Both brothers suffered terribly from gout, and Allen been given permission to wear the soft footwear whenever he had an attack—even to the White House.

"It's a good deal more difficult than we anticipated, Mr. President."

Dulles ticked off the points on his fingers. "We've instituted anti-revolutionary propaganda campaigns, terminated sugar purchases, ended oil deliveries, and continued the arms embargo. But the regime remains as strong as ever. The Soviet support is massive."

"Godammit, Allen, I won't have a communist state ninety miles off the coast of Florida!"

"I understand, Mr. President, which is why I asked for this meeting." He turned to Bissell. "Richard..."

Bissell's tone was firm. "I believe we have to take more direct action if we're to bring down Castro, Mr. President."

"How direct?"

"The use of U. S. military personnel to train and lead the Cuban paramilitary invasion you approved last March."

"Impossible!" Eisenhower threw up a hand in frustration. "If Khrushchev found out he'd never stand still for it. He'll invade and occupy West Berlin—or worse. It could trigger a war!"

"Not if we could still make him believe we had had nothing to do with it," soothed Dulles. "The cover story would remain the same. That the invasion came from a paramilitary force of Cuban exiles in Miami and was financed by a group of international industrialists who want to recover the property confiscated by Castro."

"Mr. Bissell, may I remind you that I once led an invasion. I know the kind of preparation and training required. The Cubans have neither."

"Yes sir, which is why they need our people. The training's not going well. The reports from the clandestine camps state there's been no lack of motivation and recruits—these Cubans hate Castro and love Cuba. They're prepared to die trying to get it back—but they're raw. We believe that they desperately need our professionals if they're to succeed."

"How the hell do you propose to keep our involvement under cover?"

Dulles again leaned forward. "Difficult but not impossible, Mr. President. The camps are in remote areas of the Everglades and in the southern Louisiana Delta with additional bases in Guatemala. It will remain a tightly held CIA operation on a strict need-to-know basis. It's doable. And doing nothing, as you've said, is unthinkable."

Eisenhower leaned back in his chair and stroked his chin. Overthrowing Castro was mandatory. That was all there was to it. Even if it meant doing it by a force trained by members of the U.S. military.

"I'll go along with the training. But I want no U.S. personnel on the ground during the invasion."

"Very well, sir."

There was one more problem and Eisenhower stated it.

"And Allen…you must guarantee that if I give you the go-ahead to use some of our people, this government will have plausible deniability in the eyes of the world."

Dulles nodded. "There are seldom guarantees in this arena, Mr. President, but in this case the Cuban exiles have made it quite clear in the press that they want to invade and re-take their homeland. It should not come as a shock to the rest of the world if we maintain they did so without our help."

Eisenhower let his eyes wander over the four men and again thoughtfully stroked his chin. A few moments later he reluctantly gave them a single nod. "Very well, gentlemen, proceed. Carefully proceed."

The president got up and men rose. The meeting had lasted thirty-five minutes.

As they walked away from the Oval Office, Bissell leaned toward Dulles and whispered. "Are you certain it's wise not to tell him the entire plan?"

"You heard what he said. 'Plausible deniability.' There is nothing more plausibly deniable than something you know nothing about."

CHAPTER 3

LOS ANGELES

THE DRIVE FROM MY house took ten minutes. I parked in a space near Hollywood and Vine at 8:45 and walked a half block south on Vine to the Brown Derby—legendary eatery of stars, politicians, sports figures, a hangout of poseurs, and home of the famous Cobb salad.

Valet parkers and several photographers were out front, so I pulled the fedora lower on my forehead. The press loved to blow my cover and tonight I wanted to go unnoticed. Eight months ago the *Los Angeles Times* had run a filched photo of me by the pool at the Desert Inn. I was with George Raft and Marlene Dietrich. We were mugging and striking body-builder poses. The snide caption read: *Dante Amato and friends showing off their frames. It's obvious the darkly handsome, six-three, two-hundred-pound alleged Chicago mobster could easily be one of the stars' fellow thesps.* They got it wrong. I was only six-one. I looked taller because George and Marlene were short. Most stars are. I've never figured out why.

I waited until a limousine arrived and drew the photographer's attention, then slipped by. Raucous voices, laughter, jazz, and cigarette smoke greeted me. Paul, the maître d', was chatting at a booth with the manager of L.A. Dodgers, Walter Alston, and Don Drysdale, their star pitcher. Paul spotted me and walked over.

"Good evening, Mr. Amato. He called but hasn't arrived as yet. I have his table ready."

"Thanks Paul."

"The usual?"

"Please."

Paul snapped his fingers at a waiter and led me past the Derby's leather booths toward the lone unoccupied one at the far end of the room. Along the way we passed walls covered with caricatures of Hollywood's royalty and, seated under them, a dazzling array of their living counterparts.

As soon as I settled, a Jack Daniels over ice arrived, and I sipped while watching waiters going in and out of the kitchen's swinging doors. I figured the man I was meeting would also want to arrive unnoticed, and a few minutes later he proved me right .

His name was John "Handsome Johnny" Roselli, my boss and the man who ruled Los Angeles and Las Vegas for Sam "Momo" Giancana, capo of the Chicago Mob. He was impeccably dressed and well-preserved in his fifty-fifth year—piercing eyes, graying hair, and a sharply sculpted face set off by a prominent nose. It gave him a uniquely distinguished look, but it was his aura of power that cowered influential men and attracted countless women.

He sat saying, "Sounded like I woke you up."

I nodded. "Matter of fact you did."

"Need I ask what you were doing in bed so early?"

"You need not."

He smiled knowingly, a waiter appeared, and Johnny pointed to my drink. "The same." The waiter nodded and disappeared.

"What's so 'not on the phone' that it tore you away from The Strip?"

"I finally got through to Momo."

"About what?"

"A guy who looked me up this afternoon…Bob Maheu."

"The Hughes guy?"

"Him."

I couldn't see even a remote connection between Robert Maheu, who began working for Howard Hughes in 1955, and Roselli. "What'd he want?"

"Said he's representin' a group of international businessmen. Anti-Castro Cuban exiles who lost millions when Castro took over."

"So? They weren't alone, but why'd he want to talk to you about it."

"They want it back."

"Cuba?"

"He nodded. "And they're prepared to finance a paramilitary invasion to get the job done."

"What the hell's that got to do with us?"

"Other than the fact—as you just pointed out—that we *also* lost millions when Castro took over our casinos?"

"Point taken."

"These guys've been screamin' that they wanted to invade Cuba since the revolution. Maheu says it's finally gonna happen. But before it does, the people he represents want us to take care of a little matter they feel we got experience with."

"What for christsakes?"

"They want us to whack Castro."

I was aghast. I stared at Roselli with widening eyes. "A hit?"

He nodded. "What he says they want. But they obviously wanna keep that part of their plan a secret."

"Christ! What'd you tell him?"

"I'd think about it…then called Momo."

"What'd he say?"

"That the guy's ex-FBI. So Momo wants to be sure he's not settin' us up for some kind of sting. Like nailin' us with a conspiracy rap. He said play along, but he wants Maheu checked out."

"How?"

"Your brother."

I was stunned. "Our relationship is pretty strained, Johnny. You know that. I only talk to him when…"

Roselli held up his hand and interrupted. "I know it and it's wrong. You should talk. He's your blood."

"What the hell would CIA know about an ex-FBI guy?"

"The word is he's done work for them."

I again started to object. "Johnny…"

Roselli again interrupted—this time, more forcefully. "Look… Momo wants this done. We play along with Maheu, but we check him out. We can't figure any other way than your brother. Those guys have ears everywhere. Call him. Make nice. See if he knows Maheu and if he's heard anythin' about an invasion—don't say anything about the hit."

"Johnny—my brother thinks I'm the anti-Christ. I haven't talked to him since our father's funeral six months ago. He'll want to know why I need the information. What I intend to do with it. Will it be used for anything illegal."

"No problem. Maheu said for the invasion to succeed there has to be uprisin' of anti-Castro Cubans in Cuba when the landings go down. Tell 'im Maheu's people want us to use our contacts in Havana to begin stirrin' up a counter-revolution."

"Christ, Johnny …"

"Do it, Dante. Momo's orders."

I sighed and gave up. "Okay, Johnny, I'll see what I can do. What's the time frame?"

"That's what we gotta find out. Maheu said if we wanted to go forward, I should show up here tonight and be contacted with details."

Ten minutes later the waiter re-appeared with menus. The one he gave to Roselli contained a letter-sized envelope. Roselli opened it. There was no message or signature. It contained four simple items: name, time, place, and password.

CHAPTER 4

A RED NEON SIGN flashed *Saharan Motel*, a one star venue on Sunset Boulevard two blocks west of La Brea that catered to low-budget tourists, worn-out salesmen, and hot-bed hookers. Roselli's message said our contact was M. del Valle in Room 108. I pulled into the courtyard, parked, and rang the bell.

She answered the door bare-faced, wearing a conservative suit, flat-heeled shoes, and her raven hair in a ponytail. I noticed she was about five-nine and slender—ivory skin and violet eyes.

Roselli, shocked that our contact was not only a woman, but an exceptionally beautiful one, removed his hat first.

I said, "Saludos deste Vegas."

She accepted the password, stepped back, and we entered. Closing the door, she extended her hand.

"Marissa del Valle."

We'd later learned she was the twenty-six-year-old daughter of an aristocratic Cuban family who had once owned vast sugar and tobacco plantations in pre-Castro Cuba, and had graduated from Bryn Mawr.

Roselli took her hand. "Johnny Roselli...and this is Dante Amato."

She smiled. "A pleasure to meet you, gentlemen. Your Spanish is excellent, Mr. Amato."

I thought her accent sounded Latin, but not quite. It was more subtle. I shook her hand and tried not to stare.

"Thank you. Sicilian father—Mexican mother. Growing up, they insisted we speak both."

The room was low-rent basic. A narrow table flanked by two simple chairs, a 15" black-and-white TV with rabbit ears, and a bedside table with a rotary phone. The carpet was threadbare, and the curtains hadn't been cleaned since they were hung.

She waved us toward the chairs and sat on the bed. "I take it by your presence that you wish to go forward."

Roselli nodded. "Maybe. How much do you know about this?"

"Only that the gentlemen who sent me seem to need your expertise. I'm merely a messenger. Trusted because of my family."

"Okay—But we need to know more about the set-up. Who's involved? How many? Where are they? The time frame."

"I can only tell you that these gentlemen are all anti-Castro Cubans who come from the highest echelons of politics, industry, and commerce. My father was one of them. He grew, harvested, and exported both sugar and tobacco before the revolution. Our family was one of the oldest in Cuba."

Roselli cocked an eyebrow. "Was?"

She nodded. "They were executed for 'war crimes.'"

He shook his head. "I'm sorry."

"Thank you. The men we're talking about love Cuba and are dedicated and determined to take it back…cost is not an issue. They're waiting to meet you in Miami."

Roselli studied her for a few moments, then looked at me. "Any comments?"

I wasn't sure if my answer was either logical or practical, but since Momo wanted this thing checked out, and I saw no reason to simply let this extraordinary woman walk out of my life and vanish, I shrugged. "Nothing to lose by listening."

Roselli nodded and turned back to Marissa. "Miami, huh? When?"

"Within the week." She got up and extended her hand. "Mr. Maheu will call you with a time and place."

Roselli and I got up, shook her hand, said our goodbyes and left. When we got into my Cadillac, Roselli chuckled. As I thought, he'd noticed what was under Marissa's camouflage.

"She damn sure went a long way to cover up one helluva package."

I nodded. "And I think the package knows a helluva lot more than it let on."

CHAPTER 5

BEVERLY HILLS

THE FOLLOWING MORNING I got up at five and drove to a phone booth. Roselli and I constantly swept our phones but knew we couldn't be too cautious. I lit a Marlboro and dialed my brother's home in Chevy Chase. It was eight in Washington and I wanted to catch him before he left for his office at Langley.

My six-year-old niece, eager to prove she was growing up, answered on the first ring in a happy, musical voice.

"Amato residence—Elvira speaking…"

"Good morning, Elvira… It's Uncle Dante."

"Uncle Dante!" Her voice went from happy to thrilled. "Mommy! It's Uncle Dante!"

Several seconds later, Aldo's wife got on.

"Well…to what do we owe the pleasure?" Pat's voice was cold with sarcasm. Unlike their two kids, Pat shared her husband's aversion to me.

"Hi Pat. How are you?" There was no answer. "Okay, then. Is Aldo there? I'd like to…"

"Al! It's your brother!"

I heard the phone drop. Several seconds passed before Aldo got on. "What is it Dante? I'm on my way to work." As anticipated—curt and annoyed.

"I'll make it quick, Al. Help me with what I'm about to ask, and it might do you some good down the line."

"What the hell are you talking about?"

"Keeping you in the loop if what I've heard is true."

"I repeat—what the hell are you talking about?"

"We've been contacted by…"

Aldo interrupted. "Wait a minute! Who's we?"

"You know damn well who 'we' are. Me, and the guys you love to hate."

There were several seconds of silence before Aldo responded. "Where are you?"

"In a phone booth."

Another pause, then, "Okay, I'm listening. What's this about?"

"Cuba."

"Cuba!"

"You heard me. My boss was told about a plot. A bunch of international businessmen—mainly Cuban exiles—planning to back an invasion of the island to get rid of Castro."

"Those rumors have been coming out of Miami since the revolution. They're ridiculous."

"Are they?"

"Of course! An invasion from where?"

"I don't know. But the guys behind it want our help."

"Your help? How?"

"We've still got contacts there—people who worked our hotels and casinos. We're supposed to get to them and have them agitate an uprising when the invasion comes."

"Again—it's ridiculous. Who'd you get this from?"

"Glad you asked. Bob Maheu. He got in touch with my boss in Vegas."

There was a pause before Aldo spoke again—this time quieter and more tentatively. "Maheu…? Ex-FBI. He works for Hughes."

"Any idea of his rep?"

"As far as I know he was well thought of at the Bureau."

"The word is he's done covert work for you guys."

"You know I can't confirm or deny that."

"Good enough, Al."

"Why the interest in Maheu?"

"If his story's bullshit he could be setting us up for a sting."

"Once more, ridiculous. What's his motive?"

"That's what I'm trying to find out."

"I don't see one…I also don't get his interest in Cuba?"

"Says he's representing the businessmen."

There was another pause from Aldo. My brother knew Maheu was a serious player. I figured he was trying to scope out why he'd be spreading rumors.

He murmured, "It doesn't make sense."

"We agree. That's our problem. We need to know if an invasion could actually be in the works. If it is, we'll help make it happen. We hate that bearded bastard as much as you guys. But if your outfit isn't in on it, it could be a disaster for all of us."

"When's this suppose to be happening?"

"We're about to find out. A meeting in Miami in the next few days."

"Who else knows about this?"

"On my end—five people. Three of my guys, Maheu, and a female contact we met last night."

"Okay. I'll see what I can find out. But I'm warning you, Dante. Keep your mouth shut about this from now on. You're not shaking down studios, scamming unions, and skimming casinos, pal. If this is even remotely true, it's a matter of national security. There are laws that can put you in irons for the rest of your life."

"You may not think so, Al, but my guys are as patriotic as yours. We want Castro to go down as much as you—maybe more, and it's about more than casinos. In the end we have the same goals and use the same techniques. We just get results more often. Maybe because we've got a better trained staff… "

Aldo ignored the shot, said, "Call me tomorrow," and hung up without saying goodbye.

I put down the phone and knew my brother was right. If we were caught meddling in matters of national security, we'd be in deep shit. The kind that even our high-priced, hot-shot lawyers and paid-off judges couldn't dig us out of.

And if we actually did whack Castro, it didn't matter who caught us. Either side would hang us out to dry.

CHAPTER 6

ALDO SPENT THE BETTER part of the morning going over the latest reports coming in from Vietnam. Assigned to Southeast Asia desk in the Directorate of Intelligence, he was preparing the President's morning briefing paper. The north was continuing to infiltrate cadres and weapons into the south via the Ho Chi Minh Trail. Ngo Diem had barely survived a coup attempt, and Hanoi was forming the National Liberation Front. They were dubbing them "Vietcong."

He closed the folder, sighed, and thought about his brother the mobster. Dante was eighteen when Pearl Harbor was attacked, and he enlisted in the Marines the next day. He was part of every island assault in the brutal sweep across the Pacific, and came home with a chest full of medals. He'd gotten Dante into his alma mater, Northwestern, and the plan had always been that Dante would join him in the CIA. He was an outstanding student, but in his third year he ran into an associate of Tony Accardo's he'd met in the Marines. The Chicago hood gave him a dazzling eye-opener.

In 1947 when college graduates were lucky to make two thousand a year, this guy, who hadn't made it through high school, was making fifty. Dante dropped out and never looked back.

Aldo made a lunch date with Dan Cantrell from the Latin American desk, in order to sound him out about Dante's inquiry. They were old friends, and Cantrell had even endorsed Dante's CIA application while he was still at Northwestern. When the Agency found out Dante joined Accardo after being recommended by Aldo and Cantrell, it had briefly threatened their careers.

Aldo said he didn't want to meet in the Agency's cafeteria and selected DiGiorno's, his favorite Italian bistro in Georgetown. The owner was a distant cousin who'd become close to Aldo, and knew he worked at Langley. It was crowded, and several comely ladies greeted Cantrell as they made their way to a table against the rear wall. Divorced and a fairly handsome fifty-three, Cantrell was always impeccably dressed and groomed. They sat, ordered Martinis and lit cigarettes. Cantrell, who thought Aldo's behavior strange, couldn't wait to satisfy his curiosity.

"What's with the mystery, Al?"

"I heard a rumor about something going on in your area and I'd like to know if you've heard it."

"Oh? Where?"

"Cuba."

"Really. What'd you hear?"

There was a considerable noise level in the tightly packed room, and Aldo leaned forward to keep his voice down.

"That there's a clandestine plan by powerful Cuban exiles in Miami to back a paramilitary invasion of the island."

Cantrell chuckled and waved dismissively. "Al… Those Cubans have been screaming about re-taking their island from the minute they arrived in Miami."

"I'm aware of that. But has there been any new background noise lately?"

The waitress arrived carrying a tray of Martinis, removed two, and placed them on the table. Cantrell took a sip before answering.

"There's always something new in that hotbed. For instance—in the last two weeks, the Miami Cubans consolidated five different militant groups. They're calling the new organization the Democratic Revolutionary Front—the FRF.

"You don't think it could be an omen?"

"No. E. Howard Hunt, our case officer, says most of these groups spend more time fighting each other than plotting to overthrow Castro."

"And seriously, not to insult, but it's not possible that something could be going on that you don't know about?"

"Anything's possible, Al, but there's no way these guys can mount an even marginally tangible invasion without our help and, as far as I know, we're not feeling generous. Where'd you hear this stuff?"

"It came through Maheu."

Cantrell looked surprised. It was his turn to lean forward.

"*Bob* Maheu?"

Aldo nodded. "You know him?"

"Yeah… He's done contract work for us in the past. Why the hell would he feed you a rumor?"

"He didn't. I got it second-hand."

"From who?"

"The people who got it from Maheu."

"Come on, Al. I answered your questions—now it's your turn. Who?"

"It goes no further than here."

"Sure—why not? The whole things bullshit anyway."

"My brother."

Cantrell sat back and his eyes narrowed. "Maheu contacted your brother?"

"No. An associate of his in Vegas. Then Dante called me."

"I thought you two didn't talk."

"We don't…at least not usually. I hate what he's into."

That was true. But Aldo also remembered the boy he grew up with, and the war hero he became. He'd try to help Dante as long as it didn't break laws or compromise his principles. He believed he was righteous as his kid brother was corrupt.

"What'd Maheu want from Dante's people?"

"Use of their contacts in Havana to help the anti-Castro Cubans."

Cantrell absorbed the information and glanced around. "Bob Maheu contacts the Vegas mob for help in a supposed paramilitary invasion of Cuba financed by a group of international businessmen…"

"That's what my brother told me."

"And what did his associates say to Maheu's proposal?"

Aldo paused. He'd gotten the information he needed and didn't want to say the Mob was considering the offer. "Nothing. They blew him off. But I wanted to see if there was anything to the story. They're worried Maheu might be setting them up for a conspiracy charge."

Cantrell thought a few seconds, then shook his head. "I doubt it. He's worked for us but, as you know, we have nothing to do with organized crime. That's the FBI's bailiwick. Besides, what the hell would be his motive?"

Aldo gave the same answer he'd given Dante. "None that I can think of."

The waitress arrived and they ordered refills and club sandwiches. When she left Cantrell again leaned forward.

"Look, Al…Don't mention this to anyone else, okay? This kind of rumor could ripple though this town until some wise-ass congressman who wants some headlines hears it and demands an investigation. That's the last thing the Administration *or* we want. I'll keep my ears open and let you know if anything changes, and I'd appreciate it if you'd do the same."

Aldo nodded. "Done."

After lunch Aldo returned to his office hoping that Cantrell's take was accurate—more saber rattling by the militant, exiled Cubans. But there was something about the timing, the sequence of events, and the disparate people involved that suggested he could be wrong. He feared they could be looking at the tip of an iceberg.

Cantrell had come to the same conclusions. But it wasn't just fear that was bothering him—he was pissed off. Cuba was on his beat. If there was a clandestine operation in motion that he didn't know about, he damn well wanted to know why. He'd have to tread lightly in the halls of an agency dedicated to secrecy but if something were flying under the radar, he'd dig it out.

CHAPTER 7

MIAMI

FOUR DAYS LATER, ROSELLI and I checked into the Fontainebleau. We took the elevator to a three-bedroom suite on the penthouse floor where Sam Giancana was waiting on the balcony. He'd flown in earlier from Chicago and was in his shirtsleeves with his tie loosened, sweating profusely. He looked over the spectacular beaches and waved toward the south.

"Hell of a view. You can almost see that fuckin' island from here."

Roselli nodded. "With any luck we'll get to see it again—up close."

"How was the trip?" I asked, extending my hand.

Giancana shook it, and Roselli's. "A pain in the ass. We bounced like a goddamn basketball as soon as we hit Florida. Fuckin' thunderstorms. How do people live here with that shit? And the goddamn humidity!"

Roselli shrugged. "It's summer, Momo."

"What am I—a fuckin' moron? I know it's summer. We still set for five?"

Roselli checked his watch. "Yeah. Maheu should be here any minute. He's bringin' one of the principals with him."

"The what?"

I clarified as I took off my jacket and removed my shoulder holster. "One of the financial backers."

Giancana nodded. "Good. You're pretty sure this Maheu guy's square?"

I shrugged. "What can I tell you, Momo? I checked with my brother and he checked with his people at Langley. They don't think he's setting us up." They better be right, I thought, or I'd be facing Momo and concrete boots.

The door chimes rang and I answered.

Bob Maheu entered with a man in his forties. Both wore tailored suits that gave the impression they were executives who were in shape. Maheu had an oval face, a balding head, and egg-shaped eyes. His companion was hawk-faced with tightly curled hair, intense brown eyes, and an aquiline nose. It gave him an imperious look I instinctively disliked.

Maheu introduced him to Roselli—the only man in the room he knew. "Hi, Johnny. This is Mr. Rafael Sanchez."

Roselli shook Sanchez's hand and pointed at me. "This is my associate, Mr. Amato." Indicating Giancana, he said, "And this, for the moment, is Mr. Gold from Chicago."

Giancana nodded. "Want a drink?"

Sanchez shook his head. "No thanks. Too hot."

"I agree. Have a seat."

We sat around an art deco coffee table, and Maheu led off.

"Mr. Sanchez is a senior organizer of men who have extensive holdings in Cuba and want to overthrow Castro by means of an invasion. He currently owns several petroleum leases, as well as a refinery on the island. Castro is about to nationalize the Texaco, Esso, and Shell refineries, and he knows his will undoubtedly be next."

Sanchez lit a cigarette, leaned forward, and used his hands to accentuate his points.

"My colleagues and I are prepared to finance an invasion of Cuba— that is a given. But it is obvious to us that its chances for success would be greatly enhanced if a certain event preceding the invasion took place."

Giancana toyed with him. "What event?"

Sanchez glanced at Maheu. "Castro not being there to witness it."

Giancana wouldn't let him to mince words. "You want him hit."

Sanchez shrugged. "We do. But we feel we lack the ability and connections to anyone who might accomplish this. But, with no criticism intended, we believe you gentlemen are uniquely qualified for the task. And knowing the operation will undoubtedly require a great deal of cash, we are prepared to pay generously for the undertaking."

Giancana got up, paced several steps, and turned back. "It's not that simple. In a normal situation, a close-in hit with a pistol or a shotgun would be the way to go. Here it's a no-go because the chances of gettin' away are zip. Nobody would take the job." He paused and stroked his chin. "A long-range rifle or a car bomb? Maybe. But we'd have to scout the territory, track Castro's moves, and check out the possibilities. What's your time frame?"

"We have a good bit of latitude," answered Sanchez. "The invasion forces are being trained and supplied but they're not ready yet. Also, boats have to be acquired along with planes. It will take months. In the meantime we will be at your disposal."

Giancana walked forward and extended his hand. "Okay…We'll be in touch."

Aware that the meeting had just been ended, the men stood and said their goodbyes. I led them out and closed the door.

Roselli turned to Giancana. "So?"

"It sounds legit, but somethin' about Sanchez's too pat. He didn't ask any questions. Like—who are our people in Havana—do we need help with communications—fake papers—transportation in and out. I'd've felt us out on all that. And he called it an operation. Not a hit, a clip, or a whack—an operation. It's what the Feds call their scams to take us down."

Roselli shrugged. "He could have gotten it from Maheu. He's an ex-Fed."

"Maybe. But I think he's more than he says."

I said, "You still want to go ahead?"

Giancana hesitated a few second and then nodded. "Yeah. I wanna see how it plays."

CHAPTER 8

FONTAINEBLEAU'S BEACH

I WALKED ACROSS THE shimmering sand and squinted against the glare. A brisk breeze whipped whitecaps and the air smelled of salt. I passed hotel guests enjoying the last of the sun and dropped my towel under a vacant beach umbrella. An eight o'clock dinner with Giancana and Roselli was still two hours away, and I wanted to take a relaxing swim. I started a slow jog toward the ocean but suddenly stopped and froze.

Marissa del Valle was stepping out of the surf and coming directly toward me. She pulled off her swim cap, shook her head, and a cascade of black hair tumbled over her shoulders. She was wearing a white bikini that was in stark contrast to her newly tanned skin. The way it set off her lean body and long legs was heart-stopping.

Marissa saw me, slowed to a walk, and paused a few feet away. A delicate smile crossed her lips. "Hello, again, Mr. Amato."

I resisted glancing at her cleavage and extended my hand. "Dante."

She took it. "Marissa…Did you have a fruitful meeting?"

I nodded. "We did…I take it you're here with Sanchez?" The underlying inference was obvious.

She smiled. "Yes. But only in the sense that he asked me to be available for errands as a result of your meeting."

"Were there?"

"None, as yet."

"Ah…" I waved toward the outdoor bar behind the hotel. "Then may I buy you a before-dinner cocktail?"

"Weren't you going for a swim?"

"The ocean won't go away."

She smiled acquiescence, adding a flirtatious nod. Moving to an umbrella a few yards away, she picked up her towel and quickly dried off, putting on a short beach robe. We walked toward the bar. A group of kids building a sand castle was in our path, and I took her arm to steer her around them.

"Staying in the hotel?'

"No. Rafael took a room, but we just came for the afternoon. I have a house in Coral Gables."

"Nice…"

"It is. My family bought it many years ago. Yours is in Los Angeles?"

"Beverly Hills."

She smiled and returned my comment with the same nuance. "Also nice…"

We took stools at the bar, and a bartender wearing a cutaway jacket and bowtie took our order. A Jack Daniels for me—a Mojito for her. She plucked an olive from a tray of condiments and used her teeth to slide it off the toothpick and into her mouth. I found it incredibly sensual.

"Rafael tells me you were a Marine. A war hero in the Pacific."

I laughed. "I was trying to stay alive."

"And that your brother wanted you to join him in the CIA."

I nodded. "He got me into Northwestern after the war so I could get a degree while he greased the rails to get me into the Agency."

"But you dropped out."

"I did."

"To join Mr. Tony Accardo."

"You're well informed."

"Rafael is. But in light of your present occupation I found your background interesting."

Our drinks arrived—we touched glasses and sipped. I was glad she wanted to know more about me so I filled in the blanks.

"In '47 I was looking forward to graduation and two thousand a year. I met a guy who worked for Accardo. He hadn't made it through high school, and he was making two thousand a month." I shrugged. "That afternoon I dropped out and joined 'The Outfit.'"

"And now I'm told you are Mr. Roselli's 'right arm.'"

I nodded again. "Are you aware of what Sanchez asked us to do?"

"Yes."

I was taken aback by her emotionless answer delivered with a cold stare. "And you're okay with it?"

"I am…" She sipped her drink without taking her eyes off me, and said, "I was celebrating New Year's Eve with friends in Madrid when Castro's leading elements marched into Havana. My parents phoned and forbade me to return until the situation stabilized. I obeyed, and two weeks later I was informed that they'd vanished.

"I'm sorry…"

She thanked me with a perfunctory nod. "I returned to Miami and joined the thousands of Cuban refugees who'd fled after the revolution to fight Castro. End—and beginning—of story."

"Then I assume you know why Sanchez choose to contact *us*…"

"I do."

"And you're also okay with that?"

"The assignment? Of course. I'd do it myself if the opportunity arose."

I was again taken aback. "Really… Assassination isn't a typical job for a woman."

She smiled. "It might surprise you to know that six months ago a woman tried it."

Doubt must have registered in my face because she tilted her head and said, "You don't believe me."

"I just find it unlikely."

"I met the girl who attempted it. Her name is Marita Lorenz. Her father is the captain of a German ocean liner. When they docked in Havana last year, Castro came aboard, and they had a short affair. She returned to New York City with her father, and six months ago she was recruited by us to return to Havana, resume their affair, and poison him. She agreed, but at the last minute couldn't do it. She realized she loved him."

"What happened to her?"

"As far as we know she's back in New York."

"She could have put us out of a job. In which case, I wouldn't have met you."

Marissa dipped her head in a petite bow and she smiled. "Thank you. Compliment accepted. Will you be staying long in Miami?"

"We're due to leave tonight," I lied. "But it depends."

"On what?"

"On whether you'll have dinner with me."

After a pause she said, "You're a charming man, Dante. And although I've been around charming men all my life, you don't seem to fit the mold. But I think mixing dinner with our business arrangement would be unwise."

"Is that a no?"

Another pause. "Did you tell Raphael you'd help us?"

"Yes." It was only a partial lie. But I felt sure we'd take the job and saw no sense in waffling.

She gave me an enigmatic smile. "In that case I'm sure joining you for dinner would be unwise.

I realized I'd blown it. I felt she wanted to accept the invitation and could only think of one reason she wouldn't. "Sanchez?"

She nodded. "But not for the reason you think. We're not romantically involved. However there's no question that at this point in our relationship he would not approve of an association with you for security reasons. But you should know, while I'm happy for our cause I'm disappointed for myself."

"Sanchez's attitude could change."

A small shrug accompanied her smile. "It could…"

I raised my glass. "To change."

CHAPTER 9

THE FOLLOWING MORNING, Giancana, Roselli, and I took a cab to Miami International and flew across the state to the Gulf Coast. We had a meeting with Santo Trafficante, the most powerful organized crime figure in Florida. He was a partner of the New York and Chicago mob families who built our Havana hotels and casinos.

We met at an Italian restaurant he owned in Tampa's Ybor City district—the headquarters for his illegal bolita lottery. It hadn't opened for lunch yet, and we were let in by a young janitor who was expecting us. He'd turned on a Wurlitzer jukebox whose kaleidoscopic neon was lit up and booming Bill Haley's "Rock Around the Clock." Chairs remained stacked on all the tables except the one where we sat. The place reeked of cigars and garlic, clearly catered to a low-end clientele, and was obviously chosen because it was an unlikely meeting place for high-level mob figures.

A few minutes later, Trafficante arrived with two bodyguards, left one outside, and walked in. He yelled, "Turn that fuckin' thing off!" to the janitor, and the chastised kid dashed off to pull the plug.

Saying, "I hate that shit," he walked briskly to the table and we all got up. He extended his hand to Giancana. "Hello, Momo—good to see you." He nodded to Roselli and me. "Johnny—Dante, how goes it?"

Roselli answered. "Fine Santo—makin' a living."

"Drinks?"

Giancana said, "Too early."

Roselli and I nodded agreement.

Trafficante was about five-ten, wore horn-rimed glasses, and had a receding hairline that reached the top his head. He was wearing a suit, and when he sat, French cuffs shot out of his sleeve, revealing cuff links that were large, gold, and diamond studded.

We all sat and Trafficante turned to Giancana without preamble. "You said you wanted to talk about Cuba."

Giancana nodded.

"What about it?"

"We met a guy by the name of Rafael Sanchez in Miami. You know him?"

"Yeah. He's a big shot from Havana. An oil guy. Leases and a refinery. Why?"

Giancana was as direct as our host. "He says he and some other big shot exiles wanna finance an invasion of Cuba."

Trafficante's eyes roved to Roselli, me, and back to Giancana. "There's been some quiet talk about the Sanchez people, but as far as I know nothin' definite. You think they're serious?"

Giancana shrugged. "Maybe. But I wanna know what you think?"

He again paused and considered. "It's possible. There's four or five exile groups who want to take back Cuba any way they can. They want their country as much as we want our casinos. Half the time they're fightin' each other, but it's possible they're finally makin' a move. How'd Sanchez come to you?"

"Through a guy named Maheu. A former Fed. He contacted Johnny in Vegas."

Trafficante looked stunned. He knew who Maheu was. "Why? What's he want from you."

"He wants us to whack Castro."

Trafficante again appeared stunned. His eyes narrowed and drifted to each of us once again. "A hit?"

Giancana nodded. "That's what they want."

Trafficante shook his head and smiled. "Unbelievable..."

"You think so?"

"Yeah. It's been tried before. Only ten weeks after the bearded asshole took over there was a try. It failed. Then there was a broad he was fuckin' who got recruited to poison him. Also failed. And there were supposedly a bunch more."

Giancana asked, "Were any of them pros?"

"Probably not. The broad sure as hell wasn't. The daughter of a German liner captain. Also the prick's got a first class intelligence operation and's more protected than the Pope."

Roselli leaned forward. "With all due respect, Santo, anybody can be hit. From Caesar to Lincoln, to Gandhi. All it takes is the target's schedule, lay of the land, and plannin'. We need to get someone we trust in there."

"You want to infiltrate?"

"Me? No. I'm too old for that shit. But Dante here could handle it."

This was a surprise, but I said nothing. Trafficante looked at me.

"You'd try it?"

I shrugged. It was ridiculous. "How? I don't have the slightest idea how to get in there."

Trafficante smiled. "I do."

It figured. He had strong ties to the exiles. He'd want the Havana casinos back as much, if not more, than any of us. We had huge cash flows coming out of Vegas—he didn't. He'd think a combination of the Sanchez people, the CIA and the Chicago mob would have an excellent chance of getting his cash flowing again.

Giancana leaned toward Trafficante. "How'd you get 'im in?"

"Rolando Masferrer. Former senator in Batista's government. Headed an off-the-books paramilitary outfit called *El Tigres*. They went after Castro in the Sierra Maestra."

Roselli said, "Yeah, I read about him—a ruthless sonofabitch who supposedly slaughtered over two thousand pro-revolutionary Cubans in the process."

Trafficante nodded. "I know 'im from the old days, and we're partners in a Miami restaurant. He heads one of the groups we're talkin' about, and I know he's plannin' to infiltrate some guys by boat. As far as I know, not linked to Sanchez, but if you want, I'll talk to him."

Roselli was doubtful. "The guy's supposedly extortin' money from the Miami exiles to 'help free Cuba' but these outfits usually spend their time fightin' one another other. You think he'd help us?"

"They got a fat common interest. They want Cuba back and Castro dead. They don't give a shit how. They'll figure out who gets what when it's done."

Giancana nodded. "Talk to 'im."

CHAPTER 10

Fidel Castro swept through the door of his conference room and angrily dropped into his chair at the head of a long table. Raúl had requested an urgent meeting that included Che Guevara and Camilo Cienfuegos. After Castro, they were the revolution's leading figures. All four were bearded, smoking cigars, and wearing their camouflage fatigues.

They were also young. Fidel, 33—Guevara, 31—Raúl, 29—Cienfuegos, 23. Fidel, his brother Raúl, and Cienfuegos were all native-born Cubans. Guevara was an Argentine physician.

Cienfuegos, a hero of the revolution, spoke as soon as Castro was seated. "We have a problem, Fidel."

Castro answered in disgust. "Add it to the rest. We have little else, Camilo. Demonstrations over the tribunals—outrage that there will be no elections for two years—and more front page articles calling for an end to executions."

Cienfuegos frowned apologetically. "I think this new problem will be close to the top of the list, Comandante."

Castro waved him on. "I'm listening…"

"I've been informed that Matos is about to defect and take fourteen of his officers with him."

"Matos again." Castro shook his head.

"Yes. He remains opposed to communism. He's become increasing strident. And now this."

Castro waved it off. "Huber Matos been complaining about our move toward communism since March. He hates it. In July he tried to resign. I refused him."

Cienfuegos was respectful but insistent." I believe this time he'll do it—without your permission."

"I can't believe that. Huber is a difficult man, but a dedicated revolutionary. I'll talk to him."

'Fidel—I know you love him, but he is one of the leading figures of the revolution. If he defects with fourteen of his officers, it will deal us a serious psychological and political blow."

Raúl said. "Camilo is right, Fidel. And it's too late for talk. The man is about to defect!"

Castro sighed and shook his head, distressed. "He's been with us from the beginning."

Raúl said, "Yes—but we can't allow him to defect."

Castro reluctantly agreed. "No—we can't."

Cienfuegos leaned forward. "There's more, Comandante. From what I've heard, he could be trying to lead an open revolt."

Raúl slammed his fist on the table. "Not an honest revolutionary, Fidel. A traitor!"

Guevara was just as vehement. "Fidel—I don't care what he's done in the past—arrest them all, and try them for treason!"

Castro nodded sadly. A trial for treason invariably led to a death sentence, but there was little he could do without appearing weak. He turned to Cienfuegos. "See to it, Camilo. He shifted his gaze to his brother. "Anything else?"

"Not at the moment, I …"

Insistent knocking on the door interrupted him.

Castro called out, "Come in!"

A beautiful girl in fatigues entered with a note. She was one of many that surrounded the idolized leaders and were as dedicated to the cause as the men. Handing the note to Castro, she snapped to attention, spun on her heels, and left.

He took it, and read aloud. "Word has come from our spy in Miami that there will be another infiltration attempt from Florida in the next few days. Seven or eight men."

Raúl leaned forward and folded his hands on the table. "How and where?"

"By boat, but no indication of where as yet. A soon as they set a departure date we'll be informed— hopefully with their landing site."

Guevara smiled. "We'll be waiting for them."

Castro sighed. "Arrogante. They think they're the only ones who have any intelligence at all. We will find where they are landing and greet them with what they deserve when they arrive." He looked at Che. "You can look forward to interviewing any survivors before you have them shot."

CHAPTER 11

KEY LARGO

TWO DAYS AFTER OUR MEETING with Trafficante, I dressed like a peasant and drove to the Adelphi marina, a small facility on the isolated southeast side of the key. I found the dock I was told to locate and walked toward the end. The air smelled of diesel fuel, the sun had set over the mainland, the sky was clear, and the sea flat. A perfect night for a cruise across the Florida Straight.

When Roselli and Giancana left for Las Vegas after our meeting with Trafficante, I'd returned to Miami. I wanted to call Marissa but resisted the temptation because nothing had changed since our meeting. If my trip to Cuba were successful I'd have something to report to Sanchez and an excuse to see her again.

The forty-two-foot Hatteras sport-fisher I was looking for had a flying bridge, a tuna tower, and a pair of fighting chairs on the rear deck—one of hundreds like it that were rigged for big game angling. Fifteen minutes after I arrived, eleven men approached me from the dock's parking area. Nine were dressed as peasants—obviously the infiltrators—the other two wore slacks and windbreakers. They all looked young, perhaps mid-twenties, but one was about forty and stood out. Trafficante had shown me his picture.

He signaled the men dressed as peasants to wait out of earshot and came over with the better- dressed men.

"Mr. Amato? Rolando Masferrer."

I shook his hand. "Dante."

Masferrer nodded and indicated the men. "Martine Adega and Pepe Arroyo, my drivers."

Pepe extended a hand. It was soft but his stare was hard. He was tall, wiry, and sported a neatly trimmed mustache. Martine was burly with a pockmarked face and calloused knuckles. I had a feeling he was 90 percent bodyguard, 10 percent driver, and couldn't even start a car. We shook hands but said nothing.

Masferrer hooked his thumbs on his belt. "Santo briefed me and I'm happy to help. I don't care who kills him as long as it's done. Your code name will be Mariano. Observe and learn, but stay close to me and say or do nothing without my permission. Understood?"

"Understood."

"Good." He tuned to Martine and Pepe. "I'll call you with instructions when we get situated. Send the others down."

The two men left and motioned the others to come forward. Masferrer introduced them by names I was told were aliases. Two of them looked American, but I didn't comment.

Masferrer turned to me, indicated the Hatteras, and said, "You, Luis, Miguel, and I will go on this boat. The others will follow on the two smaller boats. Masferrer shook hands with the other six, and they walked to two boats further along the dock. One was about thirty feet long, the other several feet shorter.

Masferrer said, "Luis—prepare to cast off," and led us aboard,

Miguel went to the flying bridge to start the engines, Luis untied the lines, jumped aboard, and we were off—the other two boats falling in behind us as we left the marina.

CHAPTER 12

A MAN WEARING A BLACK jumpsuit watched the three-boat flotilla leaving the marina and slipped out of his car carrying a small portable transmitter. Three hours earlier, he'd been contacted by the spy in Masferrer's organization and had followed the raiding party from Miami to Key Largo.

Walking down the nearest dock, he passed several boats before selecting a thirty-two-foot Bertram. He scanned the area to be sure he wasn't being observed and boarded. Quickly hotwiring the engines, he started them, jumped out, and released the lines. Clambering back aboard, he maneuvered toward the mouth of the marina at idle speed to be as quiet as possible and avoid drawing a wake.

Five minutes later he entered the Florida Straight a mile behind Masferrer's flotilla and followed them toward Cuba.

CHAPTER 13

CUBA

SIX HOURS AFTER LEAVING Key Largo, Miguel headed the Hatteras into a small lagoon north of Cardenas. The other two boats followed about two hundred yards back. The trip had been uneventful—I even thought pleasant if it weren't for the tension evident in the other three men.

Miguel spotted a signal light a mile from the beach and yelled down to Masferrer. "There they are!"

Masferrer picked up a flashlight and answered the signal. He saw that their two smaller boats were too far behind, and called to the bridge.

"Miguel—slow down and let the others catch up."

He called back, "Okay!" and throttled back the engines.

The relative quiet as our boat settled in the water was suddenly shattered by the roar of high-powered engines at full throttle, and a few seconds later all hell broke loose. A Cuban patrol boat, which had been shielded by the long peninsula on the west side of the lagoon, roared into view and opened fire with a machine gun. The smaller of our two trailing boats was hit, immediately set afire, and I could see the men jumping into the water.

Masferrer screamed up to Miguel. "Turn around! Head back out to sea!"

Miguel swung the boat into a violent turn and slammed the throttles forward. The twin engines—wide open—lifted the bow out of the water. I grabbed the rail to avoid being pitched overboard, and held on.

The Cubans began directing fire at their second target. Masferrer's men returned fire and took evasive action to the east. The patrol boat pursued them. Luis set a course very close to the western shore that would let us pass a hundred yards behind the Cubans, and I prayed we wouldn't run aground.

The patrol boat was closing in on its second quarry, but was being led away from our Hatteras. By the time they realized what was happening, we had crossed their stern and sped north at thirty-four knots... at least five knots faster than the patrol boat's top speed. Facing a fruitless chase of our Hatteras, the Cubans continued their assault on the boat they were pursuing until it went dead in the water and the men surrendered.

Masferrer, Luis, and I witnessed the end standing side-by-side looking over the stern. Masferrer slammed his fist against the transom. Livid with rage, he screamed over the wind and roaring engines.

"They knew we were coming! We were betrayed!"

Luis was in tears. One of the men on the captured boat was his brother. "Who, Rolando? Who would do this?"

"One of our own. It had to be. But I promise... I will find out who."

I had no doubt he would, and that there would be a lot of suffering in the wake of the hunt.

A half hour later, dawn broke as we left Cuban waters. By late morning the fast Hatteras had us back in Key Largo, and I headed straight for the Miami airport. I saw no reason to touch base with Sanchez since he had no part in the failed incursion, and I wanted to get back L.A.

Roselli had to be told that trying to take out Castro by infiltrating Cuba in small boats was an invitation to a marble orchard.

CHAPTER 14

WASHINGTON
NOVEMBER 1960

ALDO STROLLED INTO West Potomac Park and found the bench he'd been told to locate. The Washington Monument was to his left, and the Lincoln Memorial to his right—the first and sixteenth. Two weeks earlier, the thirty-fifth had been elected. John F. Kennedy had defeated Richard Nixon in one of the closest elections in U.S. history. Within two months there would be a changing of the guard.

There was a fall chill in the air, and Aldo shivered slightly. He turned up the collar of his topcoat and surreptitiously glanced around. He was sure he hadn't been followed and scanned the area behind him for the fourth time since leaving his car.

The request for the covert meeting felt a bit too Bondish for his taste, but his friend had insisted on the precautions. Lenny Mills had been Aldo's classmate from grammar school to graduation at Northwestern, and they had remained close friends. He'd recently returned from the FBI's Denver office to headquarters in Washington, but they'd only spoken on the phone.

Aldo saw him coming around the corner of the Lincoln Memorial at a leisurely pace. He still had the body of the left tackle he'd been in college and was wearing the standard J. Edgar dark suit, dark coat, and dark hat.

Ridiculous, thought Aldo. Hoods could pick out Feds during rush hour at Union Station.

Mills broke into a wide smile and extended his hand as he sat. "Good to see you Aldo—been a long time."

"Too long. How've you been?"

"Fine. You?"

"The same…But why the cloak and dagger?"

Mills was suddenly serious. "Because what I'm about to tell you could get me fired—or worse."

Aldo had never known him to exaggerate. "What's this about?"

"Your brother…more specifically, your brother and his friends."

Aldo felt another shiver. "Christ!" His first thought was Cuba.

Mills had known the Amato family since they were kids and knew Dante worked for Johnny Roselli—and that meant Sam Giancana. But after Aldo's initial shock, he relaxed. The FBI was a domestic agency having nothing to do with Cuba.

Mills took a deep breath. "The last time Sam Giancana was in Vegas to see Phyllis McGuire, there was a bug in his suite. Ironically, he'd had it placed there himself because he suspected his girlfriend was having an affair with the comedian Dan Rowan. McGuire normally stayed in Giancana's suite when she was in town, but not performing, and he wanted to catch them in the act. A maid discovered the bug and called LVPD who called us.

Aldo shook his head. "The best laid plans…"

"Exactly. But the bug hadn't caught McGuire and Rowan en flagrante and a lot of what it got was meaningless chit-chat. However, at one point it recorded Roselli and your brother in the suite with Giancana. They started talking about Bob Maheu and what they should tell him because he was pressing them for an answer—but an answer about what— they didn't say."

The mention of Maheu caused a stronger shiver to run through Aldo. This was about Cuba.

Mills lit a cigarette. "Any comments?"

Aldo shook his head. "None so far. What else have you got?"

"Aldo…" Mills went on reasonably, "Maheu works for you guys. When Hoover found out the CIA was involved with Giancana, he went batshit, and called Dulles. Dulles stonewalled him. He said it was a matter of national security. *National security*? What the hell does your brother have to do with national security?"

Aldo again relaxed. They knew something, but not everything. They didn't know the men were probably talking about the Mob's involvement in a paramilitary invasion of Cuba. "I have no idea, Lenny. None. But if it'll help, I'll see if I can find out something."

"Do that…because Hoover's a bulldog. He smells a rat. And there's no question that he'll dig until he finds one."

"Thanks for the heads-up, Lenny. I appreciate it."

"Appreciate nothing. I never talked to you." He smiled. "Take care, friend."

Aldo returned to Langley, called Dan Cantrell, and asked for another meeting. They met at cocktail hour in DiGiorno's where their first meeting had taken place and ordered a pair of Martinis. Aldo leaned forward, lowered his voice, and got right to the point.

"I got a call from an old friend with the FBI. They know something's going on between Maheu and Giancana."

Shock crossed Cantrell's face. "How?"

"A self-placed bug in Giancana's Vegas suite."

"Christ."

"The good news is that Cuba wasn't mentioned on the tape. But the FBI knows about Maheu's CIA connections so Hoover called Dulles and Dulles stonewalled him with 'national security.'"

Cantrell winced. "Oh, shit."

"How long do you think it'll be before Hoover finds out what's going on."

"Not long. But the rumors that you heard about a Cuban paramilitary invasion probably aren't just rumors. There are training bases in the

Florida Everglades, the Louisiana Delta, and Guatemala. And there're not just Cubans involved. I heard that Rafael Sanchez, an ex-Cuban industrialist, is involved. He's one of ours—an old friend of Bissell's who's been a covert stringer for us since the early Batista days. Since he was thrown out of Cuba, he's been with us non-stop and has an office at Langley. If he's involved, so are we."

"Jesus. This is crazy. If we get caught supporting an invasion of Cuba the Soviets will go nuts!"

"Yeah… But maybe there's some good news. Dulles will have to brief the new administration about the invasion plan, and if they can't convince Kennedy to go forward, they'll have to shut down. And because Hoover is pissed at being stonewalled, he'll tell Kennedy about the Maheu/Giancana connection just to bust Dulles's balls. Keeping our involvement undetected at that point will seem damn near impossible. I can't believe Kennedy would be stupid enough to okay an invasion."

"I hope you're right, Dan, but there're a helluva lot of hawks and anti-Castro sentiment in the U.S. If it comes out that Kennedy vetoed an invasion planned by Eisenhower, he's going to look like a wimp. He can't allow that this early in his administration."

A honey-dipped southern drawl interrupted them. "Dan! You sweet thang!" It belonged to a statuesque, middle-aged woman named Leonora Harrison.

Dan jumped up and kissed her on the cheek. "Leonora… Ravishing as usual."

"Then why have you been a stranger, dear boy?"

Aldo stood and Cantrell said, "Aldo Amato—Leonora Harrison."

Aldo had never met her, but knew she was the wealthy widow of a Washington power broker and that she'd had affairs with many of the capital's elite—not the least of which was rumored to be Allen Dulles. He shook her hand saying, "A pleasure to meet you."

She said, "Mr. Amato…" and then turned to Cantrell and cooed, "I'm having an impromptu little soirée at my home on Saturday and would be delighted if you'd come."

Cantrell smiled. "And I'd be delighted to attend."

She left saying, "Eight o'clock," and swept away to greet another man.

Cantrell sat down and smiled sheepishly. "An old friend."

Aldo chuckled. "She's not that old and seemed like more than a friend."

When Aldo returned to his office he grimly mulled over the facts. Dan Cantrell, who was on the CIA's Latin American desk, didn't know what the CIA was doing in Latin America. The FBI didn't know what the CIA was doing, because the CIA refused to tell them what they were doing. The new administration coming to Washington knew nothing about what either of them was doing and in Miami the anti-Castro elements would rather fight each other than share what *they* were doing.

Christ! An invasion was being planned and nobody knew what the hell anybody was doing!

CHAPTER 15

LAS VEGAS

Giancana returned to Vegas for the McGuire Sisters' closing night party being hosted by Frank Sinatra. Roselli and I flew in from L.A. to attend, and there was a message waiting for me when we checked into the Sands. Aldo had left a D. C. number for "Al Armstrong," and I went to a pay phone in the lobby instead of calling from my suite.

I dialed the number and a gruff voice answered. "DiGiorno's... Larry here..." There was a lot of background noise—voices, laughter and music.

I recognized my cousin's voice but didn't give my name "I got a message to call this number and ask for Al Armstrong."

"Oh sure..."

I was put on hold, and several seconds later Aldo came on the line. "Armstrong..."

The background noise had disappeared and I wondered why? "It's me. Where are you?"

"In Larry's office." Aldo's voice was hushed even though he was alone. "From now on, use this number if you want to reach me."

"Fine. What's up?"

"First tell me you're not going forward with the proposition."

"I can't. I told my guys it was a bad idea, but they're still thinking about it."

"Don't let them. Back off. Giancana bugged his own Vegas suite and it backfired. The queen's boys found out about Maheu and he's on your ass."

"How the hell did Queenie get involved?"

"Don't ask. But the three of you were heard talking about Maheu and an answer he wanted. The queen called *my* boss and it's all causing a shitstorm. And as of an hour ago I found out who really got you into this… and it was us."

I was shocked. "What?'

"Does one of your 'investors' have the initials R.S.?"

Aldo had to be talking about Rafael Sanchez. "Yeah…"

"He's one of ours."

I thought, *So Giancana's and my instincts were right. Sanchez is more than a former Cuban industrialist. He's CIA.*

Aldo became more solemn. "If this thing goes sour and gets exposed, my people will shuck and jive, and heads will roll. But if you get nailed, you'll be thrown to the wolves."

I knew my brother was right. I also knew he was risking his career and I softened my voice. "Thanks for the call, Aldo. I'll do my best."

"You better pray it's good enough."

I hung up and went to meet Roselli in Giancana's suite. They were having a drink and Giancana seemed to be in an effusive mood. Things must have been going well with Phyllis.

"Dante! Where you been? Have a drink."

"No thanks, Momo." I cupped my hand over my ear and frantically pointed to the phones. "There's a new Ferrari in the parking lot I want to show you guys… I'm thinking of buying one."

The men realized I was signaling the room was bugged. Giancana knew that because he was the one who bugged it. He didn't know that it'd been discovered, but he immediately moved to the door.

"Sure… Is it red?"

Roselli followed and we left the suite. I told them what I'd found out about Hoover, the bug, and Sanchez when we were in the elevator. Giancana was fuming as we proceeded to the lounge, sat at a quiet table, and ordered drinks.

Giancana remained livid, but Roselli was suddenly in high spirits. He clapped his hands together and grinned.

"This is perfect!"

I had no idea what he was talking about. "What? What's perfect?"

"Sanchez! Don't you get it? We're in business with the fuckin' CIA! We're partners! We can forget about Hoover and the Feds constantly tryin' to shut us down, lock us up and throw away the keys. If we go ahead with what they want we're as golden as Eliot Ness—untouchable!"

I'd never considered that. It was a fact, but a double-edged sword. "Johnny—if we hit them with that kind of threat, what the hell's gonna stop them from hitting us? They've taken out foreign leaders for christ-sakes."

"Yeah, but we've got the ability to hit back. Hard and for years. We know who they are and where the bodies are buried. They won't dare come after us."

Giancana thought for a moment, and then broke into a wide grin. "You're right... I love it!"

Roselli raised his glass. "To our partners!"

Giancana and I followed suit, and drank, but I still believed a hit on Castro was damn near impossible—a fact made even clearer by the failed attempt to infiltrate which I'd just been a part of. I was about to point that out when Giancana gave me an order that ended any further discussion.

"Call Sanchez."

CHAPTER 16

MIAMI

DECEMBER 1960

SANCHEZ RESPONDED BY calling another meeting with our team in Miami and I flew in from Los Angeles. Roselli came in from Vegas, but Giancana chose to remain there with his paramour.

News of Masferrer's failed attempt to infiltrate Cuba had ripped across the exile community. Broadcasts from Havana had trumpeted the capture of six men, including two Americans who had attempted to infiltrate from Florida, and Castro accused the United States of being the facilitators.

I met Roselli in his penthouse suite at the Fontainebleau, and he told me William King Harvey would join us. I poured a pair of Jack-rocks and asked, "Who's Harvey?"

Roselli answered, "CIA. Sanchez says he's the guy who uncovered that KBG spy, Kim Philby, and was also the guy responsible for burrowin' the tunnel into East Berlin that let us tap Soviet phone lines."

"Formidable spook."

"Yeah, but also supposed to be a loose cannon."

Sanchez arrived an hour later with a man who was heavy set, balding, had an oval face, mustache, jowls, and small bags under his eyes.

I thought, *Formidable spook? He looks more like a fat chef.*

Sanchez introduced him. "Johnny, Dante—William Harvey."

We shook hands, and Roselli looked at Harvey with a cocked eyebrow. "So you're also CIA?"

Sanchez's eyes widened—momentarily paralyzed by the question. His eyes shot over to Harvey, and back to Roselli. When he recovered, he stammered.

"How…"

Roselli held out his hand. "Not to worry. Your cover's safe with us."

"But…" began Sanchez.

"I'm not tellin' you how—so forget it. Let's get on with business."

Sanchez started to press the issue but must have realized it was futile and heaved a sigh of defeat. "Have you decided to accept the assignment?"

Roselli pursed his lips, extended his hand palm down, and waggled it. I figured he wanted a guarantee of the concept he'd laid out to Giancana and me. I was right.

He said, "That depends on whether you agree to get the FBI off our ass and keep them off."

Sanchez was taken aback. He had to know Dulles wouldn't want Hoover involved, so he sidestepped the proposal with his own.

"Can't be done, but we are prepared to pay you one hundred and fifty thousand dollars for the contract."

Roselli shook his head. "We don't want your money. We want the Feds off our ass—permanently."

Sanchez glanced at Harvey. Harvey's brow knitted as he appeared to be considering the ramifications. I suspected he'd either have to figure out a way to handle the demand or lie about making the arrangement.

After a several moments he reluctantly nodded, "Okay, we'll make it happen."

Roselli grinned, rubbed his hands together and waved them to the couches. "Good—have a seat—drink?"

They declined and we arrayed ourselves around the art deco coffee table. Sanchez leaned forward as he had during our first meeting. He must have thought it gave him more gravitas. I smiled.

"We've come to the conclusion that the methods we've been using to infiltrate non-professionals into Cuba to remove Castro are a losing proposition. We think we need something subtler—something that plays on his weakness."

I said, "What weakness? No one's come up with one from the time he was holed up in the mountains."

"You're wrong. There was one. A girl. She was recruited to poison him."

I remembered Marissa's story. "Marita somebody…"

"Lorenz. She couldn't go through with it because she realized she loved him, but with the right girl it could work."

Roselli laughed. "The old honey trap?" The Mob had used it many times to blackmail politicians and judges. "Good idea. But even if you find the right girl, how do you smuggle her into Cuba."

"Bill's figured out a way to get her in legally. He looked at him. "Bill?"

Harvey nodded. "We'll do it through Mexico City—with a set of false documents. Her visa will come from their Cuban consulate."

I scoffed. "Even if they buy the phony papers, what the hell makes you think the Cubans will issue a visa to someone out of left field?"

"Because the someone won't be out of left field. She'll be vouched for by Rolando Cubela."

Roselli's eyed narrowed. "Who the hell is Rolando Cubela?"

"Along with Che, and Raúl, he's been one of Castro's most trusted advisors. But…over the past year he's become furious over Castro's plunge into communism and contacted us. He wants to defect."

I was still skeptical. "I still don't see how that gets the girl into Cuba."

"Because we'll want a quid-pro-quo. We'll take him in and give him political asylum if he'll vouch for our team. Cubela will say they're relatives from Mexico he hasn't seen since they left as children—cousins who want to return to their homeland for a family reunion in the glorious new People's Republic of Cuba."

I hadn't missed the switch in pronouns. "You said, 'they—relatives—and team'. You're talking more than just the girl?"

Harvey nodded. "I don't like the idea of a girl traveling to Cuba alone. I think it'd seem more credible if she were coming with family— her brother, for instance. Once they're in, Cubela will introduce them to Castro, and nature will take its course."

Roselli nodded appreciatively. "I agree… and I take it you've got the girl."

"We have. You've met her. Marissa del Valle."

I felt my pulse skip, covered my concern, and shot my eyes to Sanchez. "She's agreed?"

"She volunteered. She has a score to settle with Castro. She'll do whatever it takes."

Roselli smiled. "Well she sure as hell's *got* what it takes. She's beautiful, smart, willing, and a native. Who's the guy?"

Sanchez turned to me "We were hoping it would be Mr. Amato."

I was speechless. A blur of thoughts flashed across my mind. *It was ridiculous. A suicide mission. Although she'd be credible in a familiar environment, I wouldn't—I had no experience as a goddamn spy. Even more disturbing was the fact that I'd already seen how effective Castro's intelligence network was. Taking the job made no sense!* I was about to point that out when I was hit with another thought. *If I accepted, we'd be together—something I wanted from the moment I saw her.*

Harvey apparently saw my confusion and said, "Think about it… You're perfect. Your friends have already accepted the contract—you look Latin—and you speak fluent Spanish."

Roselli seemed to like the idea but offered me an out. "I dunno… what d'ya think, pal?"

I quickly weighed the obvious risks against the possible rewards and came up with what I knew was a stupid answer.

"I'm in. When do we leave?"

Harvey smiled. "Hopefully, before the holidays."

CHAPTER 17

CORAL GABLES

I'D NEVER DRIVEN AN EDSEL, and when Hertz offered me the rental at Miami International I jumped at a chance to drive the latest Ford product. Reviewers had called it a flop, but I loved the look and found it handled beautifully, as I drove it to Coral Gables.

Marissa's house was a Spanish Colonial with a cascading fountain in the middle of a circular drive. *Twelve rooms or more,* I thought. The huge entryway, framed by Emperor palms, made the lowly Edsel seem out of place.

"Nice."

At the end of our meeting, I'd asked Sanchez for Marissa's phone number, and called her. She'd been expecting my call, and she asked if I'd made a decision. I told her I'd accepted and asked the name of her favorite restaurant. We made a date for El Matador, and since I knew it was a high-end Miami eatery, I'd worn a lightweight suit and tie.

A maid answered the door. I removed my hat, and she took it. We walked into a large living room looking out to a patio, interior courtyard, and freeform pool. A pre-prepared drink was on a silver tray—Jack Daniels over ice. The maid picked up the tray, presented the drink, and left.

Marissa walked in a few minutes later. She was wearing a black silk dress cut at the knee, a single strand of pearls, and heels. Her ebony hair dropped to her shoulders, and for the first time since I'd met her, she was wearing makeup.

There was no question, she was stunning. She was also charming and highly intelligent, and therefore perfect for the mission. But the possibility of her in bed with Castro left acid in my mouth.

I shook the thought and indicated my drink. "You remembered…"

"I did. And I'm very happy you agreed to Rafael's plan. Thank you." She smiled and kissed me lightly on the cheek.

The maid re-entered with a Mojito on a silver tray.

Marissa took it. "Thank you, Adelaida." Turning to me she said, "It's too beautiful to remain inside."

I followed her through a large set of double doors to a tiled patio that smelled of jasmine and was lit by cognac-colored lights. We settled into rattan armchairs facing the pool, and I raised my glass.

"To our success and safe return."

She mirrored the toast, saying, "I'm sure it will be both… Salud."

After we sipped, I leaned back and crossed my knees. "You don't seem concerned about the alternative."

"Being unconcerned with getting caught would be foolish. But if Cubela puts me next to Castro, I won't fail."

I reluctantly asked the obvious question. "By 'next to' you mean in bed with?"

Her answer was anything but reluctant. "If necessary, yes. Does that offend you?"

"Morally? No. The objection's personal."

She smiled. "Ah… Another oblique compliment. You seem to have a talent for it."

I shrugged non-committally. "You're not worried someone'll recognize you?"

"I left Cuba for boarding school in Spain when I was thirteen and didn't return for five years. But not to Cuba—to Bryn Mawr. My family lived here a great deal during those years, and we traveled to Europe in the summers. When I graduated, I returned to Spain and worked as an interpreter at the Embassy for four more years. I haven't been in Cuba for over thirteen years, and the time I spent there as a young girl was in circles to which Castro and his followers were not even remotely connected."

I sipped my bourbon and stared at her several seconds. "Have you decided how you're going to do it?"

"Kill him? No. It will depend on the circumstances. I'll have poison disguised as facial powder, and a lethal pen."

She'd have to be close to, and alone with, him, I thought, and the acid returned. "Sanchez told me how we're getting in, but when I asked him about getting out, he said the same way—commercial flight. How? The minute they find Castro murdered they'll shut down the island."

"Both poisons are designed to take effect ten hours after they're administered—enough time to fly out."

"They told me that... But how the hell do they know the drug'll have a ten-hour delay? Everybody's metabolism is different. It could be nine—eight—or less. It's an iffy thing."

"Are you having second thoughts?"

"No... I just wanted to make sure you saw the minefields. My only thoughts are about taking you to dinner and spending the holidays in Havana."

El Matador's cuisine was exceptional, and the mission wasn't mentioned. We talked about pastimes, places we'd visited, traded anecdotes, and laughed easily. In light of her obvious beauty, I asked whether she'd ever been recruited by modeling agencies. She chuckled dismissively and said fashion and cosmetic houses had pursued her from the time she was sixteen. She was uninterested.

She asked about my parents, and I told her their relationship was stormy. It saddened her, and she said hers had always been devoted. They'd hosted a huge banquet on their twenty-fifth anniversary, renewed their wedding vows, and had gone on a second honeymoon. She said it wistfully, twirling a few strands of hair next to her ear. It was an endearing habit of my mother's when reminiscing about the past. The tough would-be assassin had unconsciously become tender, and I was fascinated.

When we returned home she openly, and without the slightest reticence, admitted she'd enjoy taking me to her bedroom—then immediately said it could complicate and compromise what was ahead of us.

"However," she added, "since I have unwavering confidence in our success, I'll look forward to an wonderful celebration when we return."

Without a logical counterargument, I reluctantly agreed and left.

CHAPTER 18

MEXICO CITY AND HAVANA

WE ARRIVED AT MEXICO CITY'S Cuban Consulate on December 23, and Marissa told me that from this moment forward we should speak nothing but Spanish. We'd dressed casually, carried an array of forged papers, were expected, and welcomed like prodigals. Cubela had greased the wheels perfectly.

After agreeing to Sanchez's terms, Cubela was supplied with several backdated letters from his cousins—"Diego and Maria López y Cubela" In the most recent one they had requested a visit to Cuba. The cousins were supposedly related by the marriage of their father—Carlos López — to Cubela's father's sister—Louisa Cubela. With the letters, and a request from his influential position, obtaining the visas was a fait accompli.

Our cover story was that the López family had immigrated to Mexico in 1942 to escape the repression of Batista. In Acapulco, our father supposedly became a very successful businessman but had been killed along with our mother in an auto accident three years earlier. We were supplied with photos of our invented parents as well as newspaper articles and obituaries about their life and death. It was an all but impregnable cover story.

Our flight was leaving that afternoon, and we drove to the airport on streets festooned with Christmas decorations. I carried a briefcase with twenty-five thousand in cash, and we had several pieces of luggage. We were supposedly on an extended visit, were very wealthy, and Marissa would need a large wardrobe for the multiple situations that could arise during our stay. Check-in and boarding were uneventful, and we departed on time in a Mexicana DC-4.

The weather was a balmy 79 degrees when we landed at José Martí International Airport, and the plane taxied to a relatively quiet terminal. A portable stairway was wheeled up, and as we deplaned I noticed six soldiers standing beside a Lincoln sedan. They were all bearded, in fatigues, and carrying automatic weapons. The sedan's rear door opened when we reached the tarmac, and a man with a full beard—also in fatigues—got out and beamed at us.

I recognized Rolando Cubela from a picture we'd been shown, and Marissa rushed into his extended arms as he walked forward.

"Maria! At last!" he gushed in Spanish. "And Diego!" He released Marissa and embraced me. "Welcome to Cuba. You both look wonderful."

Marissa hugged him again and happily answered in her native language. "As do you, Rolando. It's been far too long."

"Your flight was pleasant?"

She nodded. "It was."

"And you, Diego, are as I remember you. Life has been good to you, yes?"

I nodded and answered in unaccented Spanish. "Very good."

"Excellent. Let me have your passports. They will be stamped and forwarded to your hotel along with your luggage." He indicated the car. "This way…"

That was it. No customs, immigration lines, or baggage claim.

Marissa grinned and hooked her arm into Cubela's as we walked past the soldiers to our waiting car. Smiling broadly and happily chatting, we settled into the Lincoln. The soldiers climbed into the back of an open truck and followed as we pulled away.

Rolando dropped us off at the Hotel Nacional, a short walk from the Malecón. The Nacional combined art deco, neoclassical, and neocolonial design with an illustrious guest list boasting everyone from Churchill to Hemingway, as well as organized crime's most notorious capos. It was the site of the Mob's infamous 1946 meeting that used Frank Sinatra as a courier to bring in a briefcase containing a million in cash. Chaired by Lucky Luciano and Meyer Lansky, and attended by the hierarchy of organized crime, it was the meeting that set up the international heroin trade.

Cubela told us he would pick us up for dinner at eight. He smiled broadly and said, "The dress will be semi-formal. We are entertaining the Soviet Vice Prime Minister…and Fidel cannot wait to meet you."

CHAPTER 19

WE CHECKED-IN BY SIGNING a pre-prepared registration form. Again, that was it. No questions, passports, or credit cards required. An assistant manager handed his business card to me and our keys to a bellboy. He bowed, saying he was at our service at all times—day or night. We thanked him, and the bellboy led us across the massive lobby to elevators.

I scanned the area. "Notice anything unusual?"

She nodded. "There are no Christmas decorations."

"Castro hasn't declared Cuba an atheist state yet, but lets it be known that celebrating the birth of Christ is unwelcome. He wants New Year's—the birth of the revolution—to be the day for festivity."

We were brought to suites on the penthouse floor, and our luggage and passports arrived within the hour. I changed into a dark suit, and Marissa chose a fuchsia dress that was strapless, backless, and what held it up, obvious. Her heels matched the dress, and her necklace contained a single pear-shaped diamond complemented by matching earrings. With her hair in a dramatic up-sweep, the overall look was heart stopping. There was no way a man could resist her—least of all a man with Castro's reputation. But it wouldn't be difficult to lure her to bed. She'd willingly give up her body so she could snuff out his.

She twirled in front of me and asked, "You think he'll like it?'

"He'd have to be blind not to."

"Good, because I think I might have to lure him away from Mikoyan. Castro is reportedly negotiating for everything from sugar purchases and arms to lend-lease."

"And he'll get everything he wants. The Soviets are salivating over a foothold ninety miles off the Florida coast."

Cubela picked us up at eight sharp, and I noted he'd changed into a suit. Followed by our escort, we drove to a magnificent seaside estate a mile outside Havana. It had been owned by Hernando Flores, a wealthy sugar baron whose family arrived in the eighteenth century. The government had expropriated it after Flores was tried and shot by a revolutionary tribunal for treason, i.e., counter-revolutionary statements.

The colonial mansion was behind guarded gates on sprawling, well-lit grounds dominated by towering palms. There were over a dozen luxury cars parked out front, and I noticed more armed soldiers patrolling the area. Cubela escorted us up a granite stairway and into a chandeliered entry hall, where we were met by a formally attired butler.

Cubela greeted him with a conspiratorial wink. "Good evening, Tomaso. Are we sufficiently late for the lady to make a grand entrance?"

Tomaso returned a slight bow and a smile. "They are all on the balcony."

We were shown down the long hall to a cocktail party being held on an elevated balcony that spanned the entire rear of the building. It was surrounded by a balustrade that overlooked gardens, a reflecting pool, and fountains. A small orchestra was playing languid Cuban ballads while white-gloved waiters served hors d'oeuvres and a dozen candelabra flickered in a light breeze.

There were thirty-two well-dressed male and female guests, and I immediately noticed Castro, chatting with Anastas Mikoyan, vice prime minister of the Soviet Union. Out of deference to his distinguished guest, and out of sight of his people, Castro had apparently abandoned his signature fatigues to host the extravagant dinner wearing a well-tailored suit.

Heads swiveled as Cubela led Marissa and me toward Castro and Mikoyan. There was a hush in the conversation as we passed, with both men and women gazing at Marissa. I was aware of a mixture of Spanish and Russian being spoken with the occasional voice of an interpreter in the mix.

Castro noticed us approaching. Looking over Mikoyan's shoulder, he stopped mid-sentence and stared. Mikoyan turned to see what had interrupted their conversation, saw Marissa, and smiled appreciatively.

Cubela dramatically lifted his hand toward Castro and Mikoyan as we arrived and formally announced, "The Prime Minister of Cuba, Fidel Castro, and the Vice Prime Minister of the Soviet Union, Anastas Mikoyan…May I present my cousins, Diego and Maria López y Cubela."

Marissa and I inclined our heads and then took the extended hands of the two statesmen. Castro held Marissa's hand for several seconds longer than was necessary and smiled.

"My country is honored to entertain such an astonishing beauty." He bowed to kiss her hand. "Welcome to Cuba."

Charm, I thought. The sonofabitch has charm. There was no denying it.

Marissa cooed, "Thank you, Prime Minister. The pleasure is mine."

He shook his head. "Fidel…please."

Almost as an afterthought Castro shook my hand. "And a fond welcome to you, Diego. We must find time to chat…" Turning to Mikoyan, he said, "Excuse us a moment Anastas," and took Marissa's arm to lead her to the balcony rail a few feet away, but not out of earshot.

Mikoyan might have been bemused that he'd been so abruptly abandoned, but he simply smiled understanding and turned to me for some banal conversation.

Addressing me in Spanish, he asked, "So… Was your trip a pleasant one?"

I said it was and continued to chat with Mikoyan, but I was tuned to Castro and Marissa. I watched Castro remove two flutes of champagne from a passing waiter's tray.

He handed one to Marissa, raised his and smiled. "Salud!"

Marissa tapped it and returned his smile.

"Salud."

"Your cousin has told me much about you, Maria, but since you were a child when you left Cuba, he could not have known the exquisite woman you've become."

"Thank you, but certainly there are many beautiful women in Cuba."

"There are…but a country can never be blessed with too many."

"Thank you, again."

"Unfortunately, as you can see, tonight I am committed to affairs of state…but tomorrow I insist on re-acquainting you with Havana. We will begin with a one o'clock lunch at the Bar Floridita, tour the city, have cocktails at the palace and then…" He smiled … "Return to my home for a private dinner."

There was no mistaking his intent and Marissa couldn't have asked for more. "I would be honored to be the guest of such an illustrious guide."

"Until tomorrow, then."

He again took her arm, and as he guided her back in our circle, dinner was announced. We all began leaving the patio, but when I passed through the towering double doors, Tomaso, the butler, brushed me.

I felt something slide into my jacket pocket, but Tomaso made no eye contact and kept walking.

CHAPTER 20

WE FILED INTO A FORMAL DINING room where a twenty-foot table was arrayed with Waterford, Limoges, and Gorham—a table setting from the mansion's pre-revolutionary owner.

Christ, I thought, what hypocrisy. Half the people on the island were struggling to put bread on the table, but their glorious communist leader had no problem with a capitalist display and a sumptuous banquet. All fucking governments were alike.

A waiter stood behind each high-backed chair. Above the table, three crystal chandeliers lit the room in a festive blaze. Castro, Mikoyan, and the senior Soviet dignitaries were seated at one end of the long table—Marissa and I at the opposite end with Cubela and an assortment of the lesser Soviet and Cuban bureaucrats. Notably absent from the thirty-two attendees were Raúl Castro and Che Guevara, who were supposedly traveling. I thought it more likely the dedicated Marxists didn't approve of the ostentatiously bourgeois extravaganza and chose not to attend.

Although several of our dinner partners were taken with Marissa, and eagerly engaged her in conversation, the man on my left took no interest in her. He seemed to be studying me. He was powerfully built, had a military crew cut, and his accent was Russian.

After a few benign comments about the wine, he casually remarked,

"You bear no resemblance to your sister, Diego."

I felt a chill. "Yes... People always comment on it." I laughed. "My mother withstood some good natured gossip about it as we grew up."

"And where was that?"

"Acapulco."

"Beautiful harbor. I vacationed there when I was stationed in Washington.

That damn near froze me. "Oh? The embassy?"

"Yes. I was a press attaché."

Press attaché. Shit! The guy was undoubtedly KGB. I immediately assumed Castro put him there to question me. Did they suspect something? What? How? I stayed outwardly calm, and asked, "Did you enjoy Washington?"

"Enormously. Especially the museums and monuments. Have you been there?"

I said, "No." That was easier than explaining what I was doing there.

Then it suddenly hit me. *The Washington newspapers. Had they run the pictures of me, Dietrich, and Raft in Las Vegas? Was it possible he'd seen them?* I felt another, colder chill.

"What is it you do in Acapulco?" he asked.

"Import-export. The business established by my father. I take it you're now attached to the embassy here."

"Naturally."

"Press attaché?"

He smiled. "Of course."

We were interrupted by a glass being tapped to get our attention. Castro stood up and offered the first toast of the evening followed by loud applause and an order to begin the meal. It featured Cuban and Russian specialties, was accompanied by vintage wines, and lasted two and a half hours. Unending toasts and chatter—idle, political, and comic—continued throughout the dinner.

The KBG man had joined other conversations, and at one point I surreptitiously removed the butler's note from my pocket. The message instructed me to excuse myself between the cheese course and dessert and go to the men's room—which I did at the appointed time.

The butler locked the door as soon as I entered and led me to the far end of the room. "My name is Tomaso Rodriguez. I served Fernando Flores, the former owner of this house, for thirty years."

I nodded, but was wary. Anyone or anything could be a trap in this world. "Why were you allowed to stay?"

"Because no one in Cuba knew this house and staff better. Castro wanted it to be available for functions like the one tonight. But these affairs require highly trained chefs, kitchen personnel, barmen, waiters, and maids who have worked together for years. He didn't want the uncertainty of new and inexperienced servants at high level dinners."

The story was plausible but I remained cautious. "Why'd you want to see me?"

"Because I know who both of you are…and so do they."

I was taken aback but tried to remain calm. "And who do you, and they, think we are?"

"You are Dante Amato. And she is Marissa del Valle."

I was stunned. *How the hell could it have happened?* Remaining calm became a struggle.

"You want to tell me how you know that?"

"*I* knew when you arrived and I saw the girl. Her father was a dear friend of the Flores family. He sometimes brought his daughter here when he visited. I knew who she was the minute I saw her."

"She left over thirteen years ago. Marissa was just a child."

"Yes…and she was as beautiful then as she is now. But it's not important how I know. *They* know because my daughter overheard a phone conversation between Che and Castro. Elaina is one of Che's mistresses— an unwilling one. She heard Che say that the man who was bringing Marissa del Valle to Cuba was a gangster named Dante Amato… And then Che suddenly roared with laughter and said, 'I would love to see the look on that bitch's face when she realizes you know who she is. Her father will roll in his grave when you fuck her—on Christmas Eve, no less!"

I saw red and exploded. "Christ! And there was a KGB agent questioning me at dinner. They could arrest us tonight."

"I don't think so."

"Why not?" It was getting difficult to keep my voice down.

"Because I believe that Castro will want the joy of telling her himself when he takes her to bed."

"It seems impossible. Our cover was supposed to be foolproof!"

"Castro's intelligence is superb, Mr. Amato."

I grabbed Tomaso shoulders. "I've got to get her out."

Tomaso nodded vigorously. "Tonight. Tomorrow will be too late."

The plan had been to fly out on Mexicana by day. There were no flights at night, and there was only one other way off the island. I exclaimed, "We'll need a boat."

"You have money?"

"Yes."

"There is a large fishing fleet, commercial and sport, in a marina fifteen minutes from downtown. Buy, steal, or bribe—but get out tonight. Tomorrow night is Christmas Eve."

I gratefully shook the man's hand. "Someday I hope to get a chance to properly thank you."

Retuning to the table, I made no effort to tell Marissa what had happened and gave an Oscar-worthy impression that nothing was amiss. I even engaged the KBG man in a conversation about the Soviet Union's admirable support of Cuba. When the dinner finally ended, we exchanged pleasantries with other guests, expressed our pleasure in meeting Mikoyan, then thanked and said goodbye to Castro.

Cubela once again returned us to The Nacional in the Lincoln. We were followed by our military escort, and Cubela, to his credit, even in the brief moments when we were alone, had never given any indication that we were anyone other than his cousins.

I thought his handlers in Washington would've been proud…if they really were his handlers. Cubela could be answering to Havana, in which case he was the one who'd betrayed us.

CHAPTER 21

I SAID NOTHING TO MARISSA until we were crossing The Nacional's lobby toward the elevators. I squeezed her arm and lowered my voice. "Follow me—say nothing."

She understood the warning and nodded.

When we got to my suite I opened the door, and assuming the rooms were bugged, led Marissa directly to the balcony. Under other circumstances, the glittering lights of the city and the sweep of the Florida Straight would have been unforgettably romantic—but not tonight.

I turned to her. "Marissa, they know who we are. Castro knows you're Marissa del Valle."

Marissa's eyes widened as the words sunk in. "It's not possible! How could he know?"

"I have no idea, but we've been made. The butler recognized you and warned me. His daughter overheard Che tell Castro that your father would roll in his grave when he fucked you Christmas Eve."

She shook her head. "I can't believe it! Only Sanchez, Harvey, you and I knew the plan."

"Plus Cubela, whoever made the phony documents, and Christ knows who else."

"I must be an idiot. The bastard was taking me on a tour of the city tomorrow. He had me completely fooled."

"Yeah, he's great fucking actor."

"Dammit. I could have poisoned him at lunch."

"Yeah, and we could have been dead before dinner. We've got to get to the docks, rent, buy, or steal a boat, and get out tonight. Take your papers and the cash—nothing else. No bags. Change into sportswear and meet me back here in five minutes."

"If they know, they may be watching the hotel."

"They don't know *we* know. Hopefully they're arrogant enough to think we suspect nothing. We'll take the elevator to the second floor, the stairs to lobby and leave by the pool exit."

We slipped out wearing dark slacks and sweaters, and two blocks from the hotel we flagged a cab. It was almost midnight when we got to the marina, and there was very little activity. A quarter moon hung low on the horizon, and the breeze rattled the rigging of sailboats.

The marina was large facility, fairly well lit. I noted the harbor master's shack and headed for an area out of his line of sight. The boats seemed to be separated by type—pleasure, commercial, sports-fishers. I wanted one I was familiar with and looked for a prospect among the sports-fishers.

We heard singing at the end of a long pier and turned that way. Two men were drinking beer in fighting chairs on the rear deck of a forty-two foot Hatteras just like Masferrer's. The older was wearing a captain's hat, the younger, bareheaded, probably his mate. They were both a bit toasted.

I called out in Spanish, "Captain! We'd like to hire your boat."

The man turned a bleary eye toward me, and rotated his beer bottle in the air. "Good! Come back at seven. Fifty dollars a day."

I said, "We want to rent it now," stepping aboard to get closer.

"We don't fish at night, comrades."

"We wouldn't be fishing. "I opened the briefcase, revealing stacks of banded hundreds, and the man's eyes bulged. "We'd be going to Florida."

The words seem to sober the captain, and his eyes darted to his mate. Fear spread on both their faces, and the man rapidly shook his head.

"No... no—no! We would be shot when we came back!" He lurched out of his seat and headed for the cabin. Pointing to the bridge he yelled, "Carlos! The radio! Call the harbor master!"

I grabbed him before he reached the door. A kidney punch dropped him to his knees—a rabbit punch knocked him out. I whirled and caught the mate by his ankle when he was halfway up the bridge ladder. I pulled him down and his chin struck on a rung, saving me the trouble putting him away.

"Marissa, search the cabin. He was probably going for a gun. Find it." I scooped up spare mooring lines under the transom, tied both men's hands and gagged them. The mate was wearing a filleting knife, and I grabbed it.

Marissa returned with a shotgun and a triumphant smile. "Twelve gauge insurance."

"Perfect."

"What do you want to do with them?"

"Take them with us. If we let them go they'll spread the alarm, give our descriptions, and we'll be chased by patrol boats. But there's no point in killing two innocent fishermen so I'll tell them I'll dump them en route if they resist... A lie, but they don't know that."

I picked up the seawater hose, doused the captain until he came to, then slapped his face.

"Listen carefully. We're going to Key Largo. If you co-operate, I'll pay you when we get there—if not, I'll dump you en route. Either way we're going. Nod if you understand."

The captain nodded rapidly.

I laid the filleting knife on the man's neck. "I'm going to remove your gag. If you cry out, I'll gut you like one of your fish." I hauled the terrified man to his feet and pushed him toward the ladder. "Start the engines."

The captain scrambled up, his fear apparently overcoming the alcohol. I followed him saying, "Marissa—untie the lines."

She leapt back onto the dock, and quickly untied the bow and stern lines as the first engine roared to life. Jumping back aboard, she climbed to the bridge.

The captain gave me a pleading look before he started second engine. He was probably thinking even if I let him live, if he were caught returning, he'd be shot.

I shook my head and pointed at Marissa holding the shotgun.

He crossed himself, started the second engine, and we pulled away.

Castro had only a dozen cutters covering over a thousand miles of shoreline, so I figured our chances of being spotted at night were doubtful, unless they'd been tipped off, as they were in Masferrer's case. We slipped out of the marina unnoticed and cleared the twelve-mile territorial limit without being spotted by patrol boats. In the Straight we had calm seas and arrived off Key Largo before 7:00 a.m. under clear skies and a rising sun.

I directed the captain to take us into the same marina Masferrer used for our failed infiltration in the opposite direction. I hadn't noticed any law enforcement presence then, and it was the only one I was sure I could find.

I put my arm around Marissa, and said, "We got lucky. More than a few times back there. I wasn't sure we'd make it."

She feigned shock. "Mr. Amato, are you saying you were scared?"

"Terrified."

She laughed and kissed my cheek.

During the crossing the captain was co-operative, the mate hung over and peaceful, so I left them with their shotgun, knife, and five thousand in cash.

Why the hell not? I could be magnanimous. I was using government money.

CHAPTER 22

MIAMI

SANCHEZ AND HARVEY WERE speechless. We were sitting on Marissa's patio, and I'd just finished describing the debacle that began in Mexico City and ended in Key Largo after twenty-four fucked up hours. After we landed, I'd phoned Sanchez, picked up a rental car, and drove back to Miami fuming. By the time Sanchez rounded up Harvey and met us at the house, it was almost noon.

I made no effort to restrain my fury and continued a verbal assault on Harvey while Sanchez listened with a bowed head.

"They knew who we were before we left for Mexico City!"

Harvey threw up his hands. "I don't see how! This thing was tightly held."

"But they knew... Which means that either Cubela fucked you over and betrayed us, or the traitor's one of your own people!"

"Not possible!"

"Did anyone in the exile community know about us?"

"No one."

"Who made the documents?"

"A seventy-one-year-old Albanian who's been with the Agency forty years."

"Who else knew?"

"Bissell and the two us."

Disgusted, I yelled, "Use your fucking head Harvey! Bissell's office is in Washington—you call that a tight environment!"

"Bissell's people were vetted by Angleton for Christsakes! They haven't taken a piss he doesn't know about."

"Angleton's the one who should be pissing! He missed Philby. He could've missed someone else."

Harvey sputtered, "Godammit Amato—James Jesus Angleton's the Deputy Director of Operations for Counterintelligence! He's nearly destroyed the CIA single-handedly because of his paranoia about moles."

"But Angleton missed Philby, and he would've stayed missed if *you* hadn't nailed him!"

Harvey threw up his hands. "Fine, but this is getting us nowhere. It's obvious there's a mole, so we'll give Bissell a heads-up and tell him to get Angleton on it. In the meantime Cubela contacted us as soon as he found out you'd escaped. He now says he wants cash and a position in a free Cuba for helping us get rid of Castro. The Agency's going forward. His code name's going to be Amlash."

"I don't trust that fuck!"

"Okay, but you failed, and at the moment he's the only game in town. We still want to nail Castro." He looked at Sanchez, frowned, and asked, "Anything else?"

Sanchez was still stunned. He hadn't uttered a word. He blinked and shook his head.

Marissa checked her watch and said, "Castro would have known we'd escaped hours ago, but there's been nothing on the air. I suspect he's embarrassed about our escape and doesn't want to advertise it."

Harvey nodded. "From what you've told me, you've probably wounded his macho pride. He's targeted people for less. Be careful. He knows who and where you are."

"I don't think he'll try to kill me. From the look I saw in his eyes, he has something else in mind."

Harvey scoffed. "Marissa, don't fool yourself with this one. A look is a look. But he'd kill you with a smile on his face." He tapped Sanchez's shoulder and started for the door.

I ushered them out, said goodbye, and again told them they'd been stupidly careless. When I returned, Marissa was opening a bottle of wine.

I was still steaming. "When Roselli hears this he'll go into orbit. His people don't get ratted out."

"You think he'll want to cancel the arrangement?"

"He'll sure as hell consider it. I'll find out when I get back."

She nodded, then said, "Before you leave there's something I'd like to do."

I shrugged. "Sure, whatever…"

"I'd like to make good on my promise of a wonderful celebration when we returned."

I smiled, took her in my arms and kissed her.

She eased away and caressed my lips. "I have a confession."

"Yes…"

"I was tempted to knock out the captain and attack you last night."

"The boat had no autopilot."

"We could have stopped the engines."

"We might have been pursued and captured."

"We might have died happy."

She took my hand and led me to her bedroom. We undressed each other slowly.

Later, completely exhausted, Marissa rolled on top of me and smiled.

"Merry Christmas…"

CHAPTER 23

THE FOLLOWING MORNING we were drinking mimosas on the patio, enjoying the beautiful day. The radio was tuned to holiday music, and Nat King Cole was warbling *Chestnuts roasting on an open fire…* Idyllic. Until Masferrer called at ten o'clock. He'd received word of our escapade from a source in Havana and told Marissa he wanted an immediate meeting.

I fumed, "It's Christmas!"

"In his world, politics take precedence over religion."

I was amazed. We'd just returned. There'd been no broadcast from Cuba—neither Sanchez nor Harvey had any reason to speak to him, and Masferrer already knew what happened in Havana.

I shook my head. "Christ, the spies outnumber the civilians in this war!"

"He's probably angry that his CIA friends didn't keep him informed."

"Mind boggling. My brother thinks no one in Washington knows what's going on—but in Miami and Havana they know what's going on before it happens."

"Remember Dante, the CIA has been funding and training many disparate groups for months. They all want to prove they're the most important and therefore deserve the biggest piece of the pie—and the pie is funding. They've supposedly consolidated under Manuel Artime but rivalries remain strong. They're especially paranoid about what will happen after we overthrow Castro, and who will be in control."

"Who're you with?"

"Artime. He's trying hard to maintain a dialogue and co-operation among everyone. He doesn't trust Masferrer but wants to keep a semblance of peace so let us see what he wants."

"Okay, but I have to call Roselli and see what *he* wants."

I called Roselli at his Los Angeles home and got him out of bed. I briefed him on the past twenty-four hours, and he went from groggy to infuriated to consoling. He wasn't happy that our partners had fucked up and would read them the riot act, but he also liked keeping Hoover off our ass and possibly getting our casinos back. He wanted to maintain the relationship and was sure Momo would feel the same way.

My orders were to keep our hat in the ring and make nice.

Masferrer's headquarters were in a Cuban section of downtown Miami that was awash in Christmas decorations. The location was a large converted store—unmarked, but well appointed, with a reception area and hallways leading to partitioned offices.

Sitting at the reception desk—probably more for security than reception—was the man who had been introduced to me as Luis during the infiltration attempt. He appeared drawn and cheerless—probably because his brother has been captured, and was now undoubtedly in La Cabaña prison awaiting execution.

Marissa knew him. "Merry Christmas, Timo. We are all sorry about your brother …"

He nodded his thanks.

"Is Rolando in his office?"

He nodded again, and jerked his thumb toward the hall behind him.

Luis apparently was Timo, and Timo was obviously hostile—probably because he suspected I might be the traitor who got us jumped in Cuba.

Two secretaries—one exceptionally beautiful, the other very pretty—were busily typing at desks flanking the beginning of the hallway. Their hair was fashioned in the recently popular bouffant style worn by the incoming first lady, Jackie Kennedy, and as we passed, Marissa exchanged greetings with them calling the beauty Abril, and the other girl Yolanda.

When we entered his fairly large office, Masferrer was seated at his desk and didn't get up to greet us. He wasn't happy. Martine and Pepe, the two men Masferrer had introduced as his drivers, were on a sofa.

Masferrer angrily addressed Marissa. "What were you thinking?"

She was taken aback. "What was *I* thinking?"

"Yes—you!"

I saw her face flush. The real enemy in Havana had almost nailed us, and now she was being attacked in Miami by one of her own people.

"*I* wasn't thinking of anything other than killing that bastard. It was a *CIA* operation."

Masferrer scoffed. "The CIA… What do they know about Cuba? They're neophytes in that world. Do you know what would have happened if you were captured—*before* they killed you? I'll tell you. You would have been tortured until you told them the CIA is financing us. You would have told them about the camps. You would have told them the U.S. military is training our invasion force. Your confession would have trumpeted and televised worldwide. Then…" He paused for effect. "*Then*—there would have been no way the United States could deny they were supporting us and everything we dreamed of would be lost."

Marissa took a deep breath, and I could see she was honestly contrite. "I'm sorry Rolando. I thought it was a good plan. We were betrayed."

"Of course you were! And if I'd been informed who you were dealing with I would have told you who it was before you left."

She looked like she'd been slapped. "What?"

"Cubela! I've suspected for months that he was what your beloved CIA calls a 'dangle.' I believe he convinced them he wanted to defect so he could become a double agent."

So my suspicions were accurate. My problem was knowing Masferrer had his own ax to grind. Could *he* be trusted?

Marissa managed a choked, "How…"

"How did *I* know? I have as many moles in Havana as Castro has in Miami. The problem we *both* have is figuring out who they are, and where they are, so we can feed them disinformation!"

Marissa must have realized that Masferrer's knowledge, if accurate, could have saved us from a nearly fatal mistake. She shook her head. "I don't know what to say."

"Say you'll communicate with me…" He looked at me. "And that includes *you* and *your* people. We can only succeed with the constant exchange of intelligence from all sources."

I felt humiliated for both of us but remained silent. I'd be leaving Miami—Marissa wouldn't. She'd be staying and would continue to work with Masferrer's people. Punching this arrogant asshole in the chops would do nothing to cement solidarity.

I remained in Miami though New Year's, and we treated the week as if it were the last holiday of our lives. Although we were both beginning to think that it wasn't just about the sex, we said anything about deeper feelings. I knew the loss of her family made Marissa determined not to let anything or anyone stand in the way of destroying the man who was responsible. For my part, I had a long-standing aversion to permanent relationships. Mob guys with wives always had mistresses but constantly bitched about one or the other being a pain in the ass. My parents' relationship, while committed, had always been fiery, and my brother, the dedicated cold war warrior, was relentlessly hen-pecked by a wife who wanted a better life than the one that could be had on government wages.

On January 2, Marissa drove me to the airport. I promised to come back as often as possible, and we said we'd speak on the phone often. We held each other for a long time before I kissed her gently, smiled, and boarded the plane for Los Angeles.

CHAPTER 24

WASHINGTON
JANUARY 1961

SHORTLY AFTER HIS INAUGURATION on January 21, 1961, John Kennedy assembled his advisors in the Oval Office for a discussion of an operation they'd inherited from the Eisenhower administration.

The paramilitary invasion of Cuba.

In attendance were Attorney General Bobby Kennedy, Secretary of Defense Robert McNamara, Secretary of State Dean Rusk, Undersecretary of State Chester Bowles, National Security Advisor McGeorge Bundy, and Arthur Schlesinger, special assistant for Latin American affairs.

Kennedy was sitting behind his desk in a rocking chair, and his advisors were arrayed in front of him. He held up a file labeled *Pluto*.

"Have you all read this?"

There were nods and "Yes sirs," all around.

The president said, "Dulles and Bissell have told me they're committed to the plan and believe it both viable and necessary. What do you think, Dean?"

Rusk said, "I don't like it, Mr. President,"

"On what grounds?"

"First—the operation would be a violation of international law. There is simply no way to make a legal case before the world for an American-backed invasion of Cuba."

Bundy immediately objected. "We can hardly be squeamish about the niceties of law with a communist state ninety miles off the coat of Florida… Besides which, our involvement would be covert."

Rusk shook his head. "I don't see how. An operation on this scale can't be conducted covertly. The landing and our involvement would become publicly known the moment the brigade hit the beach."

Bundy remained firm. "Perhaps, but the expected uprising of the Cuban people against Castro would drown out any criticism it caused."

Kennedy watched the back and forth.

"Expectations," sniffed Schlesinger. "I have seen no credible evidence that there will be an uprising. And I don't believe we can count on one."

McNamara demurred. "Whether or not the people rise up against Castro may be unimportant. Dulles and Bissell believe the Cuban Army will revolt. They won't want to fight against their brothers."

"Again," argued Schlesinger, "I see no credible evidence that the Cuban military will strike against Castro. They laid down their arms in the opening days the revolution—*supporting* him by refusing to fight for Batista."

Bowles nodded agreement. "And if they remain loyal to Castro, an invasion force of fifteen hundred men will have to face the whole Cuban Army. It could be a disaster."

It was becoming clear to the president that the room was still split. He, Bobby, and Bundy remained in favor of the plan. Rusk, Bowles, and Schlesinger remained opposed.

Kennedy eyes roved across the latter three. "One of my main arguments during the election was that Nixon wasn't tough enough on the world-wide spread of communism. Have those of you in opposition thought of the political consequences if it gets out that there was a plan to oust Castro, designed by the Republicans, and we canceled it?"

Rusk, the senior dissenter, answered. "We have, Mr. President, and we've discussed it. The fallout would be considerable…but not, in our opinion, as destructive as the consequences of a failed invasion… and the subsequent revelation that the United States, a superpower, was defeated by a third world country."

Kennedy absorbed the assessment for several moments before he spoke. When he did, his tone was gracious. "Thank you, gentlemen. I agree we have to verify the intelligence reports and further analyze the information as it becomes available. But in the meantime, continue supporting the preparations."

The meeting ended with Rusk, Bowles, and Schlesinger knowing that Dulles and Bissell had all but convinced the President of success, and Bundy was on board with them.

But what really scared them was Bobby—next to the president, the most powerful and influential man in the room. Although he hadn't spoken up, they all knew he wanted to invade.

CHAPTER 25

LOS ANGELES
FEBRUARY 1961

ROSELLI READ THE *U.S. NEWS and World Report* article aloud. "Dr. Miró Cardona predicts a 'general uprising' in Cuba. And after the uprising, there will have to be a U.S. military decision on whether to help the people with a mass invasion or just continued infiltration by specially trained men."

He turned to me, held up the magazine, and asked, "What d'ya think?"

Roselli was sitting in a director's chair with his name on it. I was in an identical chair, but mine was unmarked.

I said, "If he's right, we may catch a break."

We were on a Columbia Studios sound stage where Roselli had had an office since the '30s. It was one of the perks he enjoyed for arranging the mob financing that allowed Harry Cohn, Columbia's legendary and much-hated president, to take over the studio. Roselli became his close friend, and as a result had access an endless source of beautiful and available starlets.

The latest in the long line of aspirants was about to get a screen test directed by Frank Capra, a Sicilian immigrant who was the winner of six Academy Awards. Roselli had put it together and invited me to watch. Roselli wouldn't dream of forcing the famous director to hire the girl, but it didn't matter whether she got the part or not. She'd fuck Handsome Johnny out of gratitude.

Capra called, "Action!"

Roselli and I stopped talking and watched.

The test was a light comedy scene with an older actor playing the girl's boss. She sat on his lap and they began engaging in the kind of smart banter for which Capra was famous. The girl was wearing shorts, a halter, and heels—a wardrobe that allowed no confusion as to why Roselli wanted her.

Three minutes later, Capra yelled, "Cut! Excellent. We've got it." He kissed the girl on the cheek, waved goodbye to us, and left.

The girl rushed over, threw her arms around Roselli, and gushed, "He likes me!"

Roselli smiled, and patted her cheek. "Of course. You were terrific."

"You really think so?"

"Of course."

"Are we having dinner?"

"Of course."

"At the Brown Derby?"

"Of course."

"I'll have to change."

"Of course." He'd never stopped smiling.

The girl kissed Roselli on the cheek and spun away.

I said, "Cute. Naive."

Roselli chuckled. "Of course."

"What's her name?"

"Elowese Margolin."

"Not for long if she gets the part."

"Think I should take her to Vegas with us tomorrow?"

"You're bringing snacks to a banquet?"

"Good point. What's up with Marissa?"

"I phone her, but with all we've got going here and in Vegas, I haven't been able to get back there."

A production assistant hurried up and said, "There's a Mister Gold on the line for you, Mister Roselli." He pointed to a wall unit. "You can take it on the stage phone."

Roselli nodded and I followed him to the phone. Roselli picked it up. "Momo?"

"Yeah. I just got a call from Trafficante. He's gettin' nervous. Masferrer told him there's been no contact from D.C. since Dante almost got iced down south. And their January payout never showed up. He needs the cash and wants to know what's up. Has Sanchez called you?"

"No. I thought they were just waitin' for the new administration to take over."

"Maybe. But give 'im a call and see if you can find out anythin'. Do it today."

"Got it." Roselli hung up and turned to me. "He wants us to call Sanchez and find out what's up with Masferrer's cash."

"Sanchez won't like it."

"I don't give a fuck what he likes. It's what Momo wants."

"He'll shit if we call his office."

"I could care less. But use your brother to get to him. Momo wants it done today."

CHAPTER 26

BEVERLY HILLS

I DIALED ALDO'S HOME at four that afternoon—seven in Washington. Since Momo wanted it done immediately I couldn't wait until morning and use the Georgetown bistro, but I figured I could be circumspect enough to defeat a bug if there was one on his phone.

"Amato residence—Elvira speaking…"

"Good evening Elvira, it's Uncle Dante. Is your daddy home?"

"Oh yes," she enthused. "When are you coming to see us?"

"Soon."

"Promise?"

"I do."

"Daddy! Uncle Dante's coming to see us!"

A few seconds later, Aldo came on the line. "You're what?"

"Nothing. I was just telling Elvira what she wanted to hear."

Aldo knew it had to be serious for me to call him at home after I was warned not to, so he made it sound like a normal conversation between brothers and casually asked, "How've you been?"

I said, "Fine, but I need some help with the family again. Mom wants me to talk to cousin Rafi about meeting him and burying the hatchet."

"What do you want me to do?"

"He gets mad when I call his office, so tell him we should try to make mom happy, and ask him to call me at home."

"That it?"

"No... Say hi to Pat for me."

Aldo tried, but he couldn't manage to keep the sarcasm out of his voice. "I'm sure she'll love hearing it... I'll have him call."

I hung up and called Roselli, telling him Aldo agreed to be our messenger, then made myself a drink and called Marissa. After the usual warm greetings and agreement that separation was more frustrating than we thought possible, her tone changed. I'd warned her about bugs so she was circumspect.

"A lot of people are talking about invasion, Dante. It's even in the newspapers."

"The exiles have been talking about it for over two years. Everyone believes it's just saber rattling."

"I know, but it's being taken seriously."

"Castro's taken it seriously from the beginning. He's arrested everyone even remotely suspected of counter-revolutionary activity. In spite of it, over a hundred thousand Cubans have made it to Miami."

"I know... you're right." She paused. "Any idea when you might be coming back?"

"No, but I promise it'll be soon."

"I hope so." She chuckled. "I'm getting bored with my Artime dinners.

"Just don't forget who doesn't bore you,"

I could picture her smiling at the phone. What a great goddamn broad.

An hour later, Sanchez called. "Aldo caught me at home, but I'm on a pay phone."

He gave me the number, I went to a pay phone on Wilshire, and he answered on the first ring. "What's so very important?"

"The natives are getting restless. Masferrer called Trafficante and said he hasn't heard from you. He wants to know why."

"Christ! Can't any of you people read the papers? As of three weeks ago there's a whole new game in town. We've been waiting to hear who's who and what's what."

"So who is and what is?"

Sanchez sighed. "Look—tell your friends that there's a split inside the new administration, but as far as we know the president is on board with us."

"When will Miami get the money?"

"Soon. I'll bring it up with Bissell, but he's been up to his ass dealing with the State Department."

"What the hell for? I thought this was an Agency operation."

"It is. But State's got a bug up its ass because the Cubans are screaming in the U.N. Security Council that we're preparing an invasion."

"The exiles've been screaming that what they intend since the revolution."

"True, but Rusk wants to demonstrate that we don't have anything to do with an invasion, and to prove it he wants to arrest Masferrer."

"For what?

"Violating the U.S. Neutrality Act. It forbids launching a military expedition from U.S. territory against a nation we're not at war with. Masferrer was behind an aborted invasion of Cuba last October."

"They're planning one of his own for christsakes! What kind of goddamn principles do those guys operate under?"

"Don't muddle the issue with the facts."

"And Kennedy's letting this happen? I thought you said he was on board."

"He is. But he has to make it look like he's not."

What a fucking world. Washington was making Castro look like the tooth fairy. "Sanchez," I sighed, "just call Masferrer."

"Okay, but things are really heating up around here. We're not sure how deep Hoover's fangs are into this. Even though we keep sweeping our office and home phones, we can't be sure he doesn't have a spy inside the Agency."

"How the hell are we gonna talk to you? I can't keep using my brother."

"I'll arrange another cut-out. But I don't think it'll be long before we're ready and get a go-ahead. We came up with another plan and we'll be calling a meeting in Miami in a few weeks."

"Okay, I'll spread the word. But the longer we wait, the more rumblings come out about an invasion, and Castro's got big ears in Miami.

CHAPTER 27

MIAMI
MARCH 1961

THE THIRD HEAVYWEIGHT championship fight between Floyd Patterson and Ingemar Johansson on March 13 had the city going wild. Made men from all over the country packed the Fontainebleau's Boom-Boom Room, but very few knew that Giancana was once again installed in the penthouse suite.

Trafficante was with him when Roselli and I arrived. Maheu got there later with a stranger wearing a suit and carrying a briefcase, and introduced him.

"This is Jim O'Connell. Harvey sent him with the product."

We took seats around the art deco coffee table, and O'Connell opened his briefcase. He removed a matchbook-sized metal case, opened it, and showed it to us, saying, "Six pills... Botulinum, a powerful nerve toxin, soluble in liquid, or ground up can be added to food. You're to deliver them to Juan Orta, and..."

Giancana interrupted. "Who's Orta?"

"Castro's disgruntled private secretary. When Castro shuttered your gambling casinos, it ended his huge kickbacks. Like you, he wants them re-opened, and he's willing to help kill his boss to make it happen. The chef of a restaurant frequented by Castro is in his pocket. The chef will put the ground pills in Castro's food. Your job is to have your people in

Havana get them out of the country."

Roselli asked, "Where do we find Orta?"

"At the moment he's here in Miami on a mission for Castro." He showed us a photo of a bearded man with brown curly hair and thick glasses. "Normally he's clean shaven, has black hair and doesn't wear glasses. He wears this disguise in Miami because the exiles know what he looks like."

Roselli studied the picture. "How do we reach him?"

O'Connell handed him a folded sheet of paper. "He can be reached at this number." He dumped the remaining contents of his briefcase on the coffee table—ten banded packets of hundred dollar bills. "And give him this. Ten thousand in cash."

Giancana was dubious. "Is this guy reliable? Who knows him?"

Trafficante answered. "I do. I was the guy who paid him off for the Syndicate. When we got shut down, he lost one helluva cash cow. He wants it back. What's the time frame?"

O'Connell said, "Three weeks. Four on the outside."

Giancana got up. "Good enough… Johnny, you handle the meetin'." He asked Maheu, "That do it?"

Maheu nodded and left with O'Connell.

Trafficante asked Roselli, "You want me to set up a quiet place for the meet?"

Roselli shook his head. "No… I'll use the Boom-Boom Room."

Giancana exploded. "What? Christ—the fights on closed circuit TV in there! Half of Miami'll see you guys."

Roselli smiled. "It won't matter. The exiles can't make him because of the disguise, but the CIA knows exactly what he looks like. They just showed his picture. I'll get a shot of me with Orta—a guy Langley's in bed with. More solid proof that we're all in this together."

Giancana let out a guffaw. "Fuckin' genius!"

Trafficante added, "Excellent, Johnny… I don't trust those assholes as far as I can throw the hotel."

Roselli gave them a short, mock bow. "Thank you… And I'll bring

Dante and his girlfriend along so we can get a group shot for posterity."

Ten minutes later Roselli had Orta on the phone and told him to be in the Boom-Boom Room at eight o'clock. He agreed and said he appreciated the opportunity to see the fight.

I'd called Marissa before I left L.A. and told her I'd be there as soon as my meeting ended. I was at her house at five, and an hour later we were having a drink on the patio, satiated and disheveled. I told her about Orta and the poison pills. She was hopeful but, because of so many past failures, unenthusiastic.

"I'll light a candle for him… But have you heard what happened yesterday?"

"About what?"

"Who," she corrected. " You remember William Morgan and Jesus Carreras?"

"Sure—Morgan's the American who renounced his citizenship, and joined Castro. Then he defected with Carreras. They were caught."

"They were tortured for four months, tried for treason yesterday, and shot last night."

"Jesus. More revolutionary justice."

"Yes…but they were two of the very important men we were depending upon to cause havoc behind Castro's lines during the invasion. They're few but critically important allies, and I'm getting very concerned. The closer we get to D-day, the faster he's taking out our support inside Cuba. "

"There's not a hell of a lot we can do about it. The train's left the station, and unless I'm sorely mistaken, there's no stopping it."

Roselli and Orta were in the overflowing Boom-Boom Room when Marissa and I arrived. The crowd was getting ready to watch the fight on TV screens mounted around the room. Bookies circulated, taking bets in the charged atmosphere, and cigar smoke was dense enough to justify scuba gear.

Roselli introduced Marissa and me as his associates. Orta shook our hands as we squeezed around a ridiculously small table. Roselli pulled out a bottle of champagne and filled our glasses while simultaneously signaling for another bottle, then playfully clapped Orta on the arm.

"Juan's a little nervous, but I gave him the items and told him we have to see results in a few weeks."

"You sure you can handle that?" I asked.

Orta nodded his head. "Yes. It will not be a problem."

Roselli again clapped him on the shoulder. "That's the spirit! Now—how about a memento?" He signaled a house photographer, and before Orta could mount an objection, Roselli, Marissa, and I squeezed around the startled man, and the flashbulb went off.

Two hours later, Patterson had defeated Johansson, and Marissa and I were back in bed.

One month later we learned that Orta got cold feet.

For the time being Castro remained indestructible.

CHAPTER 28

WASHINGTON
THE OVAL OFFICE
APRIL 1961

"APRIL 17 IS THE LANDING DATE," said Dulles, pointing at a map of Cuba on the Oval Office desk. "About fifteen hundred men in an invasion force called Brigade 2506."

He and Bissell were giving a final briefing to the president, Bobby, McNamara, and McGeorge Bundy on the CIA plan for the invasion of Cuba. Kennedy was aware of the details and wanted something less spectacular. Unbeknownst to Dulles and Bissell, he'd consulted the Joint Chiefs and asked them to come up with a less "noisy" alternative. Rusk, Bowles, and Schlesinger remained opposed to any invasion plan, and were not in attendance.

"You're landing during the day?" asked Kennedy."

"Yes sir," Dulles replied and pointed. "Here. At Trinidad."

"Why there?"

"It's 178 miles southeast of Havana, has the advantages of a harbor, a defensible beachhead, and remoteness from Castro's main army. It also has easy access to the protective Escambray Mountains, so if for some reason, the invasion force becomes bogged down, they can retreat and become guerillas."

Bobby looked at Bissell. "And the chances of that happening?"

"Slim."

The president said, "In that case I suggest we land somewhere that doesn't create as much 'noise' and has a better chance of masking our role. A brigade-sized invasion in a populated area in broad daylight all but guarantees we supported it."

Dulles glanced at Bissell and back to Kennedy. "You have an alternative?"

The president nodded and pointed at the Bay of Pigs. "Here. It's remote and has a suitable airstrip on the beach that can be used for the brigade's aircraft after the landing."

Bissell said, "But it's over thirty–five miles from the Escambray Mountains. It would be impossible for the invasion force to retreat to them from that far away."

Bobby snapped back. "I thought you said the need for that eventuality was slim."

Bissell reddened. "I did. But the plan has always called for a second option."

Booby's response was brusque. "It's also always called for plausible deniability of any U.S. involvement. The Bay of Pigs gives us a far better chance for that. Again—the political fallout resulting from our perceived participation in an invasion is unacceptable."

The president nodded agreement. "But after the landing, gentlemen, your plan essentially remains the same. The CIA will set up the Cuban Revolutionary Council as a provisional Cuban government-in-arms once the beach is secured. We'll immediately recognize the CRC as the legitimate government—they'll request military support—and we'll respond with 15,000 marines from the aircraft carrier *Essex* task force. But in order to further ensure complete surprise and a successful landing, I want invasion to take place at night."

Dulles was temporarily speechless.

Bissell was aghast. "Mr. President, a vital part of the plan is the assumption that as soon as the population becomes *aware* of the invasion, there will be a mass uprising that will join the invading forces. A night landing in a remote area eliminates that objective."

"No—our allies on the island in addition to our radio transmitters will spread the word quickly enough."

The CIA men knew when they were outgunned. It was obvious that deniability was foremost in the president's mind.

Dulles nodded. "Yes sir. A night landing at the Bay of Pigs."

McNamara asked, "Who's your man with the exiles?"

"E. Howard Hunt. He was involved in the plan to overthrow Guzmán in Guatemala, had assignments in Japan, and was the CIA station chief in Uruguay."

Bundy said, "Let's talk about the air strikes."

Bissell nodded. "Two are planned. The first—two days before the invasion. B-26s camouflaged to look like Cuban Air Force bombers will attack the bases at Santiago and San Antonio de Los Banos. They will appear to be flown from Cuba by Cuban defectors shooting up their own airfields. It will further prove that the invasion is solely a Cuban operation." He paused, looked at Bobby and pointedly said, "And therefore will give us further plausible deniability."

It was Bobby's turn to redden, but he said, "Excellent."

Kennedy asked a perceptive question. "You're not concerned that the D-day minus two air strikes might alert Castro to the invasion?"

Dulles said, "There is that chance." But then he seized the opportunity to ingratiate himself to Bobby. "However, I think the political considerations outweigh the operational ones. "The attack will be viewed as Cubans flying Cuban aircraft and will cause turmoil in the ranks. The planes will actually be flown out of Nicaragua, and when the mission is completed, they'll return. However, at dawn on D-day, they'll fly the real missions that will take out Castro's air force prior to the landings."

When the meeting ended, no one seemed to realize the full import of what had been decided. An invasion that had been in the planning stages for over a year had been tragically revised in under an hour.

The new plan, named *Zapata*, moved the landing to an isolated and sparsely populated area at night, allowing no chance for it to be seen by Cubans who were to launch the uprising that everyone agreed was crucial to success. And since the Bay of Pigs was thirty-five miles from the Escambray Mountains, any chance of Brigade 2506 retreating to them was non-existent.

Two days later, on April 12, invasion allegations were leaked to *The New York Times*. President Kennedy responded directly saying: "First, I want to say that there will not be, under any circumstances, an intervention in Cuba by the United States Armed Forces."

Little attention was paid to his denial. Even Cuba might not have been paying attention. Because that same day the Soviet Union ushered in a new era.

Yuri Gagarin became the first man in space.

CHAPTER 29

MIAMI

"I WANT TO *BE* THERE WHEN you set up the provisional government, become president, and move inland!" barked Marissa, her voice insistent and firm.

"Impossible," responded Dr. José Miró Cardona. He vigorously pointed to his watch. "It's ten a.m. here—nine in Guatemala! The invasion force will be leaving the Retalhuleu camps in a matter of hours. In two days they board the boats in Nicaragua and set sail for Cuba."

Miró was the head of the CRC and he was with Rafael Sanchez and Jim O'Connell, who were in town to monitor the preparations. They were in the CIA's Miami headquarters known as JM/WAVE, located on the South Campus of the University of Miami. It contained a powerful radio whose sole mission was to undermine the Cuban government, had over five hundred employees, and a budget of fifty million dollars. It was the largest clandestine CIA station in the world and it was illegal. The CIA was not authorized to operate within the U.S.

Marissa said, "I can be in Nicaragua in two days."

"It's too dangerous."

Marissa remained insistent. "I won't be going ashore with the men. I'll stay on one of the transports. I've done everything all of you have asked from the beginning, José, and asked for nothing in return. Do this one thing for me."

An exasperated Miró said, "Marissa. It's possible those ships will come under fire. I lost two of my dearest friends when your mother and father disappeared. I couldn't bear also losing you."

"Thank you for you concern. But I'm aware of the danger, and it doesn't frighten me. Are you forgetting I volunteered to become an assassin? This will be the beginning of the end, and I have a right to be there."

Miró turned to Sanchez, completely frustrated. "You talk to her."

"He's right, Marissa...but I'll tell you what we'll do. Let us contact Artime. He'll be leading the invasion force, and if he gives his permission, you can go."

Marissa nodded her reluctant acceptance. "Call him, I'll wait." Leaving the office, she said, "If I'm going to be in Nicaragua in two days, I have to leave today."

Sanchez called Artime at his Guatemala camp and, after determining that everything was proceeding on schedule, told him what Marissa had requested, and why.

Surprisingly, Artime seemed amenable, and asked, "And she'll remain on the transport until the beach is secure and we move inland?"

"That's what she said."

"I don't see that it could hurt. She's motivated and proved to be both brave and resourceful during her last trip to Cuba. Who knows what we may run into when the population revolts and joins us? She could prove useful."

Sanchez was taken aback. "You approve?"

"Why not? She'll be out of the way on a transport, and as I said, she might be useful later. Does she want Amato to join her again?"

"She didn't mention him."

"Find out if he'll come along. When we re-take Havana we'll want to re-open the casinos and get things back to normal as soon as possible. He knows the former operators and can lay the groundwork for their return."

"All right, I'll call him,"

Artime said, "Alone or with him, have her fly into Managua. I'll send a plane to pick her up and take her here."

CHAPTER 30

BEVERLY HILLS

My PHONE RANG, WOKE me up at seven-thirty, and Sanchez told me what Artime wanted Marissa and me to do. I was groggy for all of ten seconds before I blew my stack.

"Are you guys fucking nuts? You want to send a woman on an invasion?"

"We don't want—she wants."

"Then you're both fucking nuts! She for asking—you for agreeing!"

"I didn't agree—Artime did."

"I don't give a shit who did. This is a CIA operation, and we both know it. Stop this insanity if you've got a brain cell left."

Sanchez sighed. "I take it you don't want to go along."

"I don't want *either* of us to go along!"

"Hold on... I'll pass along your answer."

I heard him telling Miró he was on the phone with me, and I didn't want to go. Apparently Marissa had entered the room and it was her turn to explode. Her angry voice came over the phone loud and clear.

"You asked Dante to come with me?"

"*Artime* asked me to ask Dante to come with you." Sanchez sounded pissed about being in the middle of something he had nothing to do with, and I continued to listen to the argument.

"Did either of you consider what *I* may have thought since it was my request?"

"At this point it's academic. He doesn't want to go and you don't want him."

"I didn't say that."

By now Sanchez was completely frustrated. "You *do* want him?"

"What I want is to let him know it wasn't my idea to call him. Give me that phone!" I heard the sound of the phone being grabbed and Marissa spat out, "It wasn't my idea!"

"Marissa—what the hell's going on?"

"I'm going with the Brigade. But I didn't ask for you to come along. Artime did."

I tried to remain calm. "Marissa… It's an invasion. You have no business putting yourself in that kind of jeopardy."

"After what I was prepared to do when we were in Cuba together, I would think you'd understand."

"I understand the commitment, but not your death wish!"

"Life wish, Dante. Don't fight me on this. This is my country. I don't want to give up what we have, but this is my priority right now. I'm sorry.

Her plea softened me. "All right, Marissa. I'll try to understand… How are you getting to Nicaragua?"

"I'll book the American flight to Managua and be there by midnight. Artime will have a plane pick me up in the morning and take me to the coast."

"Leave the name of the hotel where you'll be staying at the American counter in Managua."

"Why?"

"So I can meet you there."

CHAPTER 31

NICARAGUA

A B-26 FLEW MARISSA AND ME to Puerto Cabezas from Managua the morning of April 14. The plane was a "Martin Marauder," one of sixteen in Manuel Artime's air force—a World War II twin-engine bomber that was basically obsolete.

The day before, I'd had a long wait for a connecting flight through Mexico City and arrived in Managua late. Marissa was waiting up for me at the hotel, I refrained from telling her how stupid I thought the idea was, and after an unusually short reunion, we fell asleep in each other's arms. We showered at sunrise, dressed in khaki jumpsuits and baseball caps, and left for the airport.

Artime was in a jovial mood when the B-26 landed at Puerto Cabezas, and he rushed to embrace us. "Marissa—Dante! Welcome!" he boomed, "Let the adventure begin!"

Marissa squeezed his hand. "We're honored to be a part of it."

I pointed at fifteen more B-26s parked in rows and being loaded with bombs. Disturbed by the fact that there were no fighter aircraft—much less any jets, I asked, "Is that it?"

Artime nodded and chuckled. "Our air force? Yes. They're old, but they're the type flown by the Cuban Air Force and painted in their colors."

"No fighters?"

"No, but we don't think that will be a problem because we intend to destroy their air force on the ground. He called to a captain who was standing by one of the aircraft. The cowling of its left engine had been removed and placed on the ground. "Mario! Come here a moment."

The pilot walked over wearing a Cheshire cat smile, and Artime introduced us.

"Marissa del Valle and Dante Amato—Captain Mario Zuniga." Artime chuckled, "Our secret weapon."

Zuniga extended his hand. "A pleasure to…"

He was interrupted by a burst of machine-gun fire. We all turned toward Zuniga's B-26. A mechanic had just riddled the removed cowling of its left engine and was inspecting the holes. He nodded to another mechanic and they began to remount the riddled cowling on the engine.

Marissa and I turned to Artime with a questioning look.

Artime laughed. "Tomorrow, while a few other planes are *actually* bombing Cuban air fields, Mario will fly that plane on a solo, low level mission across the westernmost province of Cuba and then turn for Key West. He will climb high enough to be picked up by U.S. radar, feather the engine with the bullet holes in the cowling and declare an emergency. He'll then land at the Boca Chica Naval Air Station as a Cuban defector, flying a Cuban Air Force plane that was almost shot down while bombing his own air fields."

Zuniga grinned and bowed. "I promise to look very shaken-up for the press." His grin faded as another officer ran up waving a sheet of paper.

"Manuel! Manuel!" He stopped in front of Artime, breathing hard. "This just came in… Only eight planes will be allowed to make the D-day air strikes!"

Artime snatched away the paper and began to read.

The officer continued for Zuniga's benefit, "It's an order from Washington. The president is concerned that all sixteen will constitute a major raid and signal U.S. involvement."

Artime reddened and crushed the paper in his hand. "Always deniability!" He sighed and composed himself. "Tomorrow's small strike that allows Mario's mission to Key West will give them their damned deniability. But the critical strike that destroys their air force will be on D-day, and we'll make do with eight planes."

An hour later, Marissa and I boarded one of the transports that were preparing to take Brigade 2506 to the Bay of Pigs. There were four 2400-ton ships plus two CIA-owned landing craft carrying supplies, ordinance, and equipment that would support the 1511 man invasion force.

Our ship had seen better days, and when we reached the top of the gangplank, we were greeted by chipped paint, rust, and E. Howard Hunt, a good-looking man exuding confidence.

He smiled broadly as he extended his hand to Marissa. "Sanchez told me you'd be coming along—Howard Hunt." He was obviously disappointed that she was with me. "You must be Amato."

I had an immediate distaste for the man. "Dante will do."

Hunt ignored the remark and attempted to impress Marissa. "I'll be going ashore immediately after we establish a beachhead to set-up the government-in-exile." Turning to me, he sniffed, "I understand you're going ashore much later, after we move into Havana, to oversee the re-opening of some casinos."

"I hope to get the chance."

Hunt thought he smelled a defeatist. "You think you won't?"

I smiled. "I'm a gambler, my friend. But I don't bet on hard eights or draw to inside straights."

"You think we're facing long odds?"

"Overconfidence is risky."

"Doubt is dangerous."

Marissa interrupted the testosterone duel. "Howard… Can you tell us where we'll be berthed during the crossing?"

"One deck below. Cabins have been set up for VIPs." He glanced at me and back to Marissa. "Will you require one or two?"

Marissa smiled. "One."

CHAPTER 32

THE PRESIDENT SLAMMED the newspaper on his desk and glowered at Bissell. It was Saturday, April 15, and he sensed that his worst nightmare was just beginning.

"How the hell could this have happened?"

On the front page of the paper was a picture of Captain Mario Zuniga standing next to the bullet- riddled cowling of his B-26. As planned, while a few other B-26s were masquerading as Cuban planes with Cuban pilots bombing their own airfields, Zuniga had flown to Boca Chica. He told the bogus story that he was almost shot down in the raid but had escaped and managed to fly his damaged plane to safety.

"Mr. President," replied a humbled Bissell, "I…"

"Is your entire goddamn agency blind? Look at this picture! It's a B-26 with a solid metal nose! An *American* B-26! Didn't anyone planning this strike know that Cuban B-26s have *Plexiglas* noses?"

The press had almost immediately seen through Zuniga's lie when they identified the bomber as American and asked Zuniga pointed questions about the plane and the raid. He, of course, had difficulty answering their questions, and they'd broken a huge story.

In the Oval Office there was a massive clean-up underway. Bobby and McGeorge Bundy were witnessing the tongue-lashing. Bundy was in shock, Bissell was absorbing the full brunt of Kennedy's tirade and Dulles, inexplicably, was in Europe.

"Sir…" said Bissell, trying to remain calm. "The planes came from…"

"I know where they came from! And so does everyone else. *Here*!" The president paced behind his desk while he continued his tirade. "Castro let the world know at six o'clock this morning that his airports had been bombed and immediately accused us of the raid. Worse—Stevenson has just flatly rejected Cuba's accusation that they were our planes in the U.N. and held up *this* photograph to prove his point!"

Bundy sheepishly said, "Stevenson was totally in the dark because no one thought to inform him of the invasion."

The president said, "Unfucking believable!"

Bobby asked, "Do you think we should call it off?"

Bissell, clearly shocked by the suggestion, said, "Mr. President, the ships have already left Nicaragua."

"Ships can be turned around," snapped Kennedy.

"I know sir, but there's still a good chance for success. The damage reports indicate that a majority of Castro's air force was destroyed on the ground during the first small strike. The rest will surely be taken out on the larger D-day strike. With surprise and air superiority the invasion force should be able to secure the beaches before Castro can respond."

Kennedy fumed. "How can you say we'll achieve surprise? We just bombed his airfields!"

"Yes, sir. But he can't be sure it's a prelude to invasion, and in any event, he can't know when or where we're landing. The Bay of Pigs, as you know, is an obscure area, which is the reason we chose it." Bissell wanted to say, "the reason *you* chose it," but didn't want to further infuriate the president.

Kennedy asked, "Where are the other B-26s that conducted the raid?"

"They've returned to Nicaragua where they'll be re-loaded for the dawn strike on D-day."

At nine thirty that evening, Bundy, probably reacting to the president's fury, put in a call to General C.P. Cabell, Deputy Director of the CIA. In Dulles's absence, he was the Agency's senior man.

"Charles, as you've probably heard, the president was furious over the Zuniga fiasco. The second strike has to be cancelled."

Cabell was shocked. "What?"

"Not completely. Instead of the planes taking off and bombing from Nicaragua, they'll wait until the beachhead is secured and take off from the Bay of Pigs. There's a suitable landing strip there, which is one of the reasons the president selected the site."

"But that would mean there would be no *dawn* strike *prior* to the landings."

"True, but since the majority of Castro's air force has already been taken out, it shouldn't be important. The benefit however will be very important. It will mean that the aircraft took off from Cuba—making the strike a *Cuban* attack, thus giving the president the deniability that's so vital to him."

"Good point, but I have to take it up with Bissell—this is his operation."

Bissell was aghast when he heard the news. He sputtered, "This couldn't have just come from Bundy—it had to come from the president. He knows there a landing strip on the bay. It was one of the reasons he chose it!"

He slammed down the phone, but remembering the president's rage over Zuniga, and not wanting to confront him directly, called Rusk and asked him to phone the president and rescind the order.

Rusk listened and said, "But there will still be a second strike. For the obvious reasons, I think it's a *good* idea for the planes to take off from Cuban soil."

Bissell tried to control himself. "But it has to be *before* the beaches are secured. It's vital that it occur at dawn to insure that *not just the majority but all* Castro's aircraft were destroyed before they can take off."

Rusk said, "If you feel that strongly, I have no objection to your calling the president directly."

Knowing the president's mood, and not wanting to endure another tirade, Bissell didn't make the call.

CHAPTER 33

THE BAY OF PIGS

SHORTLY BEFORE MIDNIGHT on Sunday, April 16, while the invasion force bobbed about five thousand yards off the coast, Marissa and I watched a team of frogmen leave their transport and head for shore. We were on the *Atlántico*'s bridge and hadn't heard Hunt come up behind us.

"They're going to set up lights on the primary landing zone at Playa Girón beach," he said, trying to impress Marissa again. "To guide in our men. And at Playa Larga, twenty-two miles northwest of here, we're staging a diversionary landing in fiberglass boats."

During the crossing from Nicaragua, Hunt had continued his advances, and she'd enjoyed diplomatically repelling them.

I smiled. "I'm surprised you're not going with them."

"My involvement here," he said airily, "is infinitely more important."

Even more airily, I said, " Oh, no doubt."

Two hours later, the signal lights from the beach began flashing, and the ships started toward the landing zone. Hunt had left, but Artime had joined us.

"I can't believe the hour is here! We're doing it, my friends. We're doing it!"

His high spirits were short lived. Within minutes, we heard a humungous metallic screech as the transport directly ahead of us rolled starboard, then stared dumbfounded as it settled into a ten-degree list.

I said, "Christ—I think she's hit a reef!"

"Impossible," cried Artime, We have U-2 photos that show nothing but seaweed!"

I said, "They obviously misread them. What they must have identified as seaweed beds are coral reefs!"

The remaining ships continued inbound and began lowering their troop-laden landing craft. They started toward the landing zone and all went smoothly until they were eighty yards from the beach. Two LCIs accompanying the landing craft also ran into the reefs.

Minutes later, the radio squawked, and we heard from Playa Larga.

"This is Benitez! We've been spotted! We're taking small arms fire, but I think we can make it ashore!"

I said, "It's the diversionary force. You'd want them spotted, no?"

Artime replied, "Not yet. We wanted the main force completely ashore before they made their presence known at dawn."

An hour later the two LCIs that ran aground had to be abandoned and some heavy equipment was lost. About five hundred men managed to keep going and got to the beach. But they immediately began taking fire and were temporarily pinned down.

I shook my head. "So much for the element of surprise."

Artime pounded his fist on the bridge rail. "We were supposed to have guerillas behind the beaches to interdict any opposing force! Where are they?"

José Basulto, leader of the guerilla group in charge of the interdiction, inexplicably, like Stevenson, had never been told when the invasion would begin. Surprised that it had, and having no time to complete his mission, he drove to Guantánamo and jumped the fence. As a result, when the fiberglass boats were reported coming ashore at Playa Larga and a second invasion was reported at Playa Girón, Castro rushed tanks and troops to both beaches and there were no guerillas to interdict them.

As dawn approached, Artime, Marissa, and I heard frantic radio calls from the first battalion that had landed. They'd managed to fight their way inland a few miles but were reporting heavy resistance and a forced retreat. The men who had landed a short time later were still pinned down on the beach.

Artime was unbelievably distraught but turned to Marissa and me saying, "The sun is coming up. Our B-26s will be here in minutes and turn the battle around!"

I said, "Pray you're right. We're taking a whipping that'll..."

The roar of a jet engine interrupted me and I saw a plane dead ahead, fifty feet over the water. It was headed directly toward the bow of our ship.

I screamed," Get down!" and threw myself at Artime and Marissa, pulling them off the bridge wing and into the wheelhouse.

Seconds later, .50 caliber bullets raked the ship from stem to stern.

I yelled, "Jets! T-33 trainers armed with fifty caliber machine guns. Is anybody hurt?"

Marissa shook her head. "Just a few scrapes."

Artime growled, "I'm fine."

But the situation on the beach was not.

The brigade's air force hadn't appeared at sunup, but Castro's air force had—Hawker Sea Furies, B-26s, and T-33s.

Artime screamed, "Those planes were supposed to be destroyed on the ground!"

The planes strafed the beach and then attacked the support ships. The *Marsopa* and *Rio Escondido* were hit, and the *Houston* was crippled.

Artime cried, "The field hospital is on the *Houston*. Without it we have no way to treat our causalities."

Marissa pointed. "It's headed for the beach. I think the captain's grounding her."

He didn't quite make it. The ship smashed into coral reefs and began settling. Most of the men from the 5th battalion were able to get off the *Houston,* but they were unable to get organized ashore, and ceased to be a factor.

By mid-morning the doctors on the beaches were overwhelmed with casualties and didn't have the medical supplies that were lost when the *Houston* foundered. Radio equipment had been brought ashore but was soaked with salt water and inoperable.

Hunt re-appeared on the bridge and Artime screamed at him. "Where were the bombers you promised? Where!"

A subdued and chastened Hunt replied, "I don't know. I'm still trying to get through to Bissell. They're all at the White House."

Artime screamed, "They're sacrificing everything! Cuba! The men! God damn them to hell!" He whirled around yelling, "I'm going ashore!" and dashed off the bridge heading aft for the boat waiting to take him in when a beachhead was established.

I turned to Hunt, "You want me to try to get through to my brother? He might know what going on."

Hunt shook his head. "This is way above your brother's pay grade. From what I could find out, it's total turmoil back there with accusations and denials flying back and forth between Washington and Moscow."

The next twenty-four hours were horrible. The *Rio Escondido* was hit by a rocket that ignited 200 gallons of aviation fuel stored on its deck. It sank, and the *Caribe* began a retreat to international waters. The three lost ships were carrying the fuel, food, ammunition, and medical supplies needed for the first ten days of the invasion.

Artime radioed us at sunset. He was distraught. Castro had over 20,000 troops encircling the beachheads and his aircraft continued to control the skies, but he vowed to fight on. The brigade fought all through the night, but by mid-morning, Cuban troops, supported by tanks, took Playa Larga.

During the second day and into the night we continued to hear radio calls for help, ammunition, and medical supplies.

I said, "It's not good."

Hunt nodded. "They won't be able to hold out much longer."

Marissa seethed, "Dammit Hunt! This is your operation. Is there nothing the CIA can do?"

"Not without orders from the White House. And there's no chance they'll be coming."

On the morning of the third day we watched the final chapter.

Without direct air support, and short of ammunition, Brigade 2506 retreated to the beaches in the face of a massive onslaught from Cuban artillery, tanks, and infantry.

"It's over," said Hunt.

Marissa whispered, "God help those men."

The invasion was crushed later that day.

We soon learned that of the 1,511 troops in the brigade, 1,297 made it to the beaches. Two hundred were killed in the land battle, and about a hundred were killed at sea. Some deserted, and a few escaped with us in the *Atlántico* and other surviving boats.

One of the escapees reported that early in the fight his men had captured a Cuban militiaman stationed at Playa Larga. The man proudly admitted he'd spotted the bobbing ships around midnight of the first day and fiberglass boats coming ashore a short time later. He'd called Havana and reported that the invasion had begun.

Castro had responded instantly by sending troops and tanks. The Cuban Army—unhindered by interdicting guerillas—predicted defections—or a rebelling population—had rushed to repel Brigade 2506.

When the exiles surrendered, 1,180 were taken prisoner, and under brutal interrogation, most confessed their connection to the CIA.

CHAPTER 34

MIAMI AND CORAL GABLES

DURING THE RETURN TO Miami, I was bitterly reproachful and Hunt nervously defensive, but Marissa was despondent. I figured it best to stay over in Miami a few days. Sanchez and Harvey had returned to Washington, and Hunt flew off to join them as soon as we docked. The senior survivors immediately went to CRC headquarters to give a firsthand account of the failed invasion. News of the brigade's fate had arrived, and recriminations ran rampant in the exile community. The report that Kennedy had cancelled the vital D-day air strike sent them into a rage.

It was dark when we got to Marissa's house, and she hadn't spoken a word since the surrender. I settled her into a patio chair, and she stared into the middle distance.

I asked Adelaida to make our drinks, and I put a Mojito in Marissa's hand. Her fingers closed around the glass, but she didn't drink.

I pleaded with her softly. "Marissa… You're home now."

She said, "I know. I just want to be quiet for a while. Is that all right?"

"Of course. We'll just sit here."

The warm, night breeze in the leaves was the only noise until she turned her thoughts to Kennedy.

"They'll never forgive him…"

Knowing whom she meant, I said, "No. They won't, I think… "

"But we'll never give up…"

"I know, there'll be a new brigade and…"

She wasn't hearing me. "We'll have to do something for the widows…" The glow of the landscape lights was giving her face an ethereal quality and she seemed to be thinking out loud.

I tried to soothe her. "I'm sure that…"

"And the families…"

"Washington will…"

"Castro might execute the prisoners…"

She still wasn't hearing me. I said, "Marissa. Stop it."

"Please… just leave me. I want to sleep."

"Let me call a doctor…"

"I don't need anything. Please, I just want to sit here…"

I was about to argue but thought better of it. I nodded, kissed her on the cheek, and finally left.

Adelaida was in the kitchen. She put down the dishcloth as soon as I entered. "Adelaida, I'd like you to do something for me."

"Of course. Anything."

"Marissa's had a very bad shock."

"I know… We all have." Her eyes became moist. "My nephew was with the Brigade."

I said, "I'm sorry…" and hugged her.

"We're praying for them."

"I'm sure the government will try to get the prisoners back."

She crossed herself. "Maybe you will light a candle for them."

"I promise."

"Thank you… What is it you'd like me to do?"

"I want you and Marissa to keep each other company tonight. You understand each other's pain. I think it would help."

She nodded. "Of course. I will do it."

"Good… and maybe right now you could make yourself a drink and join her on the patio."

She smiled and I kissed her cheek. "I'll be staying at the Fontainebleau. I'll be back in the morning."

I checked into the hotel, called Roselli, and told him I was back in Miami. He'd obviously heard the news reports, and told me to stay put. He and Giancana were coming to Miami in a couple of days to meet with Harvey and Sanchez. We'd be deciding our next move. *They'd* lost a battle—not us.

The following morning Marissa looked a bit better. She and Adelaida were having coffee on the patio. As soon as she saw me, Adelaida smiled, got up, and left. I kissed Marissa on the cheek and sat opposite her.

She said, "I spoke to Miró this morning." Her voice was emotionless. "He and the CRC are furious with Kennedy over the cancelled air strikes. They believe it's the root of the failure." She could have been reading a laundry list.

I said, "I don't disagree."

"He's going to Washington, and I'm going with them."

"Oh? When?"

"Today."

"I don't think..."

She interrupted, her voice stronger. "We leave at five."

"What's Miró hope to accomplish?"

"He wants to see the president."

"Really? With the world in an uproar about U.S. involvement, an exile leader wants to show up at the White House?"

"He thinks the president will see him out of guilt for betraying us."

"You really believe Washington's going to be righteous? They just sacrificed their own men to save face."

"He wants to pressure Kennedy to lead international clamoring for the release of the prisoners."

"Noble, but..."

"I'm going because I want to do something for those men, for Adelaida's nephew."

"I understand. But do one thing for me. Listen to why I think you should stay here."

She shook her head. "Out of the question, Dante. And if you can't support me, or stand aside, I won't be able to see you for a while."

"What?"

"God is punishing me. First the fall of my country, then my parents, then our failure, and then the Brigade's."

"I didn't know you were religious."

"I was brought up in a strict Catholic family. I've not been a good Catholic, but old beliefs die hard."

I didn't know what to say. I thought the Washington trip would only result in more frustration, but arguing might be worse than letting her go.

"All right… If that's what you want. Call me when you get there. I have a brother in Chevy Chase if you need anything. I don't know if he'd want to help, but it can't hurt."

"I'm sorry Dante…"

"So am I."

I kissed her cheek and left to get very, very drunk.

CHAPTER 35

"I EARNESTLY APPEAL TO YOU, Mr. President, to call a halt to the aggression against the Republic of Cuba. The military techniques and the world political situation now are such that any so-called 'small-war' can produce a chain reaction in all parts of the world."

Dean Rusk lowered his copy of *The New York Times* he'd been reading aloud, and said, "It's an obvious threat to invade West Berlin."

Rusk was there with the president, along with Bobby, McNamara, Chester Bowles, McGeorge Bundy, and Schlesinger. *The Times* had printed an exchange of letters between Khrushchev and Kennedy that had taken place on the second day of the invasion. Kennedy had answered, "I have previously stated and I repeat now that the United States intends no military intervention in Cuba."

Bowles said, "Your answer was technically accurate for the Russians, but it reads as an outright betrayal to Miami's exiles. We'd led them to believe we'd send in the Marines if the invasion got into trouble."

Tension in the White House had been palpable in the days following the Bay of Pigs. Bobby's anger since the debacle was barely controlled. He growled at Bowles. "We could have! *If* they'd set up a government in exile as soon as they landed and asked for recognition and help!"

McNamara shook his head. "They never got the chance. Everything we'd been told would happen when the invasion began—didn't. Castro's army didn't defect, there was no uprising, no guerilla action, and his air force wasn't destroyed."

Bowles noted, "The Joint Chiefs still believe we should have reversed our order forbidding any overt American intervention," He shook his head in disgust. "A condition *they* insisted on prior to the invasion!"

Kennedy's military advisers, once it became obvious the landings were doomed, had come to him and argued that he had to junk the original plan and send in American reinforcements to save the prestige of the United States. He'd rejected their plea.

"I was right then and I'm right now," argued the president, "You saw the firestorm over one American B-26 exposed at Boca Chica—imagine the world's reaction if I sent in 15,000 Marines."

Bowles said, "Horrific. Unfortunately the CRC doesn't see it that way. Miró Cardona's called. He wants an audience."

Schlesinger frowned. "I don't think that's wise. He's a well-known exile leader and…"

"It's too late to hide, Arthur. Schedule it. I'll state my regrets and admit my responsibility to all comers."

Rusk again held up a copy of *The Times*. "There's also a story in here saying we're blaming Eisenhower for the failure since the invasion was planned on his watch, and by his people. It says the leak came from a White House staffer."

Kennedy bristled. "Find out who's responsible for the leak. I don't want to hear any more about Eisenhower being responsible!"

Bobby, in an effort to shift the blame away from his brother, stated the obvious. "But everybody already knows the invasion was planned during Ike's administration."

"I don't care. I'll take the defeat, and I'll take the blame for it."

Bobby didn't give up easily. "And the CIA?"

"A complete overhaul. Initiate an Inspector General's report on the entire Cuban affair, and when the time comes I'll want the resignations of everyone responsible for the debacle—starting with Dulles, Bissell, and Cabell."

Bundy had misread Kennedy's orders. "You want to cease any further planning to get rid of Castro?"

"On the contrary. I want to *increase* planning. But I want it done by people who know what the hell they're doing! Castro has to go. Now more than ever he'll want to put Cuba into bed with the Russians and longer he stays the stronger he'll get." He turned to his brother. "This time keep the CIA on a very short leash and give the job to the Joint Chiefs. It'll give them something better to do than second guessing their own advice. And I want you in overall charge."

It was immediately obvious to all concerned that Kennedy had no intention of allowing Castro to remain in power. His young administration had been seriously bruised by the Bay of Pigs fiasco, and he was determined to erase the stain by removing the cause.

CHAPTER 36

MIAMI

"UNBELIEVABLE... CUBELA! The guy who sucked us in the last time!"

Sanchez replied, "No. Let's get this straight, now, gentlemen. He's the guy who Masferrer *said* was the guy who sucked us in!"

I said, "What the hell's that supposed to mean?"

Giancana, Trafficante, Roselli, and Harvey watched in silence as Sanchez and I went at it. We were on the Fontainebleau's penthouse patio and they were drinking gin-rickeys. There was a thunderstorm over the Atlantic and the last rays of the sun had tossed a rainbow on the horizon. A beautiful backdrop for an ugly business.

"Look, persisted Sanchez, "Castro's basking in glory right now, and he's proudly told Cubela and everyone close to him that he'll soon declare his revolution Marxist-Leninist."

"Again, what the hell does that have to do with Cubela?"

"Cubela's a nationalist—not a communist. He wants no part of it. He's still willing to help us assassinate Castro for the right price and position in a free Cuba."

"And you've got no problem with his obvious betrayal of Marissa and me when we tried to assassinate Castro?"

"Why would he betray you? What's his motive? To capture two more would-be assassins?"

"Masferrer thinks he's a double agent!"

Sanchez pressed his point. "Masferrer has his own agenda. He wants us to think he's the only one who knows what's really going on in Cuba because he wants the lion's share of our financing. And he definitely does-n't care who he burns to get it."

I threw up my hands. "I don't believe this shit! If Cubela didn't rat us out, Sanchez, then it was someone in your shop. Are you prepared to deal with that? I sure as hell don't want to partner with an agency that doesn't mind feeding me to the sharks. You damn well better…"

Harvey held up his hands. "Relax, Dante, We're trying…"

'Bullshit! Get your head out of your ass, Harvey. There's a rat in your crib. Has your famous spy-catcher gotten even a whiff of who?"

Harvey shook his head. "Calm down, Dante. Have a drink. So far Angleton's come up dry, but he's still digging."

Trafficante nodded. "It could be Masferrer's lying. He's a business partner and I've known him a long time, but he definitely believes the squeaky wheel get the grease. The CIA's money is the grease. The squeakier he gets the more he's greased."

Roselli went to the bar, poured a tumbler full of Jack Daniels and handed it to me. He knew me. If I was skeptical, so was he. "How the hell can we still trust Cubela?"

Sanchez said, "Please, you can't be sure of anything in this business. It's just like yours…"

Giancana scoffed. "Fugetaboutit. In ours, whatever we're not sure about's gone."

Sanchez sighed. "Look, all I know is that this is the second time he's contacted us and the second time he's offered to help us take out of Castro."

Giancana shrugged. "What's to lose? If he's on the level, he helps us take the prick out. If he's not, nothin's lost—we're just back to square one."

I said, "Which genius comes up with the plan to get somebody killed this time?"

Harvey reddened. Using Cubela had been his idea. "We'll use

Cubela again, but this time we'll ask *him* the best way to go. If we like what he says, we'll proceed.

Giancana asked, "How do we contact him?"

Sanchez pointed at Trafficante. "Santo's people in Havana."

I sighed and shook my head. "What makes you guys think taking out Castro is going to change things in Cuba? Without an uprising and a counter-revolution you've got nothing but one dead Commi."

Harvey said, "Because of what we heard in Washington. Kennedy's pulling out all the stops. DOD's been told to come up with an all-out plan that includes that includes NSA, State, and the CIA. They're ordered to make up for the Bay of Pigs failure—re-taking Cuba lock, stock and barrel. That means a government friendly to us, and you getting your casinos back. Killing Castro will only be the first part of it."

That did it. Trafficante and Giancana said they were in, and that meant so were Roselli and I.

I returned to my room and left a message for Aldo at DiGiorno's in Georgetown. He returned the call from a pay phone two hours later.

"What is it?"

"Good evening to you too."

"I'm in no mood for small talk. The shit's hit the fan up here."

"The Bay?"

"Obviously. The word is that a lot of heads are going to roll."

"Yours included?"

"Cuba's not on my watch. But I have friends taking heat—including Cantrell who gave us the Maheu connection... What is it?"

"Something I'm sure you'll be happy to know. The contract on Castro stands."

"At this point, I'm glad to hear it."

"Fine. But my people don't think it'll make any difference unless—and this is what we're being told by your guys down here—there's a balls-to-the-wall effort by Kennedy to finally blow out his revolution and replace it with a friendly government."

"That's what's in the works. All the agencies are part of it, but this time the pointy end of the spear will be DOD, not us, thank God. We'll get involved, but the president isn't very happy with us at the moment."

"So you don't think its bullshit?"

"I think the president would do anything to get rid of Castro. He was saddled with the Bay of Pigs but had to take the rap for it. Now he's determined to extract a pound of flesh to redeem his administration."

I let it all sink in. "Has Marissa called you?

"No. But I know Miró Cardona wants to see the president. He'll be given the Texas two-step, but if he creates enough heat, he'll wind up at Cantrell's doorstep—if Dan's still there."

"Can you help?

"Like I said, Cuba's not on my watch… but I'll give Dan a call."

"Thanks. I owe you one."

"You owe me a helluva lot more than one."

"Say hello to the kids."

I said it to a dead phone.

CHAPTER 37

JAMES JESUS ANGLETON WAS severely frustrated by his inability to track down the spy Sanchez and Harvey suspected lurked within his agency. He'd never recovered from the embarrassment he'd experienced over his failure to uncover Kim Philby. He wasn't fired, but many felt it was due to his friendship with Richard Helms, who many felt would one day become head of the Agency. Angleton was determined not to let another mole slip under his radar. *Everyone* was suspect, and in a mental state bordering on paranoia, he finally went to see Dulles with a request.

Once again suffering from a gout attack, the urbane head of the CIA received Angleton at his Q Street home wearing silk slippers and a robe. It was early evening and he was sitting in a wing chair flanking the fireplace, with his feet on an ottoman. He gently tapped tobacco into his pipe bowl and gave Angleton a warm, welcoming smile.

"Good evening, Jim. May I offer you a drink?"

"No thanks, Allen. Sorry you're suffering again."

"Ah, it comes and goes. Very painful, but you learn to live with it."

"Nonetheless, under the circumstances, I appreciate your seeing me."

"Nonsense—have a seat. What can I do for you?"

Dulles lit his pipe and puffed appreciatively while Angleton settled into an opposing wing chair.

"You know about Marissa del Valle's attempt to assassinate Castro."

Dulles nodded. "I read the Sanchez-Harvey report. I recall a man named Amato was with her, correct?"

"It is... They think they were exposed by a traitor inside Langley."

"They also reported it was possible that this Cubela fellow called Amlash could be a double agent."

Angleton said, "Possible, but I think, not probable. Independent sources maintain he's nationalist, not a communist. And according to Harvey, Hunt, and Sanchez, our three agents closest to the situation, the accusation comes from Masferrer. He's close to Santo Trafficante, an ex-Batista supporter, and a man looking to line his own pockets."

"So you believe the spy is one of ours." Dulles's reply was a statement, not a question.

"I do. And as you know, from the beginning, the entire Cuban operation has been very tightly held."

"What are you saying?"

"This has got to be someone very high up. I'm going to need your authority to do some extraordinary things."

"How extraordinary?"

"I want to wiretap Agency phones. And I want to use the FBI to monitor the taps so that our own people have no knowledge of the operation."

Dulles was shocked. What?"

Angleton was prepared for the objection as well as the outburst and he underlined his request with a sharp affirmative nod. "Yes! Wire taps by the Bureau."

"Out of the question! The Bureau is a conglomeration of incompetent amateurs run by a publicity seeking egomaniac." Dulles was fuming. "In 1935 when Hoover formed the FBI and pursued headlines faster then bank robbers, I was quietly sending reports to Washington about the threat of Nazism. I met Hitler. I met Mussolini. The world stage, not a local sinecure in the DOJ! In 1946 when we formed the CIA he groused that another intelligence agency was superfluous. Jealousy, pure and simple. I wouldn't use his people to shine shoes."

Angleton weathered the tirade, but was on a holy crusade and pressed on. "Allen, we must have these wiretaps. Starting with Richard's!"

Dulles went from shocked to stunned. "Bissell? Ridiculous! He's been with us since OSS—he was in charge of developing the damn U-2! *I* appointed him Director of Plans! This is most certainly not your man."

"That's just what we said about Philby, Allen. I can't trust anyone until I can prove otherwise."

Dulles banged his pipe into an ashtray, emptying it, and then stared at Angleton for several moments before he spoke. His voice was low, threatening.

"Jim—number one... I don't want the FBI anywhere near this investigation. Two... Any phone taps will start at the bottom, not the top. And three...They will be monitored by you and no one but you... Understood?"

"Allen this is..."

"Understood!"

Angleton started to object again, but realized he'd lost. "Understood."

What Dulles didn't know was that Angleton had already called his contact at the FBI to discuss the feasibility of his plan. What Angleton didn't know was that Hoover already had wind of the query.

A day later, Lenny Mills called, asked Aldo for a meeting, and once again suggested West Potomac Park. Aldo agreed, found the same bench, and looked toward the Lincoln Memorial. Mills had appeared from that direction the prior November and probably would again.

The cherry blossoms had arrived late that spring, and a few remained on the ground, but with the thermometer in the mid-eighties, summer had arrived early.

Mills appeared with his suit coat slung over his shoulder and held by an index finger. If Hoover saw that, he'd be exiled to Kiska.

"Hi, ole buddy. How goes the war?"

"We lost."

"Things getting pretty hot in your crib?"

"Hell's colder."

"It's gonna get worse. Yesterday I found out Angleton asked if we could bug your phones."

Aldo was as stunned as Dulles had been. "What?"

Mills nodded. "He pulled the request this morning. Dulles must've vetoed it. No shock there. Angleton thinks there's a traitor in the agency."

Angleton suspecting traitors in the Agency was old news. Aldo shrugged. "It wouldn't be the first time."

"But that wasn't the reason I called you."

"Oh?"

"It's your brother again. Hoover's been digging for something that would embarrass your boss since Dulles stonewalled him about the Maheu-Giancana connection. He thinks he's found it."

Aldo's eyes narrowed. "Involving my brother?"

"He came up with the rumor about an assassination attempt on Castro last December. The attempt was pulled off by 'Diego and Maria López y Cubela'. They got passports at the Cuban Embassy in Mexico City."

"What's this got to do with Dante?"

"He thinks 'Maria is a girl named Marissa del Valle and 'Diego' is Dante."

Aldo eyes widened. "My *brother*?"

Mills nodded. "That's what Hoover thinks he has. If it's true, and if the Bay of Pigs doesn't bring down Dulles, this will. The CIA making deals with the Mob to take out a foreign leader? Christ! Dulles will go down and bring a shitload of people with him."

Aldo couldn't believe it and just stared at Mills.

Mills said, "For what it's worth, and off the record, I admire Dante for what he tried to do, and I wish to hell he'd succeeded. But what your brother ought to know is that from now on our agents will be on his ass around the clock."

Aldo returned to Langley in shock and arranged to meet Dan Cantrell at DiGiorno's for dinner. The bistro was overflowing with a Friday crowd bunched around the bar in the weekly mating dance of low-level bureaucrats. Martinis were the drink of choice, Bobby Darin's "Mack the Knife" came from the sound system, and cigarette smoke fogged the room.

Dan was sitting at a table along the rear wall in a comparatively quiet area. As usual, he was impeccably turned out, but his face looked haggard.

Aldo shook his hand. "Thanks for coming."

"Not a problem. I'd have probably skipped dinner if you hadn't called. I'm feeling a bit off lately."

"Aren't we all with what's been going on?"

Cantrell shook his head. "Can you believe it? The organization's gone batshit. People are reeling like headless chickens."

A waitress brought the straight-up Martinis Cantrell had ordered and left.

Aldo raised his glass in a silent toast, sipped and said, "There's more than just reeling around, Dan. I just heard Angleton's started a very serious internal investigation. He thinks we have a spy in the shop."

"So what else is new? Half the Agency thinks he's nuts."

"Maybe, but this time he tried to get the FBI involved."

Cantrell's head jerked back. "What?"

"That's what I heard."

"Where?"

"Not important. I know it's true."

"You've gotta be kidding! Dulles would never allow it."

"Oh, he didn't. Angleton wanted our phones tapped by the Bureau. Dulles said no, but you can be damn sure if Angleton's that desperate he's going to do that and more himself."

Cantrel drank his Martini in one long gulp. Dante noticed he'd paled. Dinner arrived and he ate nothing but a salad, before begging off. He made his way past the crowded bar without stopping, even ignoring a few gorgeous women waving to him.

Aldo chuckled, thinking that's a first, and finished his dinner.

Cantrell went to a pay phone and called Havana.

CHAPTER 38

MIAMI
JUNE 1961

ANGLETON'S SEARCH MAY have been part paranoia, but Masferrer's search for the man who'd betrayed him was grounded in absolute certainty. Ever since he'd been jumped by the Cuban patrol boat and lost six good men trying to infiltrate the island, he'd known the only way it could have happened.

He had to have been followed from the moment he left Miami.

When Masferrer returned to Key Largo without two of his boats, he'd informed Eni Quintero, the marina's owner, that they wouldn't be back. Quintero had dejectedly responded that it had been a bad night. A boat had been stolen and also would not be back. Rent from three slips lost in less than twenty-four hours.

Masferrer immediately thought the theft a bit too coincidental and put together a logical scenario. *Someone had followed him from his office to the marina, stolen a boat, then followed him to the island. But who?*

That afternoon he'd begun his interrogations with families and friends of the six men who had accompanied him and were captured. He assumed that one of them might have talked in spite of his mandate that they tell no one—including their wives—what they intended. Masferrer's brutal reputation proved accurate, and many innocent Cubans suffered while being interrogated by the former leader of *El Tigres*. But Masferrer came up with nothing.

He next moved to his inner circle—people who had been with him since the beginning. These included his two drivers, Martine Adega and Pepe Arroyo, as well as his two secretaries—one of whom was Yolanda Tomaso, his niece, and the other Abril Soto, his mistress. Finally, there was Luis Quevado and Miguel Olivera who were on the Hatteras with him during the failed infiltration attempt. The latter two made little sense since they were exposing themselves to capture or worse… Unless the traitor's plan was to *be* captured and then allowed to escape. It was unlikely, and they'd convinced him they were loyal, as did all the others. He didn't believe it was anyone close to him.

There was only one other possibility. The fourth man on his boat. Dante Amato. Trafficante had vouched for him but he'd joined the infiltration effort at the last minute. He'd have to take a closer look. He called Marissa, lying that he wanted to see her about Castro. She was surprised to hear his voice but made plans to meet at his office.

CHAPTER 39

TAMPA
JULY 1961

Jimmy Hoffa arrived in Tampa for a meeting with Santo Trafficante and Carlos Marcello, the New Orleans capo who ruled everything from the Big Easy to Dallas. In Trafficante's quiet, dimly lit Ybor City office—headquarters of his illegal bolita lottery—Hoffa sipped a glass of red wine, put it down, fixed his eyes on his friends, and spoke in a flat, solemn tone.

"I've found out Bobby Kennedy has a hit team of agents he calls his 'Get Hoffa Squad.' They're spending millions of taxpayer dollars to put me away."

Trafficante said, "Please, he's been after all of us. He had Carlos deported to fucking Guatemala for christsakes!"

Marcello nodded, saying nothing.

Hoffa continued, "I know that, and I spoke to Giancana. He's been hounded to a goddamn standstill since that prick became Attorney General. But if *I* wind up in jail we *all* lose. I lose the Teamsters, and you three lose the pension fund loans to build your Vegas casinos."

"We won't let that happen, Jimmy. With Havana gone, we have to be able to expand in Vegas. No goddamn government official's gonna stand in our way."

"Really? Kennedy just hit me with another indictment. And without the U.S. military supporting an invasion you don't stand a chance of getting back into Cuba."

"We're working on it. Both fronts. We're in business with the CIA."

"I know that. But Bobby still has the FBI under him and all over us. Cuba's a roll of the dice. You have to insure your bet by guaranteein' the outcome here in the U.S."

"Trafficante said, "How?"

"Santo… think. Bobby Kennedy's a snake."

Trafficante nodded. "I agree."

"A snake that's trying to kill us all."

"Again I agree."

"And how do you kill a snake?"

Trafficante looked at Marcello, then back to Hoffa.

"You cut off its head."

Hoffa nodded.

The conspiracy to assassinate John F. Kennedy had begun.

CHAPTER 40

LAS VEGAS
SEPTEMBER 1961

A LEGGY BLONDE WITH AN angelic face and heart-stopping body jack-knifed off the high board and sliced the water. She broke the surface three feet from the wall and levered herself out of the pool in one smooth motion.

The Desert Inn pool was surrounded by happy sun-worshipers before they hit the tables with dreams of breaking the bank. Johnny Roselli applauded as the beautiful diver approached his chaise and stretched out next to him. Half rolling toward him, she kissed his cheek and tousled his hair.

Johnny laughed. "You should turn pro."

She touched the tip of his nose and smiled. "There's no money in that kind of diving, Johnny."

"Point taken."

Dee Thullin was one of the highest priced call girls in Vegas, but for "Handsome Johnny" Roselli there was never a fee. It had nothing to do with his looks. It had everything to do with who he was, who his partners were, and how their friendship was more important than a fee, no matter how large.

I joined them wearing trunks, a robe, and a towel around my neck.

"Dante—you know Dee?"

"I haven't had the pleasure."

Dee smiled. "I can correct that."

Roselli chuckled. "And you would not regret the correction, my friend . . ." He kissed Dee's hand. "But for now I have to talk to Dante privately. Join us for cocktails in the lounge at five."

She kissed Roselli on the lips. "I'll be there, darlin'. . ." She got up, and with a twinkle in her eye, said, "Nice meeting you, Dante," and left.

I removed my robe and sat on the chaise Dee vacated.

Without indicating anyone, Roselli said, "He's in the chair at the end of the pool—wearin' blue trunks."

Without looking I asked, "Batman or Robin?"

"Robin. The stupid bastards haven't changed them out for a month."

We were referring to the two FBI agents who'd been alternately shadowing me since April. Aldo had given me a heads-up about the tails, and I'd spotted them within days. I'd ditched them whenever I needed to, but for the past week it wasn't an issue. My association with Roselli was well known, and we'd hired a local wire-expert to sweep for any bugs they might have placed.

I chuckled. "They must love tailing me in Vegas. They're getting great tans."

Roselli smiled and then abruptly turned to business. "I heard from Harvey. Trafficante's contact in Havana can't reach Cubela. He thinks Cubela's duckin' him, and Harvey thinks the asshole may have changed his mind."

I shook my head. It figured. "Why am I not surprised? What's the plan?"

"For the hit? None at the moment. But he says there's the new overall strategy in the works, and it'll still include us takin' out Castro."

I scoffed. "I've said it before—it better also include a regime change because that's what has to happen before we can get back in there."

"The new plan's supposed to handle that. It's comin' down from Defense, but includes the alphabet soup agencies."

"I'll believe it when it happens."

"Agreed." He sipped a tall gin-rickey. "Heard from Marissa?"

"Not lately. Why?"

"Harvey found out that Masferrer's been talkin' to her. About you."

"What?"

"Apparently thinks you could have ratted him out him when you all got jumped by the Cubans."

"You gotta be shittin' me!"

"Don't shoot the messenger. But she's quick on her feet. Asked Masferrer why you'd betray him, then agree to go with her to whack Castro?"

"Great comeback."

"It was, but I guess he got a little rough with her."

I felt blood rush to my head. "That son of a bitch! I'll take him apart!"

Roselli held up his hand. "Trafficante heard about it, and got pissed. Masferrer questioned his judgment. Trafficante vouched for you and that should have been enough. Masferrer backed off."

"I'll still take him apart."

"You should. You should also call her."

I nodded and got up. "See you in the lounge."

I went to my room and dialed Marissa's Coral Gables number. Adelaida answered and a few moments later Marissa got on the line. She sounded tentative and a bit surprised.

"Hello Dante…"

"Hi… I heard what happened. How are you now?"

"All right, I suppose—and you?"

"The same… Fuming about Masferrer."

"He's a pig."

"What happened?"

"A few bruises, but nothing a little makeup and hot tub can't handle."

"I'll return the favor in spades when I see him."

"It's not worth it, Dante. Artime still needs him. And for some reason he suddenly became very apologetic."

I knew the reason was Trafficante. "If that's what you want... but I'm sorry I caused it."

"It's not your fault, but it did allow me to make a decision I've been thinking about for some time."

"Oh?"

"I'm fed up with what's going on in Miami. All the exile groups are either suspicious of, jealous of, or fighting each other for dominance. It's tragic and I'm sick of it."

"I don't blame you."

"I need breathing space, Dante. I'm going to Madrid to visit friends and stay through the holidays. Ironically, it's where I was on the New Year's Eve when this nightmare began."

I was quiet for several moments, not knowing how to respond. "I'll miss you."

"I'll miss you too, but I think it's better this way... Until I can get my life together."

"You'll let me know where you'll be staying."

"I will."

CHAPTER 41

"YOU LOOK PAINED, DEAN. What's bothering you?"

"My concern is the same as it's always been with the overthrow of Castro. Too much 'noise' created by the attempt, and our inability to conceal our involvement."

Rusk's answer to the president was more curt than he intended, and Bobby immediately objected.

"*All* action creates noise! *Inaction* could let the Russians turn Cuba into a Soviet missile base ninety miles from Miami!"

The meeting included Rusk, Bundy, Bobby, and John McCone, who had replaced Allen Dulles after the president had asked for, and received, his resignation. Rusk was concerned that Operation Mongoose formulated by the newly created SGA (Special Group Augmented) under Bobby went too far. Charged with formulating the comprehensive plan to eliminate the Castro regime, it included a wide range of 'noisy' actions including invasion, assassination, and "false flag" operations run by the CIA, e.g. covertly attacking our own forces and blaming the Cubans— thus sanctioning retaliation. The false flag actions appalled the president.

Although chastened by Bobby, Rusk held firm. "I'm merely trying to once again point out, as I did before, that too *much* noise in Cuba could complicate our other cold war problems—not the least of which is our struggle over Berlin."

"Bundy restated Bobby's point to Rusk. "Dean—it's either pursuing all options or we'll have to learn to live with Castro."

"*That*—*I* won't have." Kennedy's voice was low, but firm.

"Mr. President," Rusk persisted, "I know you've already ruled out another invasion, but…"

"No—I've ruled out another invasion without *provocation*. If we can instigate an uprising and the counter-revolutionaries ask for help, I'll authorize it. One hundred percent."

"Another invasion?"

Kennedy nodded. "Yes."

McCone, who was aware of the Mafia's earlier involvement in assassination attempts asked, "Do we still believe that eliminating Castro prior to an invasion to retake the island would be extremely beneficial?"

Bobby turned to him with cold eyes. "No time, no effort, or manpower is to be spared—all else is secondary."

He'd ducked using the word assassination, but everyone in the room knew his meaning.

The doves in the group glanced at each other.

The silence was broken by Bundy, who changed the subject with another question for Bobby. "You're confident that Lansdale is the right man to head up the operation?"

Bobby responded with a quick but firm nod. "Brigadier General Edward Lansdale is an expert on guerrilla and anti-subversive operations. First with the OSS in Europe, then in the Philippines and Vietnam."

Bundy persisted. "He's also known as a wild card."

Bobby waved it off. "Maybe, but he has a great brain, makes mince meat out of enigmas, and has the balls of a cat burglar."

"Are we still planning to use Harvey for the Miami end?"

Bobby said, "Yes. He's been involved with the Cuban effort from the beginning, knows all the players."

After a few moments of silence, the president asked. "Anything else?"

The men all glanced at one another, but no one responded.

Kennedy got up. "Very well. Thank you, gentlemen. Let us proceed."

Rusk left the room unsettled. It was the same thing the president had said during the final days of planning before the Bay of Pigs. He was convinced they were headed toward another disaster.

CHAPTER 42

MIAMI

DECEMBER 1961

WILLIAM HARVEY BEGAN implementing Operation Mongoose objectives from JM/Wave on the U of M's South Campus early in the month. Since it included Castro's assassination, he again asked Roselli for a meeting and told him to bring me.

On the 23rd, I lost my tail and flew into Miami with Roselli. It was one year to the day that Marissa and I had departed for Havana through Mexico City, and a little more than eight months after the Bay of Pigs. We drove through a city once more festooned with Christmas decorations and bursting with holiday spirit. Roselli commented that Bobby Kennedy was also in south Florida, but he sure as hell wasn't celebrating.

Six days earlier, in Palm Springs, Joseph Kennedy had been felled by a calamitous stroke. It had left him only able to mumble a single frustrated word over and over.

"*No...*"

Roselli received word that five days prior to the stroke, Hoover informed Bobby that he had Sam Giancana on tape—bitterly railing against the Kennedys. The reason for the tirade—Joe Kennedy had made a deal with Giancana to deliver Chicago in the 1960 presidential election. Giancana agreed to the deal, and the Chicago Mob used its power with the ward healers to deliver the city. Those votes had given Kennedy the state of Illinois and put him over the top in the closest election in U.S. history. The quid-pro-quo was a promise that the new administration would leave organized crime alone and keep the FBI off their ass.

However, what the Mob actually had gotten was Bobby's unrelenting vendetta against them all and Jimmy Hoffa in particular. It was a mind boggling double-cross, and Giancana vowed revenge.

It was known by those closest to the situation that Bobby had asked for Joe's advice about how to handle Hoover's Giancana tape. The elder Kennedy knew that the tape's exposure could bring down his son's administration, and also knew what the fury of the Mob could portend. There is no doubt that he must have been under tremendous pressure.

Bobby believed it caused his father's stroke. Roselli told me he believed it as well.

We entered JM/Wave through the columned portico of the main building and were escorted to Harvey's corner office by an officious assistant. Harvey stood when we entered, greeting us warmly.

"Drink? 'The sun's over the yardarm…'"

Roselli nodded. "Jack Daniels—rocks."

"Two," I added.

Harvey crossed to a liquor caddy and began pouring three-finger shots into a pair of tumblers. Filling them with ice he said, "We've finally come up with a comprehensive plan. Operation Mongoose will retake the island. It includes political, psychological, military, sabotage, and intelligence operations." Delivering the drinks, he added, "As well as attacks on the cadre of the regime—Castro and other key leaders."

I said, "I thought that's what you were doing for two years before the Bay of Pigs."

Harvey sat and blithely waved it off. "Feeble efforts made by disparate groups of exiles, who, although we trained them, were working with uncoordinated anti-Castro cadres on the island. You were involved with one of them when you tried to infiltrate Cuba with Masferrer. This time we're using our own people. DOD, CIA, NSA, and State are all involved. The plan is to generate a revolt of the Cubans by next October—

at which point we'll invade, retake the island, and establish a friendly regime."

Roselli said, "I like it. What's our part?"

"The same as before. You take out Castro."

"How?"

Harvey smiled and looked at me. "With him."

My response was a disparaging chuckle. "Judging by my abysmal track record in Cuba, I'd think you be looking for a better choice."

Harvey shook his head. "For different reasons, once again you're perfect."

"Once again, I can't wait to hear why."

"Your service record. I looked it up. You qualified 'expert' on the rifle range and got a medal for taking out a Jap general on Saipan from over three hundred yards."

Roselli immediately understood, and bellowed, "You want to hit Castro with a sniper rifle!"

"Harvey nodded. "Exactly. Everything that's been tried so far has been up close and failed miserably. We think it's time to try something different."

I scoffed. "Assuming I agreed—which based upon *your* track record in operational planning, I probably won't—you'd still have to get me in there and into position."

"This time we fly you into Guantánamo Bay on a Navy plane."

"That doesn't put Castro in my crosshairs."

"No. From Gitmo we outfit you like a cane worker and cross you over with a Cuban contract agent. He knows how to get through the fences, and avoid the patrols from there to Havana. His name's Teofilo Cruz."

"What about the rifle?"

On the outskirts of the city there's a safe house where you'll pick it up, change clothes and get I.D. identifying you as a musician."

My forehead knitted. "A musician?"

"Yes. A trombone player."

Roselli laughed. "Perfect. The rifle's in the case."

Harvey nodded. "Exactly."

"And what happens if I run into a situation where someone asks me to play the fucking trombone?"

"You can't even if you could. There's a rifle in there."

"That's the goddamn point. If I have to open the case I'm fucked!"

"You're not on a bandstand! Why would anyone ask you to open the case?"

"How the hell do I know? I never walked around with a fucking trombone!"

The exchange made Roselli burst out laughing. "You're actually thinking of doing it. I love it! And Momo, Santo and every capo in the country will love it. You'll be their hero—the man who fired the first shot to get our casinos back! You'll be able to write your own ticket."

There was no question about it. If I pulled it off I'd get anything I wanted—a capo's hat—a cut of the casinos—and the undying gratitude of Marissa del Valle. But I'd seen the effectiveness of Castro's intelligence organization twice, and I saw no reason to believe another effort would succeed—or worse—put me in the Hallelujah Chorus.

"I'm just thinking about thinking about it...Who sets up time and place for the hit?"

Harvey said, "You—with the help of Cruz and Trafficante's people in Havana. One of them's a mechanic in Castro's motor pool. Another's a female clerk in the Agriculture Ministry. The third's a telephone company repairman. They're the ones who'll get his schedules, then you'll pick the time and sniper nest."

"It sounds thin."

"Maybe, but they say it's doable."

"When's all this supposed to go down?"

"As soon as you're ready to go."

I had no intention of spending another Christmas Eve in Cuba, and there was no one I wanted to spend it with in Miami. But I'd been invited to a rash of parties in Vegas, ending with a New Year's Eve bash at the

Sands with Frank, Dean, and Sammy. I took a few moments, mentally called myself a fucking idiot and decided.

"Okay. I'll be back on the second."

CHAPTER 43

I AGAIN HAD NO TROUBLE ditching my tail before flying back to Miami. Sanchez picked me up at Miami International, drove me to the former Opa-Locka Marine Corps Air Station, and we departed for Gitmo in a Navy P2V. Except for my lingering hangover, the flight was uneventful.

I'd called Marissa from Las Vegas at four in the afternoon on the 31st because of Madrid's time difference. It seemed strange wishing her a Happy New Year in broad daylight from poolside, and she was happy to hear from me but we didn't get into anything else.

We landed at Gitmo and checked into the Bachelor Officer's Quarters where a handsome man who looked like Harry Belafonte was waiting. Like me, he'd been told not to shave for two days and had visible stubble. He grinned and stuck out his hand.

"Teofilo Cruz. My friends call me Teo."

I took an immediate liking to his warm demeanor and shook his hand. "Dante Amato—and I assume you know Sanchez."

He nodded. "I do."

Sanchez playfully slapped Teo's arm. "We recruited him right out of Julliard in nineteen-fifty when we heard he was a Cuban national. We knew we were going to need assets in place when it was time to bring back Batista. Two years later, in fifty-two, he helped us do it."

I said, "And you also worked for Trafficante."

"I did and do. I was his bandleader at the Sans Souci. Since it's closed, I still carry out orders like the one that brought me to you." He smiled at Sanchez. "He pays better than Trafficante, but for cover I still take work playing piano when I can get it."

Sanchez laughed. "Don't you love it? Cubans, the Mob, and the Agency. One big happy family."

I ignored the remark and looked at Teo. "What's the plan?"

"The border guards change at midnight. We leave tonight at eleven-thirty when they are at the end of their eight-hour shift and least alert. Once through the fence and across the minefields…"

I interrupted. "Minefields?"

"Teo nodded. "On both sides of the border, but I have maps to get us through. From there we pick up a truck and head across the island to Havana."

"Where I get the 'trombone.'"

"Exactly."

"You know the make and model?"

Teo smiled. "The case is a King 2B—the model favored by your Tommy Dorsey. But the 'trombone' is a modified WWII M1 Garand."

"I'll have to sight it in?"

"Yes. We'll do that outside of Mariel once we've settled in Havana."

"I take it we won't be armed en route."

"No. Our papers are for cane workers. If we're stopped and searched along the way and they find weapons it's over before we've begun."

At eleven-thirty, I changed into the cane worker's clothes Teo brought, including sneakers and battered hat. We blackened our faces and departed into a cloudless night under a rocking-horse moon. Going through the northern perimeter, we negotiated the minefields with maps, and the boundary fence with wire cutters. The area over the border was dotted with scrub brush and cactus, and we eventually emerged onto a narrow road that was once asphalt, but had deteriorated into rubble and dirt.

Teo whispered, "Our truck is hidden about a mile from here."

He began a slow trot and I followed. Ten minutes later we turned into a path, walked about fifteen yards and stopped next to a clump of bushes where a camouflage net covered a truck. We quickly uncovered a battered 1940 flatbed Ford that had clearly seen better days.

I was a bit dismayed. "Will this thing make it? It's over five hundred miles to Havana."

"Over six hundred the way we'll be going, but the engine is okay and the look is perfect."

The sound of an approaching vehicle caused us to tense and Teo dashed back to the road. A pair of headlights was approaching from about a hundred yards away.

He yelled. "It's a patrol. Cover the truck!"

We quickly re-covered the Ford and ducked behind the bushes. A few moments later a jeep with four soldiers rumbled by and disappeared down the road.

Teo checked his watch. "Twelve fifteen—too soon for the midnight watch to get this far from their base. They either relieved the third watch early or they *are* the third watch and haven't been relieved yet. Either way we have to move fast. This road ends in a mile then they'll turn around and come back."

We quickly uncovered the truck and took off down the crumbling road belching exhaust smoke and kicking up an explosion of dust—both of us hoping it would settle before the jeep came back and saw it.

Four hours later, after wiping our blackened faces clean, we drove into Bayamo. There were no patrols on the dark road, and we saw little of the rural environment. We traveled through Camagüey at sunrise and were in Ciego di Avila by noon. We refueled the truck, bought tacos and beer and continued to Trinidad. Known as "a city detained in time", it boasted magnificent villas, churches, and buildings built in the Louis XVII, XVIII and XIX eras that looked the same now as they did then. The pastoral countryside was beautiful, the people smiling, friendly and waving as we passed. My impression of Castro's Cuba took a subtle shift.

Approaching Cienfuegos the right front tire blew. I was not surprised. In keeping with the desired look of the truck, it was nearly bald. Teo grumbled, refused my help, and replaced it with an equally bald spare. Since it was our only spare, I said a silent prayer to the tire god that we wouldn't have another blowout, and we resumed the journey belching exhaust smoke.

We ran into our first serious problem in Cienfuegos. The city was fewer than twenty miles from the Bay of Pigs, and there were an inordinate number of soldiers on the roads. Teo thought they were remnants of the Cuban Army that had been sent to repel the failed invasion. They watched us pass with indifference and to my surprise, I saw that they were well-equipped, well-fed, and looked professional.

Just beyond a blind curve, a civilian truck in our lane had collided with a military truck in the opposing lane, and the road was blocked. The military truck had apparently been leading a convoy of five others that were barred by the wreck. The civilian truck was a battered old Chevrolet in the same condition as our Ford, and the hapless driver was an old man wringing his hat and crying. The military trucks were brand new Russian Zils.

We pulled to a stop, and a bearded sergeant walked up to the driver's window with a scowl on his face. He was obviously having a bad day and began waving his arms and yelling at Teo in guttural Spanish.

"Imbeciles! Do you see what you incompetent idiots driving garbage heaps have done to my new truck?"

Teo answered him contritely. "I apologize for my compatriot, Sergeant. We are poor workers and can afford little more."

"That piece of shit truck didn't cause this—the piece of shit driver did! He stuck out his hand. "Your papers!"

Teo and I fumbled for our papers and handed them over. He gave them a cursory look and barked, "Get out!"

Teo got out and faced of the Sergeant. I walked around the front of the truck and stood next to Teo. The Sergeant suddenly seemed to recognize something for the first time.

"Why do you not have beards? All loyal revolutionaries wear beards!"

Teo sadly hunched his shoulders. "I had one. But my new wife made me shave it because she said it tickled and wouldn't make love to me."

The Sergeant let out a scornful grunt and glared at me. "And you? You're also pussy whipped scum?"

I shook my head. "No sir. I play the trombone at night to earn extra money, and the mustache doesn't allow me seat the mouthpiece on my lips. But I love Fidel and would gladly have one if it were possible."

The Sergeant grunted his disgust, threw our papers on the ground, and stalked away. We got back into the truck and Teo gingerly pulled onto the narrow dirt shoulder and around the wreck.

Teo said, "Very fast thinking, my friend."

I shrugged. "Thank God he didn't ask why I didn't grow a beard *without* a mustache."

CHAPTER 44

HAVANA

WE DROVE INTO LOS MANGOS, an area about ten miles southeast of old Havana, after dark. Winding through narrow streets, we finally stopped in front of a small tailor shop with two stories of apartments above it.

Teo pointed. "This is it. Second floor."

I followed him through a door alongside the shop and up a flight of badly worn stairs. There were two doors opposite one another on the second floor, and Teo knocked on the street-side door.

A gnarled old man answered, and the astringent odor of Hoppe's gun cleaner drifted out behind him. He was dark-skinned, white-haired, and no more than five feet tall. He smiled, embraced Teo, and patted his back. "Teofilo… "

Teo leaned back and cupped the old man's face in his hands. "You are well, uncle?"

"As well as any viejo can be."

Teo indicated me. "This is Dante—our friend from America. Dante—mi tio Emilio."

We shook hands and Emilio waved us into the small one bedroom apartment. A threadbare couch and two overstuffed chairs on a sisal rug took up the left half of the front room. A narrow dining table and a pair of chairs were on the opposite wall. A unique feature of the room was a six-foot workbench set on sawhorses under the front windows. On it were a vise, a lathe, a drill press, and several other tools I didn't recognize.

Teo saw me looking at it. "My Uncle's workplace. He's a gunsmith."

"The 'trombone' modifier," I said.

Teo smiled. "Yes."

We sat on the couch while Emilio poured rum into three water glasses. He passed two to us and raised his in a toast.

"May God smile on our mission."

After we drank, Emilio crossed to the workbench where he opened a trombone case containing the modified M-1 rifle. The stock had been hinged so it would fit in the case and a telescopic sight had been added. Its original metal sights, swivels, and bayonet stub had all been removed.

He returned and handed it to me, proudly saying, "As close as possible to new condition."

I examined it and nodded agreement. "And the ammunition?"

"I loaded it myself. Match grade."

I looked at Teo. "All we need is the target."

"Also in God's hands—with the help of Trafficante's people of course."

"We sight it in tomorrow?"

He nodded. "In Mariel as planned."

We left Emilio's apartment with the trombone case and drove through more narrow streets to a building almost identical to the one we'd just left. A restaurant rather than a tailor shop was on the first floor, and there were three stories of apartments. A wooden sign above the restaurant door read: "Daniela's"

Teo said, "My cousin owns the restaurant and I live on the top floor. After we lock the trombone case in my apartment, we'll eat."

We climbed the stairs to an apartment that was similar to Emilio's, except Teo's had no workbench and there were two bedrooms. In the smaller one, Teo laid out the clothes I'd be wearing—chinos, a sport shirt, sweater, and a baseball cap—and we walked down to the restaurant.

Daniela's was crowded, noisy, and dimly lit. Scores of wicker-wrapped rum bottles hung from the ceiling, and cigar smoke, combined with the tantalizing aroma of spicy dishes, filled the air. We sat at an empty table, and a beauty wearing a short skirt, low cut peasant blouse, and apron sauntered over.

She kissed Teo on the cheek and playfully slapped his arm. "Teo—you've been ignoring me! What have you been doing?"

"Counting the days when I could return to my gorgeous Laline. Say hello to my friend Dante."

She extended her hand and smiled. "Hello, Dante. You live in Havana?"

I picked a town. "No—Trinidad."

"Ah! A beautiful city." Turning back to Teo she frowned. "What are you doing in those ridiculous clothes?"

He winked. "Visiting cane plantations. I'm thinking of buying several before they're nationalized."

She chuckled and slapped his arm again. "Will I see you later?"

"Of course. When are you finished?"

"Half an hour."

"Done…" He indicated a second very attractive waitress. "And you might invite Lola for my friend Dante."

I held up my hands. The last thing I needed was questions from someone I didn't know. "Thank you—no. I have a very jealous wife."

Laline gave me the same kind of smile I'd received from Dee Thullin at the Desert Inn pool, and said, "Lola will be very disappointed." Taking out her order pad, she looked at Teo. "The usual?"

"Si, ropa vieja and a very cold La Tropical. Dante?"

"The same."

Laline brought us our beers, and fifteen minutes later returned with two steaming plates of shredded flank steak in a tomato sauce base, black beans, yellow rice, plantains, and fried yuca. It was incomparable and we devoured it. I hadn't enjoyed a meal as delicious since my mother's pasta frutti di mare.

When we finished, Teo paid the check, and said, "You told me you weren't married."

"I'm not."

"You don't find Lola desirable?"

"I find her exceptional."

"Then why not take her upstairs with me and Laline?"

"She's a wild card. I don't know who she is, who she knows, or who she talks to, and I assume you can't be sure either. Why risk it?"

He held out his apartment key. "Okay, compadre. Let yourself in."

I took the key, returned to the apartment, undressed, showered, and went to bed. I wasn't quite ready to go to sleep so I began reading a magazine. About forty minutes later I heard him and Laline laughing as they came in.

I wasn't going to get much sleep after all. I should have known.

Laline was a screamer.

CHAPTER 45

MARIEL

THE CITY ON THE SOUTHEAST side of Mariel Bay is about twenty-five miles west of Havana. On the far southwestern side, a basically uninhabited rural area was ideal for sighting-in the rifle.

Teo didn't want us traveling in the beat-up cane workers truck in our new guise as musicians, so he contacted the clerk in the Agriculture Ministry who'd been recruited by Trafficante. Her name was Carmen Orenstein, and she picked us up at 7:00 a.m, in a 1940 Dodge that looked like it just left the showroom. Cubans loved their automobiles, and in Havana old cars in mint condition were as common as Mojitos.

I thought the girl was as extraordinary as the car.

Carmen was twenty, the daughter of a Cuban mother and German Jewish father who'd fled to Cuba in 1939 to escape Hitler's concentration camps. She was tall, stunning, and coffee-colored, but had eye-popping blonde hair and blue eyes. I caught the aroma of very expensive perfume and noted perfectly tailored clothes and equally expensive spiked heels. A tan skirt-suit showed off her voluptuous figure to perfection, and I thought she was probably a showgirl before the casinos were closed. I also thought that the over-sexed Cuban premier could not have missed anyone this beautiful working in a government office.

Curious, I asked, "Do you see much of Castro at the ministry?"

She chuckled. "Fidel? Of course. I am on his list."

"Oh? What list is that?"

"His 'to do' list. There are many of us on it. No one knows for sure how many."

It was obvious, but I asked anyway. "What is it he 'does?'"

"Not what—who? He does us."

She said it so matter-of-factly that Teo and I broke out laughing.

Carmen shrugged. "He gets around to me once every two of three weeks. But it's not terribly unpleasant, and it allows me to enjoy special privileges."

That explained the wardrobe and perfume, and I asked, "Since you hate him enough to help us kill him, have you thought of trying it yourself—in bed?"

"Of course. But we are thoroughly searched before we join Fidel. *Very* thoroughly. Nothing gets by his keepers."

I said, "I heard a woman who was sent to kill him fell in love with him?"

"Yes. She was a German girl who tried to poison him soon after the revolution. But I've had a boyfriend since I was sixteen and I love him."

"What does he think of you being on the 'to do' list."

"He hates it. But he sees the greater cause… He's a telephone repairman."

Teo turned in his seat and smiled. "*The* telephone repairman. The one who also works for Trafficante."

Carmen turned onto a dirt road, and a mile later, stopped next to an open meadow dotted by trees. I surveyed the area and walked to young Kapoc with two branches that formed a shoulder height "V".

I called back to the car. "This should do it."

Carmen answered. "Good. I said I'd be in the office by ten-thirty. We have two hours."

"Teo—bring the rifle. Pace it off."

Carmen changed into sneakers and brought the trombone case along with a pair of binoculars. Teo paced off twenty-five yards carrying a folding chair, clothespins, and five shopping bags. He set up the chair and secured a shopping bag to the chair-back with clothespins. The bag had a bull's-eye drawn on it. He adjusted its position and returned to Carmen and me.

I reset the hinged stock and loaded the rifle with a clip containing three cartridges. Cradling the barrel in the crook of the tree, I placed the crosshairs on the bulls-eye. I took a deep breath, slowly let half out—held the remainder…and then gently squeezed the trigger until the rifle fired.

Carmen raised her binoculars and said, "One inch high—one inch right."

I adjusted the scope four clicks down, four clicks right and repeated the first shot's routine.

Carmen again raised the binoculars. "Bull's-eye."

I fired off the third shot with the same result and Teo walked to the chair with a fresh target. He paced off an additional seventy-five yards—re-set the chair at one hundred yards and trotted back.

We repeated the routine at two, three, and four hundred yards with me making the required adjustments when necessary. When Carmen called out a bull's-eye on my final shot, I smiled and said, "Get me anywhere up to four hundred yards away and I'll make the shot."

Teo happily agreed. "If he's anywhere in the city it will probably be less than that."

Carmen nodded. "But if the opportunity is somewhere in the open—like here outside the city—it might even be longer."

"Whatever… You set him up, I'll take him down."

CHAPTER 46

HAVANA

SUNDAY MORNING AT nine o'clock, almost two weeks after sighting-in the rifle, the jangling phone in Teo's apartment jolted me awake. I once again hadn't gotten much sleep since Teo spent the night with the very vocal Laline. After a half dozen rings it was obvious he wasn't hearing it so I trudged into the front room.

"Diga—Cruz residencia," I answered, in my perfect accent. Thank God for my bilingual mother.

The man recognized my voice. I'd met him with Teo several times. "Dante—it's Bartolo! I must speak to Teo!"

Bartolo Melendez was Trafficante's man in Castro's motor pool, and sounded very agitated.

I said, "Hold on," barged through Teo's door and shook him awake. "Bartolo's on the phone! Something's going down."

Laline stirred and rolled over, Teo rushed to the phone.

"Yes, Bartolo!"

I leaned in and heard, "He just left! He had his scuba gear with him and they headed west."

Teo was instantly alert. "You don't know where?"

"Not for sure. But I've heard he's very fond of Cayo Levisa."

"Who's with him?"

"The usual security. Two cars and a stake-truck. The lead car has four soldiers—he's in the second car with the two bodyguards who accompany him when diving—and the stake-truck is following with ten more soldiers."

"Excellent, Bartolo." Teo hung up and said, "Get dressed! We may have a chance!"

I rushed into my bedroom and began dressing.

Teo quickly called Carmen. "We may have him! Bring beach clothes." He slammed down the phone and ran to dress.

"Can we catch up and get ahead of him?" I asked.

"Maybe, but we can't take him on the road. Too many soldiers with automatic weapons, and I know there's a machine gun mounted on the truck."

"So we hit him when he goes in or comes out of the water."

"I've never been there, but that's my guess. We'll take beach clothes to be inconspicuous while we check out the site."

Ten minutes later, wearing bathing suits under sport shirts, we were on the road in the Dodge with Carmen driving. We took the main road past Guanajay, on to San Christobal, then cut north at Las Pozas on secondary roads toward Cayo Levisa.

There were few vehicles on the road and we stopped about a half-mile from the shoreline. Leaving the trombone case locked in the car, we brought our towels and walked the rest of the way. When the shoreline came into sight, my heart sank.

The beach was a lonely stretch of white sand with several cars parked on a nearby gravel lot. The two official cars and stake-bed with its mounted machine-gun were also in the lot. Beyond it, a few food stalls and shops led to a short pier. It was an unseasonably warm day and ten bearded soldiers were sipping cold drinks under umbrellas next to the food stalls. All were armed with Kalashnikovs and wearing camouflage fatigues. There was no sign of Castro, the other four guards, or the two men who accompanied him while he was diving.

But then I noticed a boat carrying seven men rounding Cayo Levisa's western tip about a mile offshore. It had to be Castro, the other four soldiers, and the two diver/bodyguards.

Teo shook his head. "Dammit! We missed him. The dive site is obviously on the other side of the Cay. Out of sight, out of range."

"It wouldn't have worked even if we'd gotten here earlier. The ten soldiers he left ashore guard him in and out of the water. The four who're with him protect him above the dive site—and the two diver/bodyguards under it."

Carmen asked, "What about on the way back to town?"

I shook my head. "No good. As Teo said, a road ambush would face the same problem we've got here. Ten soldiers with automatic weapons in a truck with a machine gun—in addition to two fast cars with four more soldiers and his two diver/bodyguards.

Teo took a deep breath and exhaled in frustration. "He'll always be too protected in the open. We'll have to catch him in the city."

Carmen thoughtfully narrowed her eyes. "He'll be recording a speech for overseas broadcast on January twenty-eighth in honor of José Martí's birthday. When he goes to the Havana TV studio, we may be able to get into a firing position as he comes in or out of the building."

Teo turned to her and nodded. "I know the area. There are possibilities, but we'll have to know when he'll go there."

"I'm sure I can find out."

I said, "Good, but if this is a big time scuba site, let's get the hell out of here before a nosey diver comes along and wonders why our car's parked a half mile from the beach."

CHAPTER 47

THE DAYS PASSED SLOWLY FOR me as I awaited more word about Castro's plans. Teo had his friends, his music, and Laline to occupy him, but I wanted to avoid unnecessary involvement with strangers and had no diversions. On the few occasions Teo brought me to jazz clubs where he played piano, I avoided contact.

On January 25, Carmen learned that the Havana TV broadcast facilities were undergoing renovation and that a temporary studio had been set up in the old city. She called Teo and gave him its downtown address. Castro would be delivering one of his long speeches live from the Capital on the 28th, but he'd be recording a short speech honoring Martí in the temporary studio that morning,

Teo and I immediately scouted the area. The address Carmen supplied was on a narrow street of densely packed neoclassical buildings with sweeping arches and overhanging balconies not far from the Plaza de Armas. There were only a few cars and pedestrians on the quiet street, but a multitude of possible sniper nests in the buildings lining it.

I paused to take in the balconies and rooftops opposite the building where the temporary studio was located, and said, "It's got possibilities, but…"

Teo took my arm and propelled me forward. "Keep walking. If there are security people already in place, we can't let them to see us reconnoitering."

We kept walking. "Good point. But I was about to say that if I were them, I'd block off the street and put men on the rooftops."

"I'm sure they'll do that, so we'll have to get into one of the apartments or offices. There are dozens with good firing angles. They can't cover them all."

"How do we get in?"

"Before they block off the street. I have an idea but I need a map."

That afternoon, Teo called Lalo Ramos, the telephone repairman who was Carmen's boyfriend. Prior to the revolution, Batista had planned to update and expand the city's phone system, and part of the plan was to place new trunk lines in the sewers under the streets. Teo told him to get the map he needed and to scout the buildings opposite the TV studio for a suitable sniper nest. He'd enter the offices and apartments saying that he was evaluating phone lines for possible replacement.

The next day, Carmen verified Castro would record the Martí speech on the 28th at 10:00 a.m. prior to going to the capital for his live performance. That evening Ramos delivered a map of the city sewer system and told us he'd found an office in a building that was perfect for our purpose. There was no alarm system, no security guard, and no one would be coming to work that morning. January 28 was a Sunday.

Teo opened the map. "This is sewer system under the streets." He pointed. "And this is the street with the TV studio and building Ramos selected."

The plan became obvious. "We're going to hide in the sewer before the hit."

"Exactly. The night before Castro records his speech, we go into the sewer two blocks away and make out way though the system until we're under the street where our building is."

"Okay, we get out of the sewer next to the building. That still doesn't put us in it."

"No, but Ynilo does."

"Who the hell is Ynilo?"

"Lalo's brother. A locksmith."

January 28, at three o'clock in the morning, Carmen dropped off Teo, Ynilo, and me two blocks from our destination. I carried the trombone case, Ynilo carried his tools, and Teo carried a crowbar. The street was deserted, but we used Carmen's car as a partial shield while Teo used the crowbar to lever-up a manhole cover.

Ynilo was a twenty-four-year-old Afro-Cuban, thin as a rail and a former high school gymnast. He quickly lowered himself into the opening, dangled a moment, let go, and reported a three-foot drop.

Teo and I followed his example and gave Ynilo a leg-up to pull the cover back into place. Using his penlight and map, Teo led us to the manhole he'd selected. With another leg-up, Ynilo used the crowbar, and we all scrambled out. I looked around the deserted street and gave Teo a congratulatory slap on the back. We were thirty yards from the building Ramos singled out for our sniper nest.

We replaced the cover, dashed for it, and ducked into the recess beneath its neo-classical arch. Huddling in the shadows, Ynilo picked the lock on the tall double doors, and two minutes later we entered a small arcade.

The building's ground floor had shops on both sides of the arcade with three floors of offices above it. We took the stairway to the top floor and found the office Ramos had selected. The upper half of the door was glass and read: "Velasquez and Sons. Expendedor de Tobacco." Ynilo picked the lock and we entered a timeworn office with high ceilings, crown moldings, and the stench of cigar butts in brim-full ashtrays. There were six desks in an open area and a glassed-in supervisor's cubicle facing the street.

Teo led us into the cubicle and glanced out the high-arched window. It gave us an oblique look at the entrance of the building housing the TV studio. The window was double hung so the bottom section could be raised. Ideal. I could steady the rifle barrel on the windowsill while I was kneeling and hidden.

Teo said, "Ramos paced off the distance between the buildings. Fifty-four yards. You can't miss. And we'll move out the second he drops."

I nodded. "Let's get some sleep."

We got up at dawn, saw the street below being blockaded and soldiers taking up positions on the opposite rooftops. I opened the window a scant four inches—far enough to clear the telescopic sight on top of the barrel, but narrow enough to escape attention.

Teo grimaced and said, "If they notice that we're finished."

"True. But if we wait until the last minute, I'd have to stand behind the window to open it. There's less chance of them seeing a four -inch opening than me standing behind the window in broad daylight to raise it."

Teo went to the office door and left it ajar so we'd waste no time opening it when we made our escape. The plan was to take the stairway into the basement, and a service lift to the back alley—hoping to be a few blocks away before the chaos following the assassination subsided. I removed the rifle from the trombone case, unfolded, loaded, and leaned it next to the window. I lit a Marlboro, Teo a cigar, Yanilo a cigarillo, and we waited.

At ten o'clock, Teo spotted two stake-bed trucks loaded with soldiers sandwiching an official limousine at the end of the street. A few seconds later, the barriers parted.

Castro.

Teo signaled me, I reached for the rifle, and Ynilo flattened himself against the wall.

Below the window, the leading truck came into view.

I rested the rifle on the windowsill…

And all hell broke loose. The office door was smashed off its hinges. Eight soldiers flew in, grinding over broken glass. They were on us before I could swing my rifle around, and a Kalashnikov connected with my jaw. I wondered why we hadn't been mowed down in a hail of bullets and a second before passing out realized why.

They wanted us alive.

CHAPTER 48

TEO WAS ALREADY AWAKE when I recovered. Ynilo was still unconscious, and we were bound hand and foot in a moving stake-bed. Ten soldiers carrying Kalashnikovs stood over us holding onto the stakes. I caught a heavy whiff of sea air and saw Teo looking between the soldier's legs. We'd rounded the southern side of the harbor and were traveling north on its eastern side. He looked terrified and probably would have crossed himself if his hands were free.

He murmured, "La Cabaña..."

I knew of La Cabaña. It was the infamous eighteenth century fortress where Che Guevara oversaw revolutionary tribunals and had over six hundred prisoners executed in the past five months.

The truck skidded to a stop inside fortress walls and I slammed into Ynilo. A soldier jerked me upright, threw me over the tailgate, and another kicked me in the ribs when I hit the ground. Teo landed beside me, and seconds later Ynilo crashed into my back. He was still unconscious when they pulled him up and dragged him into the prison by his feet. Teo and I were hauled upright, and then our legs were untied.

A bearded captain wearing fatigues appeared and strode toward us. He was short and thin—I guessed about five-six, one-thirty—and had a chilling smile on his pockmarked face. I noticed the name stenciled over his breast pocket—*Delgado*. Four burly, three hundred pound soldiers followed him.

The captain hit me with a vicious double slap and roared, "Pigs! Fools! "Don't you know that Fidel can't be killed? *Dozens* have tried and failed!" His chilling smile returned. "I will look forward to finding out why you thought you would succeed, where you came from, and who sent you." He leaned forward and playfully pinched my cheek. "The interrogation will begin after you meet our welcoming committee… Paco!"

The four huge soldiers grabbed our arms and frog-marched us away with our hands still tied behind our backs. We were propelled into the stone building, along a corridor, down two flights of stairs, and into a huge underground gallery. It had fourteen 25x35 dungeons on either side with a hundred prisoners jammed into each. I soon learned that they had to take turns sleeping on the floor. Some stood while others twisted and contorted for space until they resembled a grotesque interlocked pretzel. The stench of sewage and despair was overwhelming.

Teo and I were shoved into a smaller 15x20 dungeon at the end of the gallery with five naked men chained to its walls. One of them was Ynilo, still unconscious, and limply hanging by his wrists.

Paco, the senior soldier, grabbed the front of my shirt and tore it off. "Strip them!"

The four huge men began ripping off our clothes and seconds later I was chained to the wall next to Ynilo. Paco and his gorillas then formed a circle around Teo.

The beating began with a kidney punch. When Teo began to fall, Paco held him up and shoved him on to the next man in the circle. The second man unleashed a savage kick into Teo's groin, held him up, and passed him on to the third. When the forth man delivered his blow, the routine repeated itself.

The welcoming committee.

Five minutes later, Teo was chained to the wall and I was welcomed to La Cabaña.

I woke up hours later thinking I was being drowned. I was chained to the wall but couldn't breathe until the deluge stopped. I opened my eyes and saw that the high-pressure hose was now on Teo. He was conscious, struggling against his chains, and gasping for breath.

As soon as Paco was sure Teo had revived, he held up hand and bellowed, "Take them down!"

Teo and I were unchained, but unable to walk. We had broken ribs, innumerable contusions, lacerated faces, and swollen eyes. My mouth and tongue were distended, and I couldn't talk. There was no need to re-tie our arms. We were helpless.

The soldiers dragged us by our armpits, face down—our skinned toes trailing blood over the stone floor. Delgado was waiting in his office when we returned to ground level and were dumped into two straight-backed metal chairs in front of his desk. To weak to sit straight, we slumped forward. Paco's men jerked us upright and strapped us in with duct tape.

"So!" smiled Delgado, "I trust your visit to our dungeon was informative, yes? I assure you, it was pleasant compared to what I have planned if you do not answer my questions... He dropped the smile. "First—names!"

Neither of us spoke. I couldn't if I'd wanted to.

Delgado signaled Paco and a few seconds later, Ynilo was dragged in. He was still unconscious and they held him upright beside Delgado's desk.

Teo and I could barely see him through our swollen eyes.

Delgado barked, "Once more! Your names!"

We remained silent in a daze of pain and disorientation.

"Paco!" bellowed Delgado.

Paco unholstered his Makarov, placed the barrel against Ynilo's lolling head and pulled the trigger. An explosion of sound, blood, and brains flooded the room and we were jolted into full consciousness.

Teo began to weep. He'd known the Ramos family all his life. He'd recruited Ynilo himself. Paco's men let him drop to the floor.

Delgado said, "Once again... Your names."

Teo was shaking and began to sob convulsively. For the first time since the revolution he probably realized he'd been fooling himself. He was in no way qualified to be a CIA spy or a would-be assassin. He was simply a piano player who once led the band at Trafficante's Sans Souci Hotel.

His tears flowed and he answered, "T-Teofilo Cruz. And... and he is he is... Dante... Am...Amato."

"And who sent you?"

Teo hesitated, choked, and shook his head in despair.

Delgado pounded his fist on his desk. "Paco!"

Paco placed the Makarov against my temple.

Teo screamed, "Nooo! The CIA! It was the CIA!"

Delgado gleefully clapped his hands together. "Ah! Wonderful! Paco—bring in the camera. We must record this for posterity!"

In the next ten minutes Teo looked into its lens and revealed who we were—who sent us—and who helped us.

I remained unable to speak.

The filming ended, and Delgado happily informed us we'd be shot at midnight. Che himself would deliver the coup de grâce, and we should consider it an honor.

CHAPTER 49

CASTRO AND RAÚL CELEBRATED the end of José Martí day in a steaming hot tub with six gorgeous girls. Fidel's recorded speech had been broadcast to the world and was getting magnificent reviews. His four-hour, live performance was wildly cheered, and they had thwarted another assassination attempt by the CIA. They couldn't believe how stupid the Americans were.

A soldier with binoculars on the roof opposite the sniper nest had spotted the slightly open office window. It was one of the things they'd been told to watch for. He'd immediately radioed his superiors, and the assassins had been ambushed. The soldiers also had the good fortune to take them alive.

The huge hot tub was in a confiscated mansion in Havana's Miramar district and the women were all former showgirls. The brothers were chatting, smoking cigars, and being pampered by the adoring women.

Suddenly Castro had a thought. "Girls—wait outside—I have to speak with my brother." Indicating the phone next to the tub, he said, "I will buzz you shortly."

The girls pouted coquettishly, and got out of the tub. As they left the room, the sensual undulation of six exquisite bodies was a glowing tribute to their former profession.

Castro watched them appreciatively and took a pull on his cigar. He studied the tip and asked, "What if we don't shoot them?"

Raúl cocked an eyebrow. "The assassins?"

Castro nodded. "We have the rifle, their filmed confession, and the names of their associates."

Raúl interrupted him with a chuckle. "One of whom you are very familiar with."

Castro sighed. "Ah, the incomparable Carmen. I shall miss her."

Raúl returned to the subject at hand. "What reason to keep them alive?"

Castro shrugged. "We can always shoot them. Teofilo Cruz is a non-entity, but Dante Amato, to quote the cliché, may be worth more alive than dead. He is an American mobster. He works for Roselli and Giancana. You remember he accompanied Marissa del Valle here last year."

Raúl laughed. "Ah—the del Valles. We shot the father—you wanted to fuck the daughter—and she wanted to kill you."

Castro nodded. "Yes. A beautiful woman and I regret losing the opportunity. Another time, perhaps… But our informant tells us Amato's brother is a CIA agent."

Raúl hadn't known that. He pursed his lips. "Interesting."

"Consider… The Americans are obsessed with deniability. It caused their failure at the Bay of Pigs. But their denials exploded in their faces when the invaders confessed that the CIA had trained and sent them. And now we once again have a confession. This time that the CIA sent three assassins to kill me—one of who is the mafia brother of an agent. I don't believe they would want another embarrassing revelation. Rather than shooting Amato and releasing the film, we *threaten* to do both and see what we can get."

Raúl considered the proposal and said, "Kennedy still wants to ransom the Bay of Pigs prisoners. And eventually he'll pay a fortune for them if for no other reason than to alleviate his guilt. Amato would no doubt allow us to add considerably to our asking price."

Castro nodded, puffed and blew out a perfect smoke ring. "I

agree... But all things considered, I still think we should have an execution. He smiled, said, "Tell Che to see to it," and buzzed the girls.

CHAPTER 50

THE DUNGEON'S METAL DOOR was thrown open and slammed against the stone wall. Jolted awake, my first sensation was a brutal thirst. Teo and I hadn't had anything to eat or drink since our capture, and we were once again naked, bleeding, and hanging by our wrists.

Paco's men unchained us and we were dragged out. I shivered when we were herded into the courtyard's cold air, and I heard church bells tolling midnight. We were tied to side-by-side poles and I noticed the pockmarked wall behind us. Bullet holes made by innumerable firing squads.

Teo realized these were his last moments on earth and began praying. I was raised a Catholic, but hadn't been in church since I was an alter boy. I said a Hail Mary, turned to Teo, and mumbled, "S-sorry… we… got… you… into…" My tongue still wasn't working. I couldn't finish the sentence.

A minute later I heard marching boots. The firing squad approaching from the left with its leader calling cadence. The twelve men continued until they were opposite us, and the leader bellowed, "*Alto del detaalle!*" They were forty feet away, standing at rigid attention, and he called, "*Cara Izquierda!*"

Moments later, another figure entered the courtyard. His camo-fatigues, beret, and beard were unmistakable. It was Che Guevara. A soldier behind him was carrying a chair, which he put down alongside the firing squad. Che sat, crossed his legs, and slowly lit a cigar. He puffed content-edly, then nodded to the squad leader.

Teo and I weren't asked if we had any last words nor were we offered blindfolds. I thought, "Well, I've had one helluva run. And no one can say I didn't go out in a blaze of glory."

The squad leader slowly barked the commands. "*Listo… Panteria… Fuego!*" And twelve rifles roared and spat flame.

I heard the echo of the guns, but I felt nothing. I remained standing. Then I shivered uncontrollably and broke into in a cold sweat. Dumbfounded, I jerked my head toward Teo. He was slumped against the pole, held up by the ropes. But there was no blood. He'd fainted.

Everyone else in the courtyard was laughing.

It was a mock execution. The rifles were loaded with blanks.

I eventually learned that Che enjoyed it as a form of torture. He thought it hilarious when it caused his victims to piss their pants or evacuate their bowels. There were occasions however, when victims did neither. They died of a heart attack.

Guevara walked up to Teo and me, puffed on his cigar, and smiled. "Enjoy your stay…"

Five minutes later we were again chained to the dungeon wall.

CHAPTER 51

LAS VEGAS
FEBRUARY 1962

BLAZING SUN RAYS BOUNCED off the water while guests cavorted in the Desert Inn pool. In addition to the bevy of beautiful females, were the usual group of fun-seeking, overweight, but well-heeled men. Among them, a very happy Sam Giancana lounging poolside with a Rum Collins, Dee Thullin, and two UNLV rookies. But Momo was uninterested in the girls. He had all he could handle with Phyllis.

For Momo, it was about image. The capo of the Chicago Mob knew that being fawned over by beautiful women enhanced his notoriety and thus his power. Momo had been on a roll all day. His morning with Phyllis had begun with a fabulous fuck, he'd held the dice for ten minutes before lunch, and the afternoon brought news that his Cal-Neva Lodge problems were over. The hotel-casino that sat squarely on the California-Nevada border was supposedly owned by Frank Sinatra; however, Giancana had a large secret piece. But the Feds suspected Momo's ownership and had been after Ol' Blue Eyes' gambling license. Happily, they seemed to be backing down, and he thought it was because the CIA had told them to lay off.

Roselli approached in street clothes and gave Dee a look.

Dee gathered up her purse, "Come on girls—time to powder our noses." It only took the girls a second to register Johnny's glacial face before they followed Dee's lead and scampered off.

Roselli sat down. "I just got a call from Trafficante. They got Dante."

"Fuck! When?"

"A week ago."

"He's dead?"

"No. Trafficante said they're keepin' him alive."

Giancana was taken aback. "After tryin' to whack Castro?"

Roselli nodded.

"How the hell's he know that?"

"He got it from Harvey. Harvey thinks Castro wants to ransom him with the Bay of Pigs guys."

Giancana shook his head, "That sure as hell ain't what I'd do if somebody tried to whack me. Commies must need the money. When's the ransom supposed to happen?"

"Not soon. Diplomatic shit. According to Harvey, Washington can't be seen paying a ransom to Castro. They're gonna get a civilian to negotiate the deal which'll take time. Then they're gonna ask for donations from individuals and corporations… More time."

"Bullshit. Let's get involved."

"When they ask for civilian donations. But like the government assholes, we'll have to do it through a third party."

"Fuckin' hypocrites. We'll pony up when the time comes… I like that kid."

"Me too…"

"Anythin' else?"

Roselli lit a cigarette. "Yeah. I'm thinkin' of callin' his girlfriend."

"The del Valle broad? I thought she was in Spain."

"She was. For the holidays. The grapevine says she's back in Miami."

Giancana shook his head. "Christ. Info goes through that place like it was a pasta strainer. She probably already knows, but call her anyway."

CHAPTER 52

CANTRELL WAS STILL WAS PART of the CIA's Latin American desk. He escaped the Bay of Pigs bloodbath because he hadn't been in the loop until just before the invasion. He was now being briefed on everything Cuban.

He rushed into Aldo's office. "They've got your brother."

"Who? Who's got him?"

"The Cubans. He's alive, but he and two other men were captured trying to assassinate Castro."

"Again?"

Cantrell nodded. "Last week. In Havana."

The blood drained from Aldo's face. He'd talked to Dante when he called with Christmas greetings and sent presents to the kids. He'd said he was in Las Vegas and planned to stay there over the holidays. When he asked his brother whether he and his friends were still meddling in dangerous schemes, he'd said no. No? God*damn* it! The stupid, stupid, sonofabitch.

Aldo put his elbows on his desk and his face in his hands. "What happened?"

"Your brother, one of our contract stringers named Cruz, and a third man were caught with a sniper rifle. They were in a top floor window across the street from a building Castro was about to enter."

"Un-fucking-believable..."

"He's at La Cabaña."

Aldo shook his head. "Great. Trial and execution by Che."

"Maybe not. Harvey thinks they're holding him for ransom with the Bay of Pigs prisoners."

"That was an invasion. This was an assassination attempt. His second! I can't believe they let him live."

"They might. We still don't know. We do know that Castro needs everything from drugs to batteries. Our embargo has him rocking."

"He's got the Russians."

"Yes, but damn near everything vital to his economy—industrial machinery, trucks, cars, tractors, heavy equipment, came from *us* during the Batista years. The Russians can't supply him with replacement parts for any of that stuff and they can't replace it all themselves."

Aldo couldn't help smile at their unanticipated problem. "Have negotiations started?"

"Not yet. But I found out today that Kennedy's going to tap James Donovan, a New York lawyer, for the job. He'll supposedly be acting on behalf of relatives of the prisoners, but Kennedy will be the driving force and he won't care what its costs to get them back."

"Is there anything we can do in the meantime?"

"Not at the moment. La Cabaña's no joy ride, but if he lives through it, I think we'll get him out."

Cantrell left Langley that evening, drove to McLean, and selected one of the eight outdoor phone booths he used when calling Cuba on Fridays. They were all located at gas stations so he merely had to pull up to a pump and make the call while his tank was being filled. As usual, he dialed the home number of an undercover agent in Miami, and after giving his code name, was switched to a phone in Havana.

It was answered on the third ring. "Cubela..."

"It's me..."

"Yes, my friend, what can I do for you?"

Cantrell had met Rolando Cubela in 1953 when he was stationed at the American Embassy in Havana, and they'd become friendly. When Cubela became a power in Castro's government in early '59, Cantrell saw an opportunity and re-contacted him through a known Castro agent in Miami. The planets had aligned for him.

Dan Cantrell was fifty, had just gone through his second divorce, was broke, and knew he was never going to go much further in the Agency. He hadn't even been important enough to be let in on the plan to invade Cuba—a country on his own beat. He offered information for cash and Cubela accepted.

Cantrell lowered his voice. "Kennedy's going to announce James Donovan, a New York lawyer, as the prisoner's representative… But know he's adamantly committed to getting them out. You can ask for the moon, and get it."

CHAPTER 53

I RECOVERED FROM THE beatings in late March, but Teo couldn't stand without wincing until April. As the weeks dragged on, I knew we'd never get back to full health in La Cabaña. The inhuman conditions and terrible food simply wouldn't allow it. We'd managed to survive so far, but many hadn't.

A week after our mock execution we'd been unchained from the wall and thrown into one of the large dungeons. They'd remained vastly overcrowded, flooded by underground seepage, and infested with rats. We took our turns sleeping on the floor, were never allowed to bathe, and used bucket-toilets.

In May, we were transferred to the Isle of Pines off the southwest coast of Cuba. Castro had converted it into the Siberia of the Americas; he'd made it the detention center for political prisoners sentenced to forced labor. Conditions mirrored Stalin's concentration camps. Common criminals were made trustees and encouraged to beat political prisoners with short pipes. As a final form of terror, thirteen and a half tons of dynamite had been placed under the inmate's quarters, ready to be blown up the second there was another invasion of Cuba.

We worked from dawn to dusk in a marble quarry, and by July Teo was fading. On the 28th of the month, he was stabbed with a bayonet because a guard said he was malingering. When he was unable to stand, he was clubbed. I carried him to the prison hospital, unconscious, and an inmate doctor named Zabaleta examined him.

"It's not too deep. Infection is the danger."

"You work here. Can't you get some drugs?"

"There are none for us. Whatever there is is locked the prison doctor's office."

"What about alcohol? Can we boost any of the guard's rum?"

Zabaleta shook his head. "At night while they drink in their lounge, we're locked up in our cells. There's no way to get to it."

"How long can you keep him here?"

Zabaleta shrugged. "Until he wakes up. Then they'll put him back to work."

The guard who had brought me to the hospital stuck his head into the small examining room. "Amato! Back to your cell."

I took a last look at Teo and left with the guard. We were about to enter one of the prisons four circular cellblocks when a sergeant stopped us.

"Is this Amato?"

The soldier nodded. "Yes, sergeant."

"The captain wants to see him."

The sergeant took my arm and led me back to headquarters. The captain was seated behind a large desk smoking a cigar. Like almost everyone in Castro's government he was bearded, wearing camo-fatigues and comparatively young—mid-thirties at most. The name stenciled on his shirt was *Velasquez.*

He got right to the point. "I've been asked by the premier to personally evaluate your condition. What is it?"

"My what?"

"Your condition! Are you deaf? Are you sick?"

I was still furious over what had happened to Teo, and I lost it.

"Of course I'm sick you asshole! Are you blind! We're all sick! Half of us are dying! But why the hell would your glorious fucking leader give a shit!"

Velasquez remained calm. "That's none of your concern. But by your reaction, I can see you are well enough,"

"For what?"

"Also none of your concern. Sergeant! Throw him back in his cell!"

Two days later, Teo was transported to the mine with me and the rest of the prisoners. We worked all day, but when we returned to our cell I noticed a redness around Teo's wound and immediately called for Zabaleta. The doctor arrived and confirmed that the wound was infected.

Four days later, Teo was dead.

CHAPTER 54

SEPTEMBER 1962

"Amato! Follow me!"

I looked up and saw the sergeant who'd brought me to Velasquez weeks earlier. I climbed out of the pit we were mining, and the remaining men paused to watch the unusual interruption.

The other guards quickly threatened them with rifle butts, and shouted, "Not your business—back to work!"

I brushed the marble dust off my filthy clothes and squinted against the noon sun.

"What's going on?"

"Shut up and get in the jeep."

Ten minutes later I was pushed into one of the prison's infamous interrogation rooms and stripped. The room was equipped with a single metal chair bolted over a drain in the cement floor. I'd heard about it, and knew I was about to be strapped in the chair and tortured with a high-pressure hose like the one they'd used at La Cabaña. I steeled myself and prepared for the worst.

A guard with a hose appeared at the door and I waited to be strapped to the chair. He hit me with a stream of cold water, but it wasn't a high-pressure blast—it was the garden variety.

The guard then shouted, "Turn around! Slowly!"

I was shocked. They weren't punishing me. They were washing me! I slowly rotated and the stream was run up and down my front, back, and sides. When the hose was shut down, I was thrown a towel.

"Dry yourself!"

I did, and was more astounded when a barber appeared.

Using the photo from my false identity papers, the barber shaved my beard and cut my hair. When he'd finished, another guard appeared with clean slacks, a shirt, shoes, and socks.

By now I was convinced I was about to be the star of publicity stunt—hauled in front of television cameras and paraded before the world as an example of the humane treatment prisoners received in Communist Cuba.

Velazquez had a cigar clenched between his teeth and seemed to be in a jovial mood when I was shoved into his office. He was standing in front of his window with a grin on his face and his hands clasped behind his back.

"Do you have any idea why you are here?"

"Yeah. You're gonna haul me in front of a camera."

"Really! Why is that?"

"Why the hell else would you clean me up?"

Velazquez took the cigar out of his mouth and pointed it at me. "Because you, Amato, are one of the luckiest men alive."

"I don't feel very lucky."

"You should. You are lucky…but *my* country is the beneficiary."

"What the hell are you're talking about."

He grinned. "You're to be released!"

I was too stunned to speak.

Velasquez continued. "Did you not wonder why I wanted to see you weeks ago? It was at the personal request of Premier Castro—to assure him that you were well enough to be seen." He took a long pull on his cigar slowly and let it out—pausing before he spoke. "You, my friend, have been bought like the whore you are."

I remained stunned. "We've been ransomed?"

"Not we—*you*. Your corrupt government is hiring a lawyer to negotiate a price for the Bay of Pigs scum. In your case, it was your friends who paid for you...one million American dollars—hard currency we need far more than your life."

I was speechless.

"I shall miss the pleasure of watching you rot, Amato."

"Who paid th..."

"Salvatore Giancana."

He raised his hand and waved me off with an effete flutter.

Two hours later I was flown to Bayamo. A jeep took me to Guantánamo Bay and Sanchez was waiting in the BOQ. It was the same room where he, Teo, and I met eight months earlier.

Sanchez smiled and said, "Welcome back... You look like shit."

CHAPTER 55

BOBBY WALKED INTO THE Oval Office looking dour. He'd just left a meeting with the Joint Chiefs. He found his brother at his desk, eating lunch and reading *Thunderball*, the latest James Bond novel. The president held up his sandwich.

"Roast beef—rare and au jus. Want one?"

"No thanks, the Chiefs spoiled my appetite." Bobby sat in front of the desk. "Suddenly they're nervous. You approved Operation Mongoose last November, and they've had ten months to prepare. Now, suddenly they're waffling."

"They don't think we'll be ready by next month?"

"No—our forces are fine and the word from all the exile training camps is that they're straining at the bit."

"Then what's the problem?"

"They're concerned there won't be an uprising of the Cuban people when the exiles come ashore. It didn't happen during the Bay of Pigs and they're not convinced it'll happen this time."

"An uprising has always been a concern, but we've been publishing anti-Castro propaganda, arming militant opposition groups, and establishing guerilla bases in the country for ten months."

"True. To be exact, we've carried out seven hundred and eighty counter-revolutionary actions, seven hundred and sixteen of which involved sabotaging important economic targets."

"Bobby, what is it they want?"

"A guarantee that if there's no uprising when the exiles land, we'll go in, support the invasion, and re-take the island."

"How? We'd have no excuse to invade."

"True. So here's their list of possible provocations for an invasion."

Bobby handed him the folder. As Kennedy read the contents aloud, his face turned crimson and voice rose in disbelief.

"Sabotage of a space mission... Shooting down one of our own airliners... 'Terrorist' attacks on Cuban exiles in Miami... Blowing up one of our own ships like the 1898 USS Maine..." He looked up at Bobby, aghast.

Bobby nodded. "All false flags to place irrefutable blame on Castro and cause the American people to insist we retaliate."

"I vetoed all this at the outset!"

"I know."

"Get this out of here! Who'd it come from?"

"Lansdale."

The president threw the document on his desk. "The Chiefs must be insane to think I'd approve any of this!"

"I told them that, but they insisted I convey their concerns."

"There will be no need for you to convey my concerns to them. I'll do it myself. Get them in here!"

"Done—but there's another thing that bears on whether we should go forward, John."

The President waited while Bobby took a deep breath and crossed his legs.

"We've had disturbing reports out of the exile groups in Miami. Their Cuban spies report a build-up of Soviet troops and technicians on the island. As many as two thousand."

"Jesus! What kind of technicians?"

"Missile."

Kennedy stared, then said, "How good is the information?"

"British and French intelligence back it up. We've checked."

The President rubbed his chin and turned to stare out the window. "All right—there's nothing about the invasion timetable that's carved in stone. Notify all concerned that we're on hold until further notice."

Incredibly, in the face of what Castro knew were preparations for a second invasion of his island, he'd remained certain that he held the trump cards in any upcoming confrontation. He had good reasons to be confident.

On September 8, the first shipment of MRBMs—Soviet Medium Range Ballistic Missiles—had arrived in Cuba. And a second shipment of MRBMs had arrived one week later on the 15th.

CHAPTER 56

Harvey was waiting on the tarmac when the Navy P2V landed. Sanchez and I deplaned, Harvey stuck out his hand and frowned.

"Christ—you look like shit."

"That seems to be the consensus."

"Bad?"

"I'm alive. Teo and Ynilo aren't."

"You can tell me everything over a drink."

A limo took us to the JM/WAVE headquarters, and once in Harvey's office—buffered by three fingers of Jack—I was debriefed. Sanchez reported on my original meeting with Teofilo at Gitmo in January and my release last night. I laid out everything in-between. It took two hours. When Harvey was sure he had it all on tape, he shut off the recorder and asked if there was anything he could do for me.

"I need a phone and a car."

"Done—you've got a motor pool car, and you can use my phone. We'll take a walk." He signaled Sanchez to follow him and they left.

I called Roselli at home, then at his Columbia Studio office, and finally got him at the Friars Club playing Gin Rummy. He sounded happy when he answered, and I knew he was winning. He always won. He had a spy above the ceiling that read the other guys' cards and transmitted them to a confederate seated behind Johnny's opponent. The confederate then used subtle hand signals to let Johnny know what to discard.

I said, "A million bucks is a lotta lettuce…"

"Dante! Welcome back! Where are ya?"

"Miami. How the hell did you do it, Johnny?"

"You just said it. The prick wanted the million more than your ass in a hole. We got to him through Sanchez who got to Cubela."

"Cubela again."

"Yeah. But this time he came through."

"How the hell do I thank you?"

"You just did, but Momo was behind it and everybody kicked in—from The Big Tuna right on down the line and includin' a few associates looking to be made."

I was genuinely moved. "I'll call Momo, but at some point, I'll want to thank him personally."

"Wait a coupla days. He's in Monte Carlo with Phyllis."

"Okay, and thanks again, Johnny. You guys hauled my nuts out of one helluva fire."

"When are you comin' home?"

"Not sure. A few days maybe."

"Del Valle?"

"Yeah."

Roselli said, "I called her when we found out they weren't gonna to shoot you. She knows you're alive and that we've been tryin' to get you out."

"That's another one I owe you."

"Buy me a Jack when you get here. Ciao."

I hung up, dialed Marissa's home, and got Adelaida. She was overjoyed I was back, but I told her not to say a word to Marissa, I was on my way, and to be sure she answered the door when I got there.

A half hour later Adelaida let me in and whispered that Marissa was on the patio. I nodded, walked to the open double doors and stopped. She was sitting in a rattan chair facing the pool with her back to me. There was newspaper in her hands and a Mojito on the arm of the chair.

Wanting to soften the shock of my sudden appearance, I gently knocked on the doorframe.

Marissa turned, saw me, and her eyes widened.

I smiled and shrugged. "I was in the neighborhood, so..."

She shot out of the chair, sent the Mojito crashing to patio, rushed into my arms, and the words gushed out. "Dante! I never thought they'd let you go! I knew your friends were trying to ransom you, but didn't believe it could actually happen. You're here—you're really here!"

I held her tight. "Back—almost literally from he dead—but back."

She arched back to look into my eyes. "Johnny Roselli called me. That's how I knew what they were trying, but..."

"I know. He told me."

"I cried for days because of the way I left you. I'm so sorry..."

"Don't be. I understood."

"My God, Dante, why did you do it?"

I smiled. "You were headed for Spain and I had no plans for New Year's Eve."

She stopped and registered my gaunt appearance. "Oh, Dante, you..."

"I know. I look like shit. Everybody's been great to point that out."

She smiled. "A Cuban prison hasn't affected your sense of humor."

"Nor my libido."

She kissed me and led me to the bedroom.

CHAPTER 57

WASHINGTON
THE OVAL OFFICE
OCTOBER 1962

THE CHAIRMAN OF THE Joint Chiefs stood in front the president's desk, stone-faced. He could hardly believe what he placed before Kennedy, and he knew nothing in the world would be the same from this moment on.

Kennedy shook his head, "Max, tell me what I'm seeing isn't real. Jesus Christ. Those are Soviet SS-4s."

Maxwell Taylor replied, "Affirmative, Mr. President. And they're in all likelihood nuclear-tipped."

"I want the whole former SGA on this and my staff in here now. This is fucking insane! Does Khrushchev really think I can allow this? He's knows I've *got* to respond. What the hell is he thinking!"

EXCOM, the Executive Committee formed on the 15th of the month, convened immediately. A fitting U.S. response was the question. All members of the National Security Council were present, along with all the president's close advisors. It was agreed the response had to be "vigorous," and almost everyone believed that meant an all-out bombing of Cuba.

Kennedy demurred. "Surgical, guys. I want this solely against those missiles."

McGeorge Bundy agreed. "Politically, it's a punishment that fits the crime."

Taylor spoke for the Chiefs. "The Chiefs want to go further. They also want to take out Cuba's air defense sites and especially their bombers. They want to prevent—or at least limit—our losses in the event of a possible retaliatory air strike against U.S. bases in Florida…but I don't necessarily agree with them."

Bobby, one of the more hawkish members of the group, interjected. "Why? There's no question that we all agree our response can't appear weak! It has to be that of a great power. Bombing their offensive and defensive weapons does that."

"I understand that, but…"

Kennedy cut them off. "I don't believe we have to make a decision yet. There are two things in our favor. One—those missiles are not yet operational. And two—we know they're there—but they don't know we know."

Another U-2 flight the following day revealed IRBMs—intermediate-range ballistic missiles. Those could strike *anywhere* in the continental United States.

Kennedy examined photos of the newly discovered launch sites. "What are we talking about here?"

Taylor responded. "They're SS-5's. Each one carries a yield sixty-six times as powerful as the Hiroshima bomb. They can be in Washington in ten minutes. Seattle in half an hour."

Kennedy shook his head and sighed. "We have to get them out of there. But bombing could get us a retaliatory response that triggers more escalations. We don't want a nuclear war, Max."

Rusk said, "The only options are bombing, invasion, or diplomacy. But diplomacy takes time that allows the missiles to become operational. "

Undersecretary of State George Ball offered a different alternative. "Assume for the moment, no bombing, no invasion. What about a different kind of diplomacy? The president publicly announces the presence of missiles in Cuba. He orders a blockade to prevent the introduction of more missiles. Then he demands Khrushchev withdraw the missiles already there?"

Kennedy thought about, and liked it. He then made the first move in a nuclear chess game.

On October 22, 1962, the president addressed the nation. There were nuclear missiles in Cuba, and he was implementing a naval blockade. The U.S. defense readiness alert was set at DEFCON 3.

Castro mobilized his nation's military forces.

At the height of the tension, on October 26 and 27, the White House received two letters. In the first, Premier Khrushchev offered to withdraw Soviet missiles from Cuba if the United States ended the naval blockade and pledged not to invade the island. The second letter echoed the first, but added a demand that the U.S. remove its nuclear missiles from Turkey.

Bobby met with Soviet Ambassador Anatoly Dobrynin and an agreement was reached: Removal of the missiles under UN supervision in return for a public pledge by the U.S. not to invade Cuba. The commitment to remove the U.S. missiles from Turkey, however, would be secret.

Khrushchev was informed of the Dobrynin-Robert Kennedy agreement and met with his advisors. He decided he was not prepared to start a war over Cuba and drafted a response that accepted the terms, even thanking President Kennedy for his "sense of proportion and understanding."

The president then sent Khrushchev a letter confirming the agreement, and on the 28th Premier Khrushchev's acceptance letter to JFK was broadcast on Moscow Radio. The Missile Crisis was over, nuclear war had been averted, and the world breathed freer.

But not everyone was happy.

In Miami the anti-Castro exiles felt betrayed for the second time. Kennedy's promise not to invade Cuba dashed their hopes of ever re-taking their homeland. A militant faction formed, and within hours, the new group joined the fledgling conspiracy to assassinate the president.

CHAPTER 58

MARISSA AND I HAD WATCHED the Missile Crisis unfold from her home in Coral Gables. When tensions grew, I took her to Las Vegas for what I said was a short holiday. It was actually a move to get us out of south Florida before a possible war. Miami was an odds-on favorite to be one Castro's first targets.

I'd called Aldo when I was ransomed, and he was honestly relieved that I'd made it back. The kids were delighted to hear from me and even Pat had a few warm words. I mentioned that I no longer had any tails and Aldo checked with Lenny Mills. Mills confirmed that I'd dropped off the FBI's radar when I disappeared in January. They certainly hadn't known I was in Cuba and probably thought I'd been whacked in a petty Mob dispute.

When Marissa and I checked into the D.I., I ordered box lunches and a bottle of wine.

She asked, "Where are we going?

"To meet some friends for lunch. Put on shorts and sneakers."

I rented a convertible, and we headed west across the high desert. The sky was cloudless, temperature eighty, humidity zero. Thirty minutes later we were swallowed by the three thousand foot walls of Red Rock Canyon. I took the loop road and climbed up to Willow Spring, a crystal clear oasis in the middle of sandstone, juniper, scrub oak, and agave.

Marissa laughed. "The restaurant, I presume."

"Yep. You just have to bring your own food. Spread the blanket."

She spread it next to the spring where squirrels and chuckers were drinking. I laid out the food and opened the wine. We sat next to each other, and she was suddenly startled.

"Dante, look!"

"Ah, Our friends have arrived."

Two wild burros were approaching. They were brown, less than five feet at the shoulder and fearless. Marissa was wide-eyed.

"Say hello to Eli and Watson. We're old friends."

"How did you know they'd come?"

"They hear the car."

I got out the carrots I'd ordered with lunch and held one out to Eli. He nibbled it and I gave a carrot to Marissa.

"Give it to Watson."

She laughed and gingerly held out the carrot. Watson took it and she was delighted. "Dante, again! Give me another one!"

I was taken by how quickly she was smitten with the animals.

She fed Watson another carrot, and said, "Does Roselli know about this?"

"No. If he did, he'd have me committed."

We continued the routine until the carrots were gone, then patted their heads before they ambled off. We finished lunch and the wine watching a desert tortoise drink at the spring.

I took her hand. "I want to show you something."

We walked a short way to a ledge and rounded a large outcrop of sandstone. Wide open desert stretched below us as far as the eye could see.

She sighed. "I love it. It feels like the middle of nowhere."

"Almost." I turned her toward the opposite direction. The towers of Las Vegas hotels dotted the horizon.

She slowly shook her head. "Hard to believe it's so peaceful here with a city that close and the world in turmoil."

I nodded. "Hard as believing that forty-eight hours ago I was in a Cuban prison… You got me through down there, Marissa. You balanced the insanity." A gust caught her hair, blew a few strands over her face, and I brushed them away. "I lived so I could have you in my life."

She smiled. "I haven't been out of it since the Saharan Motel."

We returned to the D.I. changed into swimsuits and found Roselli at the pool with Dee Thullin. I sat, and the girls headed for the pool. Every eye in the area followed them.

Roselli smiled. "You're not gettin' serious with her are ya?"

"Probably."

"Fine. Just don't marry her. Set her up in a nice apartment."

"Either way my mother won't like it."

"Why not? The girl's Latin."

"She's Cuban."

"That's not Latin?"

"Yeah. But Mom's Mexican. Old school."

"What the hell's that mean?"

"Think bias. Sicilians versus Italians. The French and Dutch in Belgium. North and South Korea. *Our* north and south for christsakes."

"So have her tell your mother she's Mexican."

"She won't lie. She a very proud Cuban."

"And she has to tell that to your mother?"

"The second it comes up."

A waiter interrupted us. "Mr. Roselli… Mr. Giancana just checked into the hotel and would like to see you and Mr. Amato in his suite."

Roselli handed the waiter a ten. "Tell 'im we'll be right up."

I got up, went over to poolside and called out, "Marissa—Johnny and I have a quick meeting—see you in the suite."

She waved and nodded. I rejoined Roselli, we put on terrycloth robes, and headed for the hotel.

I said, "I thought Phyllis was out of town."

"She is. It must be somethin' else. It's gotta be important or he would've used the phone."

A man we knew was leaving Giancana's suite as we entered. He smiled and greeted us. "Johnny—Dante."

Roselli asked, "Clean?"

"As a whistle." He waved and closed the door behind him. Romeo Romero was the local wire-expert we hired to sweep rooms ever since Giancana's bug had been uncovered during the McGuire/Rowan escapade.

Momo was in his shirtsleeves, pouring scotch over ice at the suite's bar. He held up the bottle.

"Drink?"

Roselli said, "Jack—rocks."

I said, "Two. What's up Momo?"

"Grab a seat."

We sat around the coffee table and Giancana joined us with our drinks.

"I just came in from Tampa. Marcello was there with Trafficante. They wanna move on Kennedy."

I looked at Roselli. I had no idea what Momo was talking about.

But Roselli did. He'd heard about the meeting Hoffa had with Trafficante and Marcello over a year earlier.

Roselli raised an eyebrow. "Now?"

Giancana nodded. "They want him gone, they want it soon, and I agree. Everyone with half a fuckin' brain agrees."

I was aghast. "They want him hit?"

"That's it. And we should've done it the minute he unleashed his fuckin' brother on us. We didn't and it was stupid, but now the timin's perfect."

Roselli glanced at me. It was his turn to have no idea what Momo was talking about. "How so?" he asked.

"Castro is crazed about Khrushchev backin' down and pullin' the missiles out of Cuba. But he blames Kennedy for talkin' him into it. Kennedy insisted on them being hauled out of there in return for a promise not to invade Cuba. Castro didn't give a shit about an invasion. He thought he could handle it. There were tactical nukes in Cuba, and if it were up to him he would have used them on the beaches."

Roselli still wasn't following. "How does all that make the timin' right?"

"Because it figures that now more than ever Castro would want to see Kennedy dead. If an assassin sent by Castro killed Kennedy, this country would go nuts. They'd demand an invasion, and we'd send in the Marines to kick the shit out of Castro's crummy army. We'd get our casinos back, but that ain't the home run. The real biggie is we'd get Bobby off our backs. Johnson'll be president and he hates the prick. He'll throw his sorry ass out as Attorney General the first chance he gets, and we're home free."

Roselli whistled his appreciation, but then said, "Great—but who's this assassin that Castro's sendin' to whack Kennedy?"

"There is none. Not yet. But there will be—a guy who'll be set up to look like he's doin' it for Castro."

Roselli cocked an eyebrow. "A patsy?"

Giancana smiled and nodded. "A patsy."

"How do we find 'im?"

"With our friends in the CIA."

Roselli was genuinely surprised. "They're in on this?"

"Not the headquarters bunch, but some of the guys we've been workin' with in Miami and a lot of the contract people who've been trainin' the exiles for years. They're pissed because they've been told that after all the effort, sacrifice, and trainin' there ain't gonna be no game."

"What are we supposed to do?"

"As soon as they find the patsy, we work out the plan for the hit. Most of the CIA guys don't know shit about a settin' up a hit, which is the reason they hired us in the first place."

"From where? Here, Miami, where?"

"We'll see. But keep a lid on this. The fewer who're in on it, the better."

Giancana noticed that I was staring blankly. "You okay?"

I blinked and snapped out it. " Yeah…fine. I'm good."

But I wasn't good. I wasn't against killing. I'd done that for years in the Pacific. I'd offered to kill Castro. And even knocking off a dangerous threat in a mob dispute seemed okay. But assassinating the president? I wasn't sure I could be a part of it. And as soon it the crossed my mind, I wondered if I'd have a choice.

CHAPTER 59

THE PRESIDENT'S FACE WAS crimson. "He did what!"

Bobby continued, "He sent six-man infiltration teams into Cuba during the Missile Crisis. Three of the CIA teams are still on the island."

They were alone in the Oval Office, and Bobby had been as furious as his brother when he'd heard the news. But in order to advise him wisely he thought it best to remain calm in the face of his brother's rage.

"You're telling me he deliberately disobeyed my orders?"

Bobby nodded. "William King Harvey has proved once again why he's known as a wild card."

The president paced, fuming. "What the hell was he thinking? We're on the verge of a nuclear war, and this stupid sonofabitch is trying to burn down a few tobacco fields?"

Bobby shook his head. "Actually they tried to ambush Castro when he was on his way to a memorial service for fallen guerillas without his usual bodyguards. They hid in the trees and peppered his motorcade as it approached the graveyard. The driver and his passenger were killed but it wasn't Castro, it was his double... The team escaped."

"Unbelievable!"

"It gets worse. One of the other teams blew up an industrial target and *was* captured. They admitted to twenty-five sabotage missions in Cuba since the beginning of the year and said their CIA overseers in Miami were Rip Robertson and Robert Wall… They both work for Harvey."

"Get him out of there!" roared Kennedy. "I don't care what he's done in the past with the Berlin tunnel and Philby! He's a loose canon and I want him out!"

Bobby nodded. "I'll call McCone and see to it. In the meantime Castro says the missiles are being removed, but he refuses to allow either international inspectors or our aerial inspection. He says he'll shoot down any of our planes flying over the island."

Kennedy thought for a few seconds before he spoke. "Order the low level photo flights suspended but continue with the U-2s flying high enough that he can't get to them."

Bobby nodded. "There's still the matter of the Russian IL-28 bombers on the island."

Kennedy was settling down now that he was dealing with issues he thought he could control. "We'll say that we'll resume the naval blockade if they're not out of there within thirty days."

"What about the Migs?"

The president thought for a moment, then said, "I think we have to accept the fact that they're keeping Soviet trainers in Cuba, so let them keep the Migs. Our biggest problem remains verification that all the missiles have left the island."

Bobby smiled humorlessly. "The clever bastard announced that he'd allow international inspection if we'll allow the same for all the bases where Cuban exiles are being trained on U.S. territory."

"He's playing to world sympathy. He knows about our training bases and knows we can't allow inspections because they'll prove we're still planning an invasion."

"What's our excuse?"

Kennedy smiled and sat at his desk. "The deal we made with Khrushchev. He agreed to pull out the missiles in return for our promise not to invade *dependent upon verification by inspections* that the missiles have been removed. No inspections—no promise."

The fact that he had options calmed the President. He felt he'd made several intelligent decisions, among which was his order to have William King Harvey sacked. But sacking Harvey was to have deadly repercussions in the future.

When Harvey took over the JM/WAVE station he'd brought in David Morales, a Mexican-American nicknamed El Indio because of his dark skin and Indian features. He was a hard drinker and a bully who was involved in the CIA black operations known as Executive Action. He soon became Chief of Operations and was involved with Roselli in the plots to assassinate Castro. And like Harvey, he became a close friend of Roselli's.

Along with others in the clandestine community, Morales was infuriated over Kennedy's attacks on the CIA and repeated betrayals of the Cuban exiles. When his friend William Harvey was sacked it was the last straw.

He called Roselli.

CHAPTER 60

MIAMI
DECEMBER 1962

MARISSA AND I DROVE through thousands of cheering, flag-waving exiles as we approached Rolando Masferrer's house three blocks from the Orange Bowl. The streets were still festooned with Christmas decorations five days after the holiday, but the jubilant mood was about an equally joyous occasion.

Castro had accepted a ransom of fifty-three million dollars' worth of food and medical supplies for the release of the 1,113 Bay Pigs prisoners he'd been holding in Cuban jails. On December 24 the remnants of the 2506 Brigade had returned to Miami, and now, on the 29th, President Kennedy was about to welcome them back in the Orange Bowl. Radio and television stations were reporting that over 40,000 people had flooded the stadium.

Marissa and I flew in to witness the event as the guests of Manuel Artime, the leader of the Brigade. Artime had announced that Jackie would address them in Spanish—the president would welcome them, and then be presented with the Brigade's flag. Based on our admiration for Artime, and having watched him valiantly storm the beach on the night of the invasion, we gladly accepted the invitation. Roselli had also been invited but had arrived through Tampa because of a meeting requested by Trafficante and Marcello.

When we arrived at Masferrer's Mediterranean style home I noticed sentries in a parked car out front. Luis Quevado and another man.

We waved and entered the house.

Masferrer's large living room featured high-arched windows, a beamed ceiling, and rough stucco walls. Sitting with him were Manuel Artime, Rafael Sanchez, Johnny Roselli and David Morales. His two bodyguards, Adega and Arroyo, hovered in the background next to a wide interior hallway.

Artime jumped to his feet when we entered and happily hugged Marissa. "Ah! Much more pleasant surroundings than the last time we met, no?"

"Thank God you're safe," she exclaimed, "We didn't think we would ever see any of you again."

"There are many of us who no one will ever see again, but those of us who survive are planning to make Castro pay for that—and then realize the mistake he's made by letting us go. And we'll do it with or without Kennedy's help." He turned to me. "Dante, it's good to see you. We cheered you from prison when we heard of your attempt to assassinate the pig."

I shook his hand and said, "Thank you."

Artime chuckled. "You turned out to be a very expensive man, amigo. A million dollars! My God. The rest of us were not even worth fifty thousand each!"

I smiled. "My patrons may be richer than yours. What kind of shape are your men in?"

"As good as can be expected—but overjoyed to be back." He indicated the other men in the room. "You know Rolando, Rafael, and David."

I'd only met David Morales on a few occasions but had heard a lot about him, and I was wary. Marissa and I nodded to the group. Masferrer looked at me with cold eyes. I guessed he was still pissed over what he thought was the ill-advised attempt Marissa and I made on Castro over two years earlier. It wasn't. I didn't know it, but it was because Masferrer still hadn't uncovered who'd betrayed him, and he continued to suspect me. I still wanted to punch his lights out for what he did to Marissa, but out of respect for Artime, I passed.

Masferrer checked his watch and turned to Artime. "We'd best be going, Manuel. Erneido Oliva will be waiting for you on the reviewing stand."

Artime turned to Marissa and me explaining, "Our men respect and admire deputy commander Oliva so greatly that they selected him to present the Brigade's flag to the president. A great honor for a valiant warrior." He waved to those of us who wouldn't be going with him and said, "We'll see you at the stadium."

Artime started for the door with Masferrer, and his two bodyguards. Sanchez, Roselli, and Morales remained.

Roselli said, "Dante—would you mind havin' Marissa go with them? I need you for a quick meeting."

I nodded and said, "Go with them, I'll see you there."

She left with Artime's group, and Roselli motioned for the rest of us to sit. He launched into the reason he asked us to stay as soon as we settled and without preamble.

"This afternoon we'll be in reserved seats close to the action. Take a close look at Kennedy's security detail and make mental notes. How many—where they're positioned—how they scan the crowd—their hand signals. They'll be easy to spot because they'll be wearin' dark glasses and have wires comin' out of their ears. Watch everything."

I felt my heart sink. I knew what was coming.

Roselli lit a cigarette and continued. "I've just come from a meetin' with Trafficante and Marcello. We figured the best way to hit Kennedy would be either at an outdoor speakin' event like the one today or durin' a motorcade."

Morales and Sanchez, who knew I had tried to take a shot at Castro, glanced at me then back to Roselli.

Morales said, "A sniper."

Roselli nodded. "We're gonna check out what he's got with him today, but between the two choices we think a motorcade might be the best option."

Morales said, "A tougher shot. He'd be a moving target."

Roselli nodded again. "True, but we'll come at him with more than one shooter, and it'll create confusion. We figure from buildings along the motorcade route—nests on floors above street level."

Morales smiled. "I like it."

Roselli wrapped it up, saying, "Good. We'll start linin' up expert shooters, and from now on every time Kennedy appears in public we'll be there to take notes. By the time we set up a patsy to take the fall, we'll be checked out on his security details, and decide the time and place to make the hit."

I'd been right about what was coming. The plan was in full swing, and I still had no idea what I could do to stop it and remain alive. The good news was that they still had to find a patsy who could be set up to make it look like the hit came from Castro...not easy. I figured I still had a shot at doing nothing.

CHAPTER 61

SPEAKING FLUENT SPANISH, the beautiful Jackie addressed the crowd at the Orange Bowl. She called the Brigade's ransomed prisoners: "The bravest men in the world." The president was then presented the Brigade's flag and announced, "I can assure you that this flag will be returned to this Brigade in a free Havana." Forty thousand people erupted in an explosion of wild, tearful cheering.

It was an ill-conceived remark in light of Kennedy's deal with Khrushchev *not* to invade Cuba. But the event was designed to reflect a warm rapport between the president and the Brigade, and it seemed to work. Beneath the surface, of course, there ran a vein of bitter resentment among those who felt the occasion was a display of hypocrisy.

The president's Secret Service detail ushered him out when the ceremony ended, and well-wishers flooded the reviewing stand to press the flesh of the Brigade's leaders.

Masferrer's beautiful mistress, Abril Soto, was seated in the first row of seats below the reviewing stand. She'd worn a stunning red skirt with a matching low cut blouse. He was watching proudly when he saw a familiar figure embrace her.

Eni Quintero. The man who owned the Adelphi marina in Key Largo. Masferrer watched her quickly say something to him, then move away.

An hour later, the jubilant crowd broke up and headed for parties that were about to take place all over Miami. Masferrer had a short conversation with Adega and Arroyo, and then fetched Abril to slowly make their way through the teeming streets.

As soon as they were in his living room, Masferrer grabbed Abril's arm and violently spun her around.

"How do you know Eni Quintero?"

She was taken aback, but recovered quickly.

She blinked and said, "Who?"

He slapped, then roughly shoved her onto the couch. "Eni Quintero—the owner of Adelphi marina!"

Abril touched her reddening cheek, but still managed to remain calm. "I do not know what you are talking about."

"I saw him embrace and talk to you and hour ago."

"You must be mistaken. I knew a lot of the people at the ceremony. Many of them embraced me."

"This one was Eni Quintero!"

"I don't know an Eni…"

A second openhanded blow to her temple cut off her words, sent her reeling, and she passed out.

Masferrer roared, "Martine—Pepe! Carry her to the kitchen!"

The two bodyguards each grabbed an arm and pulled her off the couch so violently she was jerked out of her high-heeled mules. They dragged her down the hallway into a modern kitchen, then as they'd been instructed, hoisted her onto a large center island, and tied her hands and ankles.

Masferrer went to the stove, turned on a burner and held a ten inch serrated knife over the flame until it was red-hot. Pepe threw a pitcher of water into Abril's face and revived her. Her eyes fluttered open, and when she realized she was trussed up, her eyes darted around in panic. Masferrer leaned over and placed his face close to hers. He smiled, and she felt the heat of the glowing knife close to her ear.

She sputtered, "R-Rolando, p-please, I…"

He touched the knife to her neck in the tender area behind her left earlobe. She screamed and arched upward in a spastic convulsion. The stench of her burned flesh filled her nostrils, and tears and pitiful moans followed. Masferrer showed her the knife.

"How do you know Eni Quintero…"

"Rolando…" she sobbed, "I d-don't know…"

The knife touched the area behind her other earlobe. The result was the same—accompanied by a long agonized scream. She began shaking uncontrollably and Masferrer again placed his face next to hers, positioning the knife over her eye.

"How do you know Eni Quintero…"

She screamed—snapping her head back and forth and sobbing uncontrollably.

A few seconds later Abril began to talk. It took less than five minutes for her to tell Masferrer everything he wanted to know.

She'd been in the Sierra Maestra with Castro from the early days of the revolution. When they'd won and were about to enter Havana, thousands of Cubans fled to Miami. Castro seized what he saw as an opportunity and ordered her to join them and become a covert agent in the exile community. As one of the original, and most beautiful, exiles in Miami, it didn't take her long to get Masferrer's attention. She soon was not only working for him but had become his mistress.

She knew Eni Quintero because she'd found rental receipts for slips in the Adelphi marina in Masferrer's desk and decided to investigate. Knowing he had to use boats to launch his raids into Cuba, she suspected the Adelphi was probably where they were kept.

She secretly drove to the marina, met Quintero, and told him she was thinking a buying a boat and renting a slip. Completely taken by her, he invited her to join him for a drink. From that point it was easy. She got him talking and found out that Quintero was fiercely anti-Castro and gladly allowed his marina to be used by infiltrators.

It did not take a genius to know Masferrer had to be one of them.

Although she'd seldom been able to discover Masferrer's plans because he was so careful, she overheard a conversation between Martine and Pepe on the night he was planning to leave with three boats. She had him followed to the marina and then across the Florida Straight to Cuba where his position was radioed to the patrol boat and he was intercepted.

Masferrer's emotions were a mixture of disgust and sorrow for the loss of a beautiful mistress. He leaned over her a last time.

"And who was it that followed me, darling?"

Abril gave him the name, weeping.

He nodded to Pepe and Martine.

Abril and the man she'd named were never seen again.

CHAPTER 62

SANTA ANITA
JANUARY 1963

TWENTY THOUSAND SCREAMING fans urged their horses down the home stretch of the first race on a very fast track. Seconds later, three of them thundered past the wire in a photo finish. I'd bet two of the three to win and smiled.

Roselli and I had returned to Los Angeles after spending New Year's with Marissa, Artime, and the hierarchy of the anti-Castro community. Opening day at Santa Anita was the following week, and we'd agreed to meet for a relaxing day at the track.

Roselli was late, and when he finally showed up I was enjoying lunch in the restaurant overlooking the finish line. I told him he'd missed the first race, but Roselli didn't seem to care and was smiling broadly when he sat next to me.

Furtively glancing around to be sure we were out of anyone's earshot, he said, "We've got our patsy!"

I'd been hoping the effort to find a guy willing to take a shot at the president would be futile. Especially since he had to have a background that allowed him to be set up as a Castro-sent assassin.

I covered my alarm, and in a stage whisper asked, "Who'd you talk to?"

"Momo. They found a guy in Dallas."

"They?"

"Contract CIA. Two P.I.s from New Orleans. Guy Bannister and David Ferrie. Bannister was career FBI until he retired in fifty-four. Ferrie works with him as a shamus and he's also Marcello's pilot."

"And the guy can be connected to Castro?"

"Yeah. His name's Oswald. Ferrie knew him from his Civil Air Patrol days. He's an ex-marine with an undesirable discharge and—get this—he defected to Russia in fifty-nine and didn't come back until last June."

"He escaped?"

"They let him out. It don't figure, but they did. The word from Bannister is that the FBI's watchin' 'im because they figure the Commies let him out to spy for them. Bannister also found out that some higher-up CIA guys in D.C. are watchin' 'im—but the way they handled it is a little fucked up. Banister said they didn't even open a 201 on him until December of '60."

My eyes narrowed. My brother had told me what a 201 file was. "A *little* fucked up? A 201's standard operating procedure as soon as someone defects. This guy was a defector with an undesirable discharge, and the CIA doesn't open a 201 on him for over a year? How the hell can that be? That's not strange, it's fucking inept!"

"Momo agrees, and it gets even weirder. Four months after Oswald got back to the States, he got a job at place called Jaggars-Chiles-Stovall. A guy by the name of George de Mohrenschildt set it up. He's a White Russian immigrant with CIA connections. The company's a photo lab that does map work for the Army Security Agency—putting captions, arrows, and notations on U2 photos—includin' the ones taken last October that showed missiles in Cuba."

I couldn't believe it. "The guy's a defector and then he gets a sensitive job?"

Roselli shrugged. "Crazy, no? But Bannister told Momo that if the CIA got Oswald a job at the Lab, it might not be that crazy. *Because* it's a sensitive job, they could be danglin' him hoping the KGB will recruit him.

That would let them know how the KGB approached prospects and turned them into spies, which they'd obviously use for their counter-espionage."

"Christ! What a group."

Roselli shrugged. "Again Momo agrees. Who the hell knows? Bannister told him the CIA may even have sent him over there in the first place."

"He thinks the *CIA* sent him to Russia?"

"Again, who the hell knows the whole story? Bannister thinks the guys in D.C. don't know half of what's goin' on in the trenches and vice-versa. It could've been that the top guys in D.C. didn't want their plan to send Oswald to Russia to flow down the line—if it *was* their plan. The point is—*our* CIA contract guys are the ones in the trenches and they figure they can create a trail of evidence that'll link Oswald to the hit when it goes down."

I was aghast. "How the hell does a guy with possible connections to the CIA, and with an FBI spotlight on him, figure to be set up as a spy *or* a patsy?"

"I know it seems fucked up, but that's not our problem. All we gotta do is wait for them to get it done."

"Christ, Johnny, the reason it seems fucked up is because it is. I think there's something weird here."

"Don't think. Ferrie and Bannister say they can pull this off with the help of Sanchez, Morales, and some of Marcello's people. This Oswald guy's already got a track record of lovin' Commies so all they have to do is keep saltin' the pot. They'll tell him he's been recruited as part of a secret CIA team that hates Kennedy for what he's doing to the Agency and Cuba, and at some point they'll get him to order a rifle. It's perfect. The guy was a Marine—a marksman for christsakes."

I'd qualified as a Marine sniper and knew all about the designations. "'Marksman' doesn't mean shit. 'Marksman' isn't 'expert'. It's the lowest rung on the ladder. My niece could get 'marksman' sucking her thumb."

"Who gives a fuck? All he's gotta do is be there and pull a trigger. The experts will take the real shots."

I again felt a sinking feeling because we were another step closer to an event that I wanted no part of. My thoughts were interrupted by a combination of screams and moans from the fans as the race results were posted. I checked the board and saw I had the winner. I showed Roselli my two hundred dollar ticket at eleven to one odds.

Roselli smiled. "You are one lucky son-of-a-bitch."

I stifled a wince. The last time I'd been called lucky I'd been in a Cuban prison for eight months. Christ! I thought, *they're going to assassinate the president—leader of the free world, a war hero, and the first Catholic elected to the presidency.* I wanted no part of it. But how the hell could I figure a way to stop it without getting myself killed?

CHAPTER 63

ALDO WAS APPALLED. Yesterday he'd been on a high after reading a report just in from Vietnam saying that if the war continued to go well it might be possible to withdraw one thousand American troops by the end of the year. Good news from Vietnam, and now he'd heard what should have been good news from Cuba. But, apparently the Cuba situation was incapable of producing anything you could call "good."

In an interview with ABC's Lisa Howard, Fidel Castro agreed that "a rapprochement with Washington" was desirable. It was a totally unexpected development. Howard informed the CIA, and Kennedy was briefed. Following up the opening should have been child's play, but the president was waffling.

Aldo stormed into Cantrell's office without knocking. God, how many times had he done that this year.

"What the hell is going on?"

Cantrell looked up from the dossier he'd been reading.

"I see you've heard."

"I have. And I repeat—what the hell is going on?"

Cantrell shrugged. "There seem to be three schools of thought. The president's ambivalent about going forward because there's an election next year, and he doesn't want to seem weak on Cuba. But he's giving it serious consideration. Bobby's adamant that Castro can't remain in power. And the CIA is strongly opposed to Howard looking like she's negotiating with a communist dictator on behalf of the U.S."

"Where's State in this?"

"A usual, they're split between the hawks and the doves, but overall they don't particularly like it because it allows Castro to remain in power."

Aldo threw up his hands. "Christ!"

Cantrell asked, "Have you heard Nixon's latest tirade?"

"No."

Cantrell opened the dossier and read aloud. "'We have courageously dared a blockade to keep the peace, withdrew a blockade to avoid a war, pledged the Cuban exiles that their flag would fly in Havana, then pledged ourselves not to re-invade, then offered the exiles service in our armed forces which are *forbidden* to invade, then instituted aerial surveillance to determine whether or not we *need* to invade'" He put down the paper. "I hate to admit it, but Nixon's right. Our Cuban policy's been a disaster."

"So we're going to ignore a shot at resolving what has been, is, and will continue to be a powder keg in our backyard."

"Maybe—it's up to Kennedy. It's frustrating, but that's the way it is."

Aldo left the office and slammed the door.

Cantrell smiled. He wasn't frustrated at all. Disagreement within U.S. policy circles meant he had something to sell. The following day he selected one of his phone booths and made his Friday call to Miami. The call was forwarded to Cubela, and he passed on same information he'd given Aldo to his Havana paymaster.

Once again, nearly as soon as it happened, Castro knew everything going on in Camelot. But this time Castro wasn't the only recipient of the information. Ted Shackley, the new head of JM/WAVE, found out about the president's attitude because of his high level contacts in Langley. Therefore, David Morales, his second in command, also knew. And anything Morales knew, he passed on to his close friend, Johnny Roselli.

When Roselli got the information, his biggest concern was that

Kennedy was actually considering a deal with Castro—a deal that would keep him in, and their casinos out, of Cuba. They couldn't let that happen. He called Giancana, Trafficante, and Marcello, and they determined that they had to accelerate their plans. The president had to be killed before a deal with Castro could be made.

A seemingly unrelated incident took place earlier in the month. However, it was anything *but* unrelated. There had been an attack on Edwin Walker, a retired general Kennedy had fired for spewing extreme right-wing propaganda to his troops. The attacker had ordered the rifle through the mail from Klein's Sporting Goods in Chicago. Incredibly, he'd meticulously documented his plan with hand-drawn maps, photographs of Walker's residence, and political statements. He took one shot at Walker, narrowly missed the general's head, and escaped. Lee Harvey Oswald had taken his first step toward becoming the perfect patsy.

CHAPTER 64

"HARRY" RUIZ-WILLIAMS, the man Bobby trusted to deal with the often-fractious exile leaders, entered the DOJ flushed with excitement. The second he appeared in Bobby's waiting room, he was ushered into the office. Bobby was at his desk with his jacket off, tie pulled down, and shirtsleeves up.

He bounced up to greet the man who'd become a close friend, and embraced him. "Harry—you said 'extremely important'—good news or bad?"

"Better than good," Harry gushed, "almost unbelievable! I've just been contacted by the leader of the Cuban Army—the third highest official in Castro's government!"

"Almeida?" asked Bobby, astonished. He waved at a chair in front of his desk and resumed his seat behind it.

Harry sat. "Yes. Juan Almeida wants to lead a palace coup."

Bobby went from astonished to shocked. "My God… Do you think he's serious?"

"I do. We've known for some time—certainly since the Missile Crisis—that there's been a split at the top. The pro-Soviet faction is led by Fidel and Raúl, the anti-Soviet faction by Che and Almeida. The latter two are determined not to let Cuba become a Soviet puppet state, and Almeida has decided to do something about it."

"Amazing. There are always splits at the top. Here it's over how to get rid of Castro. There it's over the Soviet's dominance."

"But this could remove their split, no?"

Bobby steepled his fingers under his chin, and said, "U.S. and world newspapers have been full of coverage about strains in the Cuban economy, bickering political factions in their ruling elite, and our crackdowns on the exile groups. In light of that, if Almeida replaces Castro, it could seem free of U.S. involvement."

"I think so, Bobby. It's a model for plausible deniability. Almeida wants to assassinate Castro and pin his death on someone else—perhaps a Russian or Russian sympathizer—in which case he wouldn't be seen as staging a coup but merely taking over the reins before they became Russian puppets. He'll use his stature and control of the Cuban Army in the first hours and then appeal for U.S. help saying he wants to prevent a Soviet takeover."

Bobby beamed. "It's perfect! We'd be able to use force to support him without risking Soviet retaliation." He sighed happily and spread his hands. "It seems too good to be true. What does he want from us?"

"Money. And a concrete guarantee that we'll come in with our military to support the coup once he's eliminated Castro."

"No problem. You think he can he pull it off?"

"I think he's the one man who can.

"Because he's a black Cuban?"

"Yes. Over sixty percent of the island's Cubans are either black or mulatto, but Almeida's the only highly placed black man in Castro's government. The people respect, admire, and are very proud of him. I think they'd follow his lead."

"The money's easy, but how do we give him a concrete guarantee?"

"To be determined, but it will have to come directly from the president."

"And the timetable?"

"He thinks he can have everything in place by December first."

"Good, God. This is fantastic. Our long-range plan is to make an election campaign tour in late November. Six or seven cities. It would be beautifully symbolic if, when the coup's announced, we were in Miami. I'll see if we can swing back there after we leave Dallas on November twenty-second."

CHAPTER 65

MIAMI
JUNE 1963

IN THE EARLY SIXTIES, THE Rat Pack was riding high and Vegas was exploding as America's hippest city. My responsibilities there and in L. A. had kept me busy, but not busy enough to keep me from Miami and Marissa. Our relationship had intensified since the holidays, and I began to consider the unthinkable. I'd always thought of myself as a bachelor and been very happy in the role. But that'd changed when I met the incredible Miss del Valle.

Her primary loyalty was the Cuban cause—mine, the Mob. My middle-class childhood in a Catholic home, although plagued by constant parental bickering, was fairly normal. Growing up, I was aware—as was everyone in Chicago—of "The Outfit," but I thought little about organized crime until I signed on and became committed to them.

But now they wanted to assassinate the president—not Bobby— the prick who was our real enemy, but the president. I was fully aware of what would happen if I were suspected of opposing the family but decided to deal with it when and if the time came. They were adamant about setting up the patsy, and there was still a chance they wouldn't be able to do it.

I was sure Marissa wouldn't agree with my position. If she believed assassinating the president would be a step in re-taking Cuba, her natural instinct would be to turn a blind eye and condone it. At Artime's request, she was even about to leave for Nicaragua again. He was forming a new three hundred-man army with the seven million dollar budget he'd gotten from Shackley's CIA JM/WAVE station in Miami. It was a brazen enterprise for an organization that was prohibited by law from operating on U.S. soil.

Commuting to Nicaragua was a nightmare so I was determined to talk her out of going. The question was, would I go so far as making a commitment to make her stay. I'd opened the subject with Roselli one night while we were having a nightcap in the D.I. lounge. When I brought up the possibility of marriage, he stared at me, said, "Excuse me?" and then gave me the name of a Beverly Hills psychiatrist. So much for helpful advice.

I called Marissa, booked a flight, and landed at Miami International as the sun was setting. I rented a convertible, lowered the top, and picked up a bouquet of White Mariposa. It was the Cuban national flower and supposedly symbolized purity, rebelliousness, and independence. I figured they fit her perfectly.

I'd called from the airport and Marissa was waiting at the open door with a smile. Her ebony hair fell to her shoulders, and she was wearing a simple, black spaghetti-strap dress and heels. Elegant.

She took the bouquet. "They're lovely. Is it an occasion?"

"It may be."

"Ah! I can't wait to hear." She turned her head and called out, "Adelaida…" Turning back she said, "I've made an eight o'clock reservation at Boccaccio. We're late and they stop serving at nine."

Adelaida appeared, Marissa handed her the bouquet, hooked her arm into mine and we left. With the convertible's top down, and eighty degree weather, it was a delightful trip across the MacArthur Causeway to Miami Beach. The restaurant had a sprawling deck overlooking the Atlantic, and Marissa secured us a table on the far rail. Lightning trees blossomed on the horizon and Domenico Modugno was singing "Volare" in the background.

We were the last couple on the deck when our dishes were cleared and cognac delivered. Marissa smiled, sipped, and looked over the rim of her snifter. "You've been about to say something all evening but always managed to stop before you started."

"That obvious?"

"Since you brought the Mariposa bouquet."

I chuckled. "So much for a poker face."

"Why not just start at the beginning."

"Okay... The Saharan Motel on Sunset Boulevard—the night we met."

She laughed. "I remember feeling guilty for not wanting you to accept our offer. I didn't think I could mix business with pleasure."

"Any regrets?"

"None."

"Then what comes next?"

"Next?"

"For us."

She was a bit taken aback. "In our relationship? We've never talked about it."

I nodded. "Question... Do you love me?"

"Of course."

"And I love you and think we should talk about what to do about it?"

She put down her glass. "Dante, what's happened? Why now?"

I glanced around. The deck was deserted, but I lowered my voice. "For one thing I don't want you to go to Nicaragua."

"It's not forever. Artime says he only needs me a while."

"For what? He's training an army, Marissa."

"And he's training it in a foreign country. He wants a diplomatic representative in Managua to stay close to Somoza's government. Have you forgotten I worked in our Spanish Embassy for four years?"

"No. It's just that it'll be damn hard for me to get to you."

She smiled. "I haven't said yes. If I can find someone else as qualified, I won't go. Now... You said 'for one thing.' There's another?"

"Yes. At the end of the day, are you and I are more important than everything we've been involved with from the moment we met?"

A look of honest confusion crossed her face. "I don't understand…"

"Are you prepared to stop at nothing to support the exiles in their determination to take back Cuba?"

She answered without hesitation. "Of course. We both are. We tried to assassinate Castro for God's sake. *You* twice!"

"Suppose I asked you to become part of something that would all but guarantee re-taking Cuba, but I think is beyond reason."

"What could be beyond reason if it means freeing Cuba?"

"A plot to assassinate the president of the United States?"

Her eyes widened, but she said nothing and I continued.

"Some of your people and mine have agreed to assassinate him as part of a plan to re-take Cuba."

It sunk in slowly, then she shook her head, more confused than ever. "We all hate him. He's betrayed us. But how could killing him let us re-take Cuba?"

"It would supposedly have been ordered by Castro, thus the American public would be infuriated and insist the U.S. invade in retaliation."

"My God…"

"Yes… But the question is—would you agree to be a part of the assassination plot that triggers it?"

She looked out over the ocean for a long time before turning back. "No one man is more important than a free Cuba. Not even the president."

"Then you approve…"

"Yes. Just as I approved killing Castro…" She leaned forward and took my hand. "But what does this have to do about how we feel about each other or if you and I are more important than any of this?"

I sat back and lit a Marlboro. "Because I don't approve, Marissa, and I wanted to know how you'd take it when I told you."

She studied me a moment, not quite believing what I'd said. "I don't understand. This is the man who betrayed us—first at the Bay of Pigs and again after the Missile Crisis. He supports us with one hand and crushes us with the other. His brother is hounding your people, and your people want nothing more than to get their casinos back. Why would you *not* want him dead if it gets us both what we've been fighting for?"

I mashed out my cigarette and said, "Maybe it makes no sense, but I don't see him as an enemy. Castro and Bobby—yes. But not the president. It goes too far. Much too far. There are limits even in this rotten world."

Marissa was shaken by my resolve, and seemed to be weighing her answer. "What do you intend to do?"

"I'm not sure. I don't think I can stop them. For the moment I'll just try to stay uninvolved."

"What will your friends think about that?"

"I won't be making it obvious. But they'd be as livid as your friends."

"Livid? If they suspect what you're doing, they'll kill you."

"Probably. What will you do?"

She took a deep breath, shook her head, and her eyes glistened. "First...not tell anyone how you feel. But I'm surprised. I love you, Dante, but a life together is built on trust and common goals. Suddenly that's changed."

She looked away and I suspected she'd made a decision. "You'll go to Nicaragua."

"Yes."

"I'm sorry."

"I am too, my love."

I took her home and immediately left for the airport and a flight to L. A.

Roselli met me for dinner the following day and happily reported another phase in the "patsy set-up" was in place. Bannister had told Oswald to open a one-man Fair Play For Cuba chapter in New Orleans, and he was passing out pro-Castro, activist literature.

"Jesus," I thought, "Oswald was getting sucked in like a hungry guppy."

Bannister also reported that three people were monitoring his activities. Two of them worked for us, one didn't. The first was Jack Ruby, a man who'd been a strip club operator, gunrunner, and minor mobster. He was currently running a Dallas nightclub secretly owned by Carlos Marcello. The second was David Ferrie, Bannister's partner in the set-up, who was reporting Oswald's activities to David Morales. The third was an FBI agent who was adding Oswald's latest undertaking to the Bureau's growing file.

CHAPTER 66

NEW ORLEANS
AUGUST 1963

GIANCANA WANTED AN update on the patsy, so Roselli and I flew-in to see Carlos Marcello. We met in his marble, two-story mansion overlooking a Metairie golf course about seven miles northwest of the city.

Marcello was a fireplug whose iron grip on The Big Easy was so absolute that all visiting Mafiosi had to have his permission to enter the city—including the bosses—and Giancana had called ahead to request our meeting. We settled on his patio, and Marcello began the briefing with a revelation that made no sense.

"I don't get it," Roselli said, with a glance toward me.

"We think it was one of the kid's dumb ideas," replied Marcello. "He didn't clear it with anyone."

Roselli was aghast. "So we're tryin' to set him up as a *pro*-Castro fanatic, and Oswald walks into Bringuier's office and offers to help in the fight *against* Castro?"

Marcello nodded. "As ridiculous as it sounds, that's just what he did."

Bringuier was a big shot in the Student Revolutionary Directorate, an *anti*-Castro, anti- communist group of militant exiles.

Roselli's eyes narrowed. "Why?"

Marcello shrugged. "The kid thought he was bein' smart, but he ain't no brain surgeon. He knows the FBI is on him, so maybe he figures he's throwing them off with this anti-Castro bullshit."

"Christ!" exclaimed Roselli.

"Don't worry. Bringuier didn't buy his story for a minute. When he saw Oswald passing out the Fair Play For Cuba shit in New Orleans, Bringuier got into a scuffle with him. They got arrested, and Oswald spent the night in jail. Then, accordin' to my source at the station, Oswald tells the cops he wants to talk to the FBI."

Roselli was even more disturbed. "About what?"

"The Fair Play For Cuba thing… More of him thinkin' he's bein' smart. An agent named Quigley showed up and interviewed him?"

Roselli shook his head in disbelief, looked at me, and threw up his hands.

"Do we know what Oswald told him?" I asked.

"Yeah. When he got bailed out, Bannister asked him what he said to Quigley. Oswald said he threw the Fed another curveball to confuse the issue even more. He told the Fed he ain't anti-Castro—he's pro-Castro and was tryin' to infiltrate Bringuier's DRE outfit."

Roselli snapped, "The kid's ridiculous! He's all over the fuckin' place!"

I was with Roselli. "Does Bannister think the Fed bought it?"

Marcello said, "Who knows? But they're not stupid, and the kid comes off as a nut. Bannister told me he thinks the FBI's interest in Oswald is about the usual pissin' contest between them and the spooks. The CIA ain't got no jurisdiction in the U.S., so Hoover is tryin' to find out if they're runnin' Oswald as a double agent. If they are, he can bust Langley's balls with it."

Roselli stroked his chin and smiled for the first time. "Ya know—it might work for us. The Feds *think* he's pro-Castro, and that the CIA could be runnin' him. But they'll never prove it because there's no way they can connect the kid to the CIA and back to us. So when we hit Kennedy and the kid's the obvious shooter, we're both in the clear."

Marcello said, "You're right. And from that angle, it gets better. Oswald is gonna debate Bringuier on WDSU radio. Bringuier will be tearin' Castro apart and Oswald's gonna be singin' his praises. By the time the show's over the kid'll be nailed solid as a pro-Castro fanatic."

Roselli said, "Great. But the guy still worries me because he's all over the fuckin' place."

Marcello said, "Also works for us. Like I said, the kid's a flake. I know about him because his uncle is 'Dutz' Murret. 'Dutz' is one of my top bookies, and he's also the guy who had the kid bailed out. 'Dutz' is more like a substitute ole man to him, and the kid's mother once dated a lot of my guys. The word is he has delusions about bein' some kinda secret agent. He thinks what he's doin' with Bannister and Ferrie is super secret undercover work for the CIA—which is what they told him and want him to think."

I hadn't said much during the meeting, but I noticed a Fair Play for Cuba pamphlet on Marcello's desk. I picked it up and read it. I'd been trying to come up with an inconspicuous way to somehow derail the assassination plan and saw something that might help.

I held it up. "This one of Oswald's?"

Marcello looked at it and nodded. "Yeah."

"You said there was no tie to us and the CIA."

"That's right."

"Did you notice the address of Oswald's Fair Play For Cuba office on this?"

Marcello glanced at Roselli. My tone told him something was wrong.

"No. Why?"

"Because the address is 544 Camp Street. It's the same building that Bannister's office is in."

Marcello responded warily. "They're not the only ones in that building."

"No, but there's just two others—union offices for the restaurant and railway workers.

Marcello waved it off. "Fine, No big deal.

"Then how about the fact that Bannister is a CIA contract player. If we pin the hit on Oswald there's no chance the all out investigation won't turn up this connection.

Marcello nodded. "Maybe, but it's circumstantial."

I took one last shot. "True, but you also said 'Dutz' Murret had one of his guys bail out Oswald. 'Dutz' works for you and that ties you back to Oswald."

Marcello waved it off. "Again, circumstantial. But there's nothin' we can do about that now. We ain't got the time to set up someone else. We go with the patsy we got."

CHAPTER 67

ON THE FIRST OF THE MONTH, Lenny Mills was promoted to ASAC—Assistant Special Agent in Charge of D.C.'s FBI Field Office. The day he took over, he was briefed on a continuing, and highly classified, counter-intelligence operation.

Jason Manly—the Special Agent in Charge—called him into his corner office, ordered coffee and said, "You know who James Jesus Angleton is…"

Mills responded, "Of course."

"Right after the Bay Of Pigs he contacted my predecessor, Dwight Davies, who was also my roommate at Yale. Angleton wanted help in tracking down a mole at Langley by using us to wiretap his own people."

Mills not only knew about the contact, but had reported it to Aldo Amato. It could have gotten him fired then, and certainly would now, so he played dumb and appeared shocked.

"Dulles was the DCI then. He allowed it?"

"No. The next day Angleton again phoned Davies and called it off. Obviously Dulles had shot down the request. But Davies had already informed Hoover of it. Predictably, Hoover ignored the cancellation and put a half dozen men on it—always, and ever ready to discover something that would embarrass Langley."

A secretary arrived with a coffee carafe and two mugs on a silver tray. Manly said nothing until she'd poured and left, then sipped appreciatively and continued.

"We basically got nowhere with the investigation because none of our phone taps paid off. Not at Agency offices or agent's homes. Angleton was conducting his own deep cover probe, and although he also was getting nowhere, he was still sure there was a mole. He was equally sure that the mole knew he was being hunted and was being extremely careful."

Mills said, "Shades of Philby."

"Exactly. But seven months ago, one of our guys in Quantico read about a psychiatrist in New York named James A. Brussel. He'd helped the NYPD track down a mad bomber named George Metesky who'd terrorized the city from 1940 to 1956. Brussel read Metesky's letters to the press and did what he called a 'profile' on him. The cops nailed the guy in '57."

Mills was intrigued. "By using a profile?"

"Right. So we figured we'd take a shot and sent him files on all our possible suspects. Brussel said he was looking for a middle-aged or older man, fairly high up, but going no further in the Agency. Someone who'd had some personal setbacks in his recent life. And voilà! He came up with three suspects."

Mills didn't see how that was possible. "All with the same profile?"

"Not exactly, but with characteristics that fit the profile of someone who Brussel thought could be turned. We've since eliminated two of the suspects and zeroed in on the third. He's fifty-three, going no higher at the Agency, and got his second divorce three years ago. It left him broke."

"Fine but that doesn't prove he's a spy any more than the other two who you said had similar characteristics."

"No, so as of three months ago we had them all tailed. It wasn't that tough because none of them were undercover agents, and they didn't have the field craft to spot the surveillance. We came up with nothing on two of them. But we think we might hit pay dirt with the third."

"How?"

"On Friday nights he's made calls from eight different phone booths. All the booths are over ten miles from his house, and he's obviously got phones in his home and office. Initially it had us stymied since we clearly can't tap every phone booth in the Washington area. But two weeks ago he used one of the booths again." Manly made a pistol out of his fingers and brought down the thumb. "Bingo! We bugged all eight. If he uses one of them again we'll nail him." He paused to sip his coffee and then seemed to come up with a non sequitur. "You're a close friend of Aldo Amato, right?"

"Yes… What's he got to do with this?"

"The suspect's name is Dan Cantrell. He's on the Agency's Latin American desk. Amato is on the Southeast Asia desk and he's a close friend of Cantrell's. We'd like you to talk to Amato and ask him if he's seen any change in Cantrell's behavior since his divorce."

Mills said, "If Amato's a close friend of Cantrell's aren't you worried that he might tip him off."

"No." He smiled and explained, "If Amato *doesn't* tip Cantrell he'll make the usual call and we'll record it. If Amato *does* tip Cantrell, he won't make the call because he'll think we're closing in. It'll be enough to bring him in and sweat him."

CHAPTER 68

LEE HARVEY OSWALD HAD decided to visit Cuba. His intention was to contact the Castro government, reveal all work he was doing for the cause, and offer his services. He'd get a visa from their embassy in Mexico City.

When he told Guy Bannister about his plan, Bannister thought it was just another one of his hair-brained schemes. But then he encouraged Oswald. He could document the trip and further enhance the trail of evidence tying Oswald to Castro. He called David Ferrie and told him to fly to Mexico City with Rafael Sanchez.

They were in a rented car the next morning when Oswald walked out of the Hotel del Comercio. He was registered as O.H. Lee. Ferrie immediately ducked down. Oswald knew him, and he was very recognizable because he suffered from alopecia areata, a rare skin condition that caused the complete loss of his body hair. To compensate, he wore a reddish homemade wig and greasepaint eyebrows. It made him look bizarre.

Oswald remained on foot, but they followed him by car to the Cuban Embassy, and Sanchez, who'd never met Oswald, went in after him. An hour later, Oswald stormed out looking very agitated. Seconds later Sanchez ran out and jumped into the car.

"Follow him!"

Ferrie asked, "What happened," and pulled out after Oswald who remained on foot.

"He applied for a *transit* visa to Cuba claiming he wanted to visit Havana on his way back to the Soviet Union."

Ferrie paled. "Holy shit! That's not what he told Bannister he was doing! If he gets it and winds up back in Russia, we're fucked!"

Sanchez said, "Yeah—who knows what goes through this guy's head! But I don't think they'll give him a visa. The gal who took his application told him that Soviets would have to approve his trip to the USSR before he could get a visa to transit Cuba, and it could take up to four months. Oswald got angry with her, and she called the consul. When the consul showed up, he got into a shouting match with him and stormed out."

"Where's he going?"

"Probably to get some passport photos, which they told him he also needed."

They followed Oswald to a large drug store that had a photo booth, then back to the Embassy where Sanchez once again went in after him. Oswald came out a half hour later, Sanchez followed, and got in the car.

"The Cuban consul's still insisting that he needs the Soviet's permission to enter the USSR before they could issue him a Cuban transit visa, and they got into another argument."

"Why the hell doesn't he just apply for a visa to Cuba?"

"Who knows with this flake? He's still all over the goddamn place."

Sanchez and Ferrie stuck with Oswald for the next three days—twice following him into the Cuban Embassy and twice into the Soviet Embassy. Sanchez waited until Oswald left the former the last time, then entered. He greased the greedy palm of the Cuban Consul's assistant and asked how Oswald was progressing with his transit visa.

The man said, "I was in the room at the time. Our consul told this repulsive young man that as far as he was concerned, he would never give him a visa and that instead of aiding the Cuban Revolution, he was doing it harm."

Sanchez got back in the car and reported what he'd found out. He laughed, adding, "It's as if we were writing the script. The poor bastard's managed to get his attempts to get into Cuba and Russia seared into everyone's brain in both embassies. Everyone who's seen him, including the consuls, their assistants, and the fucking KGB, will remember who he is, where he was, and why he was here. Our patsy's set-up like a duck in a shooting gallery."

The following day, Sanchez and Ferrie watched Oswald board a bus from Mexico City to Laredo, Texas. They flew back to New Orleans where Ferrie reported to Marcello and Sanchez reported to Morales.

As usual, everything that Morales learned he passed on to Roselli, which was then kicked up to Giancana and Trafficante.

Their plan to set up Oswald as the patsy had worked better than they could have wished. All that remained was a time and a place for the hit.

CHAPTER 69

CHEVY CHASE
OCTOBER 1963

LORENZO'S SHOOTER KNOCKED Elvira's out of the ring with a resounding
"crack!" and therefore, in accordance with the rules of Ringo, won all the
marbles. Aldo Amato was about to applaud when his six-year-old daughter
jumped up and whacked her brother's arm.

"Cheater!" she yelled.

"Am not!" He yelled back.

She whacked him again. "Are too! You didn't knuckle-down and
you inched up!"

He whacked her back. "Did not!"

Aldo laughed and separated them. "Enough! He did a bad for inch-
ing-up, and you did a bad for whacking him."

They'd finished dinner an hour earlier and were in the backyard of
the Amato's middle-class house in the Washington suburb. It was a usually
balmy Thursday evening, but before the players could settle down and
continue the game, Aldo's wife called out from the back door.

"Aldo—Lenny's here to see you."

Aldo was surprised. "Oh? Thanks, Pat... Tell him I'll be right there."

Aldo got up and brushed off his pants. "Play nice or no *Beverly Hill-
billies* on TV or Yoo-Hoos and Ju Ju Bees at the movies for a year." He
liked making ridiculous threats and the kids giggled.

Lenny Mills was waiting in the living room, casually dressed. He'd obviously stopped at home to shed his standard suit and fedora before coming over.

"Got a couple of minutes, Aldo?"

"Sure… Can I get you a drink?"

"No thanks. I thought maybe we could take a walk."

Aldo's antenna went up. "No problem…" He called out, "Pat—Lenny and I are going for a walk. Be back in a bit."

Pat stuck her head around the corner. "Is anything wrong?"

Mills said, "No, Just some Bureau crap, and I've been on my ass all day."

Pat laughed and disappeared. The two men went out the front door onto a quiet street lined with split-level houses.

Aldo asked, "What's up?"

Lenny lit a cigarette. "You're a friend of Dan Cantrell's…"

Mills unannounced arrival and request to take a walk caused Aldo to answer warily. "Yes…"

"A good friend?"

"I suppose—but actually more of a fellow worker bee. I'm Southeast Asia—he's Latin America. We don't socialize much because Pat doesn't like his choice of female friends since his divorce."

"Speaking of, have you noticed anything unusual about him since the divorce?"

Aldo stopped and turned to Mills. "What's this, about, Lenny?"

"In the simplest terms, we think he could be a spy."

"Dan? You've gotta be kidding."

"There's a lot a circumstantial evidence, Aldo. We've been following him."

"Christ! What the hell have you got?"

"Enough to make us keep digging and we'd appreciate your co-operation…"

"Well sure—but it doesn't seem possible."

"Anything's possible, Aldo. So I have to ask you—is there anything in his behavior that seemed different from around the time of his divorce?"

"Lenny—he's befriended me—gave me a head's-up when my brother was captured in Cuba. He's a solid guy who's been with the Agency longer than I have…"

"So was Philby. Aldo—I know this is hard on you, but because Cantrell is on the Latin American desk, if he's the spy Angleton's been looking for he's very dangerous to our efforts."

Aldo sighed, lit a cigarette and looked away for several seconds before turning back to Mills. "As far as I can see there's been nothing I'd consider unusual for a guy who was in a bad marriage that wound up in a worse divorce."

"What wouldn't you consider unusual?"

"Well… Like after the divorce he started dressing very sharp and I suppose expensively—but that figures because he was back on the singles'-circuit and has some high flying friends."

"Like who?"

Aldo resumed walking. "Well…like Leonora Harrison for one. I know he sees her and mixes with her crowd—but again—why not? She a rich, attractive widow who throws great parties attended by D.C. big shots."

Mills nodded and moved to a new area. "Angleton's hunt for a mole hasn't been a secret. Has he ever discussed it with you?"

"Sure. A few times, but everybody at the Agency talks about Angleton's witch hunts."

"What about the time I told you he'd contacted us to wire tap Agency personnel. Did you talk to Cantrell about that?"

Aldo realized that he had, and remembered Cantrell's reaction. He'd paled and begged off the rest of their dinner together. "Yes—and I suppose he did seem a bit taken aback by it—but again—so was I. Anyone would be in light of the rancor between our two agencies."

Mills stopped and faced his friend. "Okay, Aldo. Thanks for putting up with my questions. Just doing my job. Let's head back."

There was nothing more that Mills had to ask. The purpose of the interrogation was not to find out if Aldo knew of anything incriminating against Cantrell. It was to see if Aldo would tell Cantrell that he was under scrutiny and cause him not to use the phone booth the following night—or not tell him so they could record his conversation. Mission accomplished.

The following Friday, Dan Cantrell left his house at 7:35. He was nattily dressed in a Brooks Brothers suit, Ferragamo shoes, and silk shirt with onyx cuff links. He was on his way to attend a soirée at Leonora Harrison's townhouse in Georgetown. But first he had to make a stop across the river in Arlington. Leonora's event had been called for 8:00 and she detested tardiness, but his Friday call had to be made on time.

He pulled up to the gas station's pump, ordered a fill up, and crossed to the outdoor phone booth. The call to Miami with the ensuing password and transfer to Havana was normal, and Cubela came on the line.

"Rolando—There's a plan called Operation Mongoose being drawn up to attack a wide variety of targets in Cuba, and it includes assassination attempts on the Cuban hierarchy. I'll call you with details as soon as I have them."

"Thank you, my friend. The usual transfer will arrive in the Caymans on Monday."

Cantrell paid for his fill up inside the station and returned to his car. Before he could get into the driver's seat, an unmarked van containing the phone-tap's recorder skidded to a stop in front of his car and blocked it. Four FBI agents jumped out and pinned him on the hood.

While he was being handcuffed, Lenny Mills said, "Daniel Cantrell, you're under arrest for espionage against the United States of America."

Mills read him his rights, and Cantrell was unceremoniously thrown into the van with a look of absolute terror on his face.

CHAPTER 70

DURING THE LAST WEEK IN October, Roselli came up with the vital piece of information that was key to the assassination plan. He reported it to Giancana, who immediately said he needed a face-to-face sit-down with Marcello and Trafficante. He had not been able to have any face-to-face meetings with his fellow conspirators in months, time was growing short, and he felt frustrated and isolated.

Roselli told me about the request, but not what caused it, and said we had to figure out a way to get the three capos together. I knew a meeting in Chicago was out of the question because of the FBI's relentless surveillance. All Momo's phones were tapped, and the Bureau was using nine men to tail him in two twelve-hour shifts, twenty-four hours a day. If he went out, the agents were right behind him, and they made no effort to conceal their presence. They called it "lockstepping" and it was driving Momo nuts.

It was obvious a meeting in Chicago was out of the question. But since Trafficante could move and Marcello had dependable safe havens in New Orleans, I figured Marcello's Big Easy was the logical choice. Roselli agreed and then came up with a way to get Giancana out of Chicago using knowledge he'd gained from his thirty-seven years in Hollywood.

We set up a casting session.

The character actor we ultimately hired was Fred Naspo. He bore a close resemblance to Giancana except for the fact that he was thirty pounds lighter and had a thinner face. So we brought in Tyler Dann, an expert make-up man, to fashion cheek implants that filled out Naspo's face and add a small wax addition to his nose. He completed the transformation with strap-on padding that Naspo would wear under his suit.

Neither Naspo nor Dann questioned why we asked them to create a second Sam Giancana. No one in show business questioned Johnny Roselli. We placed all the elements for the transformation in a suitcase and then had Naspo fitted out with a second impeccable disguise. Dann turned Naspo into a fiftyish woman who had a graying wig, sensible shoes, and sagging tits.

Roselli named her "Aunt Philomena." The plan was as simple as it was ingenious. FBI wiretaps would pick up calls about "Aunt Philomena's" impending visit to Giancana's home as well as Giancana's appointment with his lawyer later that same afternoon. On the selected day, Naspo would arrive at the house as Aunt Philomena. He would then change into his Giancana persona and leave the house as Sam—on his way to the scheduled meeting with his lawyer. The FBI would follow Naspo, and Giancana would dash off to Midway Airport where Roselli and I would have a leased airplane take us to New Orleans.

With all the elements in place, we loaded up Naspo and the disguises and flew to Chicago. The following day the plan worked perfectly.

CHAPTER 71

ON THE FLIGHT TO THE BIG EASY, Roselli told me the information he'd brought to Giancana. It stunned me, and I knew if I was going to act, it had to be soon.

Trafficante and Marcello were waiting at Marcello's Metairie mansion. They were sitting on a balcony in a jasmine-scented breeze on a sun-drenched day. It was another idyllic backdrop, and when the greetings were over, a servant brought us drinks.

Giancana lit a cigar and addressed Marcello. "Two days ago I got a message from Hoffa. Kennedy's about to hit 'im with another ton of indictments, and Jimmy knows he can't beat 'em all. Sooner or later he's gonna do time. That means he loses the Teamsters, and we lose the pension fund. The little shit is buryin' us all, and it's only gettin' worse." He thumbed his chest. "Me? The prick's got the FBI so far up my ass I can't operate." He looked at Trafficante and pointed. "You're in the same boat tryin' to run your Bolita operation." He turned to Marcello. "And you, he's got you facing a Federal rap, that, if it sticks, gets you deported."

Marcello nodded. "We get it. What's your point?"

"We're runnin' outta time, and we gotta move. You're the point man on this patsy thing, right?"

Marcello nodded.

"Are we wrapped up?"

"It's a done deal. Oswald's swallowed the bait. All we gotta do is decide on a time and place for the hit. The kid'll be put into position, and he'll take the fall."

I hid deep, anguished breath. There went my last hope. With the byzantine events surrounding Oswald in the past few months, I'd hoped he was smart enough to figure out he was being played. He hadn't. I knew what Giancana was about to say and realized my hopes were history.

"I've got time and place for the hit."

Marcello leaned forward expectantly. No one wanted Kennedy dead more than he did.

Giancana glanced at Roselli and signaled him to elaborate.

Roselli said, "Chicago—November second. Kennedy is going to the Army-Air Force game at Soldier Field. Morales got his whole campaign schedule verified from a Washington contact. He'll be in Chicago on the second, Tampa on the eighteenth, and Dallas on the twenty-second. There'll be motorcades in all three cities, but we're gonna nail him in Chicago."

Trafficante said, "Shit! That's three days from now. How the hell do we get everyone in place in time?"

Roselli overrode the question. "No pun intended—we gotta take a shot. But if we miss him we'll still have two more chances—Tampa and Dallas."

Trafficante sighed and conceded the point. "How much do we know?"

"Enough. We figured out the most logical route for the motorcade to take from the airport. On the final approach to the stadium and the players' gate—which we also figure they'll use—there's an industrial area with a lot of buildings on streets where they'll have to slow down for the corners. We'll put our shooters in the buildings over those turns. They'll have high power rifles with scopes." He paused and smiled. "Morales and Sanchez have a four-man Cuban team ready to go."

Trafficante said, "Fine, but what about Oswald?"

Marcello said, "Ferrie will fly him in with the shooters and Ruby."

Giancana didn't recall hearing the name. "Who's Ruby?"

Marcello said, "Jack Ruby's one of my guys. Not too smart, but loyal and a versatile guy. He run guns to Cuba and was the bagman we used to try and get Santo out a Castro prison. Now he runs a club for me in Dallas."

"What's he got to do with this?"

"He's backup. We've always figured that after the hit went down, we'd tip off the cops to where we'd set up Oswald. They'd find him, and a cop we'd paid off would shoot him tryin' to escape. There's no way we want him questioned. But if for some reason the cop didn't take out Oswald, Ruby would grease him. He's our insurance policy."

I became even more depressed. The plan was as well thought out as any I could have imagined.

Giancana said, "So that's it then? We go for it on the second?"

Marcello and Trafficante looked at each other and nodded.

Marcello pronounced, "That's it. Chicago on the second."

Giancana declined Marcello's offer to stay at the mansion, saying he wanted to enjoy a night in New Orleans without FBI tails. Roselli and I said we'd stick with Momo, and Marcello graciously sent two men with us as bodyguard/guides to the hot spots.

We checked into the Roosevelt—known as the "Pride of the South"—a half dozen blocks from the heart of the French Quarter. It boasted the famed Blue Room, Sazerac Bar, and was Huey Long's headquarters in the 1930s.

After dinner, Trafficante and I skipped a night on the town and had a nightcap in his suite. He called his office for messages and to let them know where he was staying and was told that Manuel Artime had flown in from Nicaragua. Artime wanted a meeting with him, Morales and Sanchez. He agreed, said he'd arrive in the morning, and as an afterthought for my benefit, asked if Marissa del Valle was with Artime. He was told she was, and he relayed the news to me.

I didn't sleep much that night. I knew I had to phone in a warning that there'd be an assassination attempt on the president. It meant I would become a traitor...a rat. Christ! I couldn't believe it. No one would've ever believed it. Betraying Trafficante and Marcello didn't bother me. I hadn't even met them until the whole Cuban business began. And Giancana had always seemed a somewhat distant capo in Chicago. What was killing me was turning on Johnny Roselli—the man who'd catapulted me to the top echelon of our family and was my closest friend. He was my real family, closer than my own brother. There was acid in my mouth, and I hadn't even picked up the phone yet.

The following day after a rollicking night on the town, Roselli and Giancana flew back to Chicago. They executed a flawless reverse of the Aunt Philomena gambit, and Momo was spirited back into his home without the FBI ever having realized he'd left.

CHAPTER 72

CORAL GABLES

I FLEW TO MIAMI WITH Trafficante since I hadn't talked to Marissa in four months and wanted to see if anything had changed. We split up at the airport and I called her.

"Dante?" She sounded surprised.

I said, "Welcome home."

She was even more surprised. "How did you know?"

"Somoza called and said he missed you."

She laughed and asked, "Where are you?"

"At the airport. I'd like to see you."

She only hesitated a moment. "Well, yes... That would be nice."

My spirits rose. "Is now too soon?"

She laughed again. "No."

"Good. I'll be there in twenty minutes."

I should have been ecstatic. But as I headed for the car rental booths, the decision I'd made to reveal the assassination plot was tearing me apart, and on the flight from New Orleans I'd decided how to do it.

Tomorrow was November 1, and in the morning I'd phone Aldo and inform him of Chicago attempt on November 2. My timing would be perfect. I'd tell Aldo the sniper nests would be on the final approach to the stadium, but I knew the Secret Service would want to check out the entire motorcade route. They'd insist on it—it was their M.O. And it would be impossible in less than twenty-four hours. They'd have to cancel the motorcade, and the attempt would never take place.

I rented a car, made the short trip to Marissa's house, and pulled into the circular drive. Marissa answered the door wearing an off the shoulder white summer dress—no jewelry, leather sandals, no stockings—and looked as stunning as I'd ever seen her.

I tried to decide whether taking her in my arms and kissing her was appropriate but vetoed it, and simply said, "Sorry, no flowers, I thought…"

"No matter, Dante, you're here. Let's go out on the patio."

The reunion had been tentative, perhaps a bit awkward, but warm, and I was encouraged.

We sat by the pool and she said, "Adelaida is making ropa vieja for lunch."

I sadly remembered that it was the meal ordered by Teo Cruz when we arrived in Havana to assassinate Castro.

"Great… a favorite."

"When will you be going back?"

"Tomorrow. I have to meet Johnny in Chicago… You?"

"As soon as Manuel finishes his business. We came here because he wants Trafficante, Morales, and Sanchez to use their influence to get us more local support in Nicaragua. In return they can offer to help Somoza put down the Sandinistas."

I shook my head. "Everybody's got a problem."

She smiled. "If they didn't, we wouldn't be here.

"Point taken."

"So, Dante… You know what I've been doing—what about you? Have you managed to resolve the conflict between you, your friends, and our cause?"

"There is no resolution. I'm still opposed to what they want to do."

"So you'll still distance yourself from the their plan."

"No… I'll try to stop them."

Marissa's hand went to her throat—shocked and dismayed. "My

God, Dante, it will get you killed."

"If they find out—yes. I'm hoping I can make the effort, and stay in the dark."

She wistfully shook her head. "I don't know whether to hope that you can't stop them, or if you do, pray that you can stay in the dark."

"You care what happens to me?"

"Of course I care. I love you, Dante. It's just that I haven't been able to figure out what to do about it."

I leaned forward, took her hand and gently squeezed it. "For better or worse, this situation will be over in a few days. No matter what happens, one way or the other, I want us together."

She paused a moment and tentatively said, "That almost sounds like a proposal.

I nodded. "It was. On whatever terms you want."

Her smile indicated she had no choice in the matter. "What I want is you. For better or worse, I accept."

CHAPTER 73

MIAMI
NOVEMBER 1963

As PLANNED, I LEFT FOR THE airport on the morning of the 1ˢᵗ and called DiGiorno's to leave a message for Aldo. I figured he was about to leave for his office, and Pat was probably driving the kids to school, but there was no way to use his home phone and disguise what I had to tell him.

I could hear the chatter of DiGiorno's large breakfast crowd when Larry answered, and I gave him the number of my phone booth. Larry said he'd deliver the message and hung up.

I opened the folding door, tried to get comfortable in the claustrophobic booth, and drank some beverage-machine coffee that tasted like acid in a cup.

Twenty minutes later, the phone rang. "Aldo?"

"Yeah. I'm in a phone booth."

Engines roared in the background and he asked, "Where the hell are you?"

"Also in a phone booth. Miami International."

"More cloak and dagger?"

"Call it anything you want, but I'm about to give you a piece of information that could get me killed."

"What the hell are you talking about?"

"The president. There's gonna be an attempt to assassinate him in

Chicago tomorrow."

I heard a noise that sounded like Aldo sagging against the booth, and he said, "What?"

I punched out the words. "This is not a drill, Aldo. There will be an attempt to assassinate the president in Chicago tomorrow."

I could hear him breathing hard. It took a few seconds but he finally asked, "Who's …?"

"That's not part of what you have to know."

"Christ, Dante! Where did you get this?"

"Also not part of what you have to know. They'll attempt it while he's in the final part of the motorcade from the airport. Snipers in buildings—from windows above the ground floor when they get close to the Soldier Field players' gate."

I imagined him pinching his nose and closing his eyes in dismay. "You have any idea which ones?"

"Where the cars have to slow for a turn."

Silence. I thought something had happened to him. "Aldo?"

A moment later, he answered. "All right, Dante, I'll put out the word. But if you're involved in the conspiracy, you'll go to prison for the rest of your life."

"I'm familiar with prisons, brother… And I have no intention of going back to one. Stop Kennedy from going to Chicago. Tip the *Tribune*, but if you want to see me alive again, don't tell them or anyone else where you got the information."

I hung up and leaned my forehead against the phone. I'd crossed the Rubicon.

CHAPTER 74

CHEVY CHASE

ALDO LEFT THE PHONE booth, got into his car, and lit a cigarette. He took a long pull, inhaled, and shook his head. He was torn between two horrendous choices. He'd taken an oath when he joined the Agency that he would defend the nation against all enemies, domestic and foreign. What he'd just heard was the epitome of that oath, and duty demanded that he inform his superiors.

But if he did, they would force him to reveal his source, and the FBI would pick up his brother. Dante was a known member of the Giancana family, and there was every reason to believe they were involved. He didn't know why his brother had blown the whistle, but he had, and if he associates found out, they'd kill him. He couldn't let that happen.

He decided that Dante was right—an anonymous tip to the *Chicago Tribune* telling them about the attempt and the details that would force a call to local authorities, the FBI, and Secret Service. He went back to the phone booth, got the number from information, and dialed. After being transferred three times, he finally reached the managing editor and gave him the information Dante had supplied. The editor then did exactly what Aldo and I knew he'd do.

He alerted the locals, FBI, and Secret Service.

The Feds, as well as local authorities, had already been investigating other threats to the president since his visit to Chicago had been announced. But when the latest one came in from the *Tribune*, they compared the information they were given against the motorcade's scheduled route, and it matched.

They notified the White House.

CHAPTER 75

CHICAGO

Roselli and I decided against staying with Giancana, and we checked into the Blackstone Hotel. If we were spotted, Roselli didn't want the FBI to report we'd arrived at Momo's house hours before the president was assassinated.

On the morning of the 2nd, we were in our suite watching TV coverage of crowds lining the motorcade route. Suddenly, Pierre Salinger appeared on screen and somberly announced the president was cancelling his trip to Chicago. Ngo Dinh Diem had been assassinated in Vietnam, and the president had to remain in Washington to deal with a possible crisis.

Roselli jumped up and screamed at the screen. "Unfucking believable! We bust our ass to set this up, and a gook halfway around the world gets whacked and fucks it up!"

I stifled a sigh of relief and shook my head. Diem's tragic, but fortuitous, assassination had made the canceling of the campaign stop understandable.

But we later learned what was only known to his closest advisors. Although Kennedy had been aware of the planned coup in South Vietnam, he had understood that Diem would be allowed to flee the country. He was not supposed to be killed. Kennedy was genuinely shaken by

Diem's murder, but under normal circumstances he still would have made the campaign swing through Chicago. It was the assassination threat that actually caused him to cancel.

The Kennedys wanted the threat kept secret because they were worried that cancellation for that reason would make the president appear weak and perhaps even cowardly. Their relationship with the press was excellent, and newspapers had often refrained from printing stories they felt would compromise the national interest.

During the Missile Crisis, details about back door negotiations with the Soviets were known and had been kept secret, and, for three years, members of the press had routinely covered up the president's extra-marital affairs.

The *Tribune* was merely turning a blind eye.

CHAPTER 76

On November 3, Roselli and I arrived in Florida in time for lunch with Trafficante. I was in veiled high spirits, but Roselli was still livid. He was determined to make what had failed in Chicago succeed in Tampa. He knew that another fluke like Diem's assassination on the day Kennedy was supposed to be whacked could never happen again.

The new target date was the 18th, the date of Kennedy's campaign swing through Tampa. It meant we had over two weeks to plan and put players in position for a second shot. And I knew Roselli was more confident than ever because we were in Santo's backyard.

Trafficante was waiting for us in the recently renovated headquarters of his Bolita operation in Ybor City. The area, northeast of downtown Tampa, had deteriorated after WWII, but Santo's hundred-year-old Spanish Revival building was pristine, and his Mission Style office opulent.

Marcello was with Trafficante, and we greeted them with the usual hand shakes and embraces. Our host poured drinks, and we settled into comfortable chairs. Shaking his head in disbelief, Trafficante opened the conversation with, "The sonofabitch has to be the luckiest guy on earth. How the hell would you figure that one? Halfway 'round the world, some asshole gets whacked and we get fucked."

Roselli emitted a disgusted grunt. "Yeah—but we can make it

happen here."

Trafficante glanced at Marcello and swept a disconsolate hand toward him.

Marcello nodded, and looked at Roselli. "Maybe, but we got a problem."

"With what?"

"Not what—who. Our partners—the Cuban exiles. They don't want Kennedy hit until after December first."

Roselli angrily responded, "Why the hell not?"

"Because Morales and Sanchez came up with a piece of news that changes everythin' for them."

In the next few minutes, Marcello revealed what the two JM/WAVE agents in Miami had learned. Their friends in Langley who had access to AMTRUNK—the CIA's small part in Juan Almeida's planned palace coup—had uncovered it. They informed Morales that the coup was to take place December 1 with the full knowledge and support of the Kennedys.

Trafficante said, "So the exiles don't want Kennedy killed two weeks from now. They need him alive so he can order a U.S. invasion after Almeida's coup. They want that invasion bad. They've been through the Bay of Pigs and know they can't re-take Cuba without the U.S. military."

Roselli exploded. "Christ! It's a Chinese cluster-fuck!"

Marcello held out his hands and patted the air. "Relax. We been thinkin'… Let's say Kennedy lives, the invasion comes off, the coup works, and Almeida takes over. What's the guarantee that Almeida's new regime would be friendly to us? The guys still a Communist."

While Roselli and I processed the statement, Trafficante lit a cigar and studied the tip before continuing, "Getting our casinos back isn't half as important as gettin' Bobby off our ass and stayin' out of prison. With Kennedy dead, Johnson becomes president and throws Bobby out of office. That means the heat's off, Hoffa stays free, and the pension fund cash keeps flowin'. With that cash we can build all the casinos we want in Vegas." He puffed his cigar, let the logic sink in, and said, "Fuck the

Cuban casinos."

Marcello said, "It makes sense. And there's one other thing. Sanchez and Morales say that because of Kennedy's involvement in the Almeida coup, there can never be a really thorough investigation of the assassination. It would uncover Kennedy's promise to support it with U.S. military."

Roselli didn't see the point, and for the moment, neither did I. He said, "That would stifle the investigation?"

Trafficante answered, "Yes—because Kennedy's told the world that invadin' Cuba is something he *wouldn't* do. Twice! Once after the Bay of Pigs, and again after the Missile Crisis. If it came out he'd planned to go back on his word, there would be a world-wide shitstorm. Kennedy would be discredited and his legacy destroyed. That won't be allowed to happen. So... if we kill him, the investigation won't go anywhere past Oswald, and we're home free." He folded his hands. "That's the whole story."

Roselli glanced from Trafficante to Marcello, and smiled. "So the hit's on?"

Marcello said, "Absolutely. Fuck the Cubans."

It was that simple. They were going forward, and they'd left me no choice. I'd have to rat them out—again. The first time damn near tore me apart, and I'd had a bad time looking Johnny in the eye. I had no idea how the hell could I'd keep facing him... Now I was even thinking I wouldn't be in this shithole if I'd finished college and joined Aldo in the fucking CIA! I snapped out of it when I heard Trafficante asking Roselli a question.

"You figure another motorcade?"

Roselli nodded. "It makes most sense. Same as in Chicago. We'll scope out the route and put our shooters in a couple of buildings so we can hit 'im from more than one angle. They'll be above ground level and we'll pick a spot lookin' down at a corner where the cars hafta slow down for the turn."

"The same team you used in Chicago?"

Roselli shook his head. "No. They were Cubans. You said they don't want Kennedy dead because of Almeida's coup. Morales is the only guy in Miami we can trust. I'll keep 'im in the loop and he'll keep us informed about what's goin' on down there, but we'll bring in our own hitmen and keep exiles out of it."

Marcello concurred. "Shooters won't be a problem. I've got plenty of buttons who'll jump at a big payday."

I asked, "Do we know the route the motorcade'll take?"

Trafficante said, "Not yet. But it'll begin at Lopez Field and head for downtown. They'll have to get to Howard Avenue to wind up at Hesterly Armory where he's makin' a speech."

Roselli asked, "What about the patsy?"

Marcello said, "Same deal as Chicago. We'll spot Oswald close to the real shooters."

"And Ruby?"

"Same again. Close by in case Oswald ain't taken out by our cop."

Trafficante nodded approvingly. "It's a good plan. I'll assign a cop on my payroll to make the hit on the kid. I'll also put a team on scoutin' all the logical routes from Lopez to the armory. It'll be the one that can handle the most spectators."

As the meeting broke up I asked, "You need me for anything in the next couple of days?"

Roselli smiled. "You figurin' on a trip to Miami for a little squeeze?"

Marissa and I hadn't told Roselli or Artime that I'd proposed. We'd agreed to wait until things became more settled in our world. But Roselli enjoyed needling me about Marissa, and I knew his good-humored jibes were the result of his warm feelings. It made me feel even more rotten but I forced a smile.

"I was. But I'll check in."

Roselli clapped my arm. "Have a good time."

Shit. He had no idea he was making the rancid lump in my stomach get worse. I used one of Trafficante's phones and Marissa answered on the first ring.

She exclaimed, "Dante! Thank God. Are you all right?"

"I'm fine."

She sighed and sounded relieved. "I heard the news. You're still in the dark?"

"I am, and in Tampa. I can be there in a couple of hours and take you to dinner."

"Dante—I'm sorry… I can't. I have to meet Artime. We're leaving at six."

"Back to Nicaragua?"

"Yes. He said we have less than a month to get ready but didn't say why."

I'd just heard why but asked, "Where are you meeting him?"

"We're flying out of Tamiami airport."

"I know where it is. I'll meet you there at five. I want to see you."

She tried to be sensible. "We won't have any…"

I said, "See you at five," and hung up.

Trafficante's men drove me to the Tampa airport. On the way I pondered what I'd heard that afternoon. The Soviets had a lot at stake in Cuba. They'd invested a tremendous amount of time, effort, resources, and money in the island. In addition, there were several thousand Soviet troops and technicians still stationed there.

If the coup succeeded, and Almeida turned his back on them, the Soviets would suffer an enormous political defeat. They could very well decide to fight by supporting an alternate government official who was loyal to them—even though he was lower in the hierarchy than Almeida. It would start a civil war. With the U.S. supporting Almeida and the Soviets supporting his opponent, it would be a proxy fight between two superpowers that could easily escalate into a major conflict.

But if Kennedy were assassinated, none of that would happen because there would be no coup. And I thought Marcello, Trafficante, and their CIA friends were correct about what would follow the assassination. There would be no thorough, in-depth investigation. And if necessary, there would be a cover-up.

CHAPTER 77

I RENTED A CAR AT MIAMI International and drove to Tamiami airport, about fifteen miles south. Marissa was sitting in the private terminal wearing a jump suit and had a small valise next to her chair.

She rushed to hug me when I came through the door saying, "You're crazy, you know that."

I shrugged. "I was in the state and it wasn't that far. Artime's not here yet?"

She shook here head. "No, but he sounded very excited when he called. Something's happened."

"I'm sure he'll tell you on the plane. It's about a coup in Cuba on December first."

Marissa was surprised. "By whom?"

"Almeida."

Her surprise turned into shock. "You can't be serious! He's been with Castro from the beginning."

"Yeah. But he's a patriot, and he's adamantly against letting Castro turn Cuba into a Soviet puppet state. He'll kill Fidel and Raúl, and take over the reins of government. Then he'll ask for U. S. support, and get it—with an invasion."

Marissa's face lit up. It was what the exiles had always hoped for.

"That's wonderful!"

"No. It's not. It won't get back Cuba for you or your friends."

"But…"

"Castro would be gone, but Almeida is anti-Soviet—not pro-exile. He considers everyone in Miami Batista's people who fled Cuba after the revolution. He'd never want you back. He's just a different kind of communist than Castro. My guess is he'll want to set up a communist state on the Yugoslavian model—independent of, but aligned with, the Eastern Bloc."

Marissa joy seeped away as she absorbed what I'd said. "If the president is not assassinated, there'll be a coup. But whether it succeeds or fails we won't be able to return to Cuba… And if the assassination succeeds, there will be no coup. And we still won't be able to return."

I nodded. "I've always been against the assassination, but now, for a different reason— the exiles are against it."

"And you'll still try to stop it."

"Yes."

She stared at me for several seconds, then said, "If you succeed, Kennedy will live, the coup will happen, and an invasion will follow."

"Yes."

"Many Cubans will die."

"Along with many Americans."

The door banged open and Artime walked in. His face lit up when he saw me with Marissa, and extending his arms, said, "Dante! An unexpected pleasure, my friend. You're well?"

I said "I am," and we embraced.

The roar of engines announced the arrival of a Douglas C-54 on the ramp and interrupted our reunion. It had been retired by the U.S. Air Force and purchased with JM/WAVE funds. It waited with its engines idling.

I indicated it. "No more B-26?"

Artime sighed. "It's just as old but a lot more comfortable. He smiled ruefully toward Marissa. "Sorry to keep taking her away from you."

I said, "I understand… Have a good flight," then turned to Marissa. "Until next time…"

She nodded, kissed me, boarded the plane, and as they taxied out, I went to a phone booth.

Unlike Chicago, I wanted to give the Tampa FBI office over two weeks to deal with the new assassination threat. They needed the time. I knew another Ngo Dinh Diem event wasn't in the cards, and Kennedy couldn't afford to cancel two appearances in a row.

After the usual transfer up the line to the ASAC, I told him that there would be an assassination attempt on the president on the 18th. The agent was initially skeptical until I began supplying details. The attempt would come during the motorcade. It would happen when the cars had to slow down for a turn, shooters would be in windows above street level, and weapons would be high power rifles. I assured the shocked agent it wasn't a hoax, and he hit me with questions about details. But I knew he was trying to keep me on the line and hung up before the call could be traced. I went to another booth just in case and dialed Roselli's hotel in Tampa. The phone rang six times before he picked up, sounding pissed off.

"Yeah!"

I chuckled. "Good morning."

"Do you know what fuckin' time it is?"

"Have a late night?"

"It's always a late fuckin' night when there's nothin' to do but jump broads… Roxy—get me a tomato juice and vodka from the mini-bar."

"Roxy?" I smiled. You had to love Johnny. And again I felt the pain of regret.

"Yeah. Why the fuck are you calling?"

"I told you I'd check in—I'm checking."

"At seven in the fucking morning?"

"Marissa's on her way back to Nicaragua. I just drove her to the airport."

"Congratulations. You coming back?"

"I'm catching a ten o'clock plane."

"Only if you buy a fuckin' watch!"

He slammed down the phone, and I couldn't help it—I broke out laughing.

CHAPTER 78

DALLAS

MARCELLO CONTINUED TO HAVE Jack Ruby keep his eye on Oswald. With the Tampa attempt getting closer, he wanted to be sure they still had him under control. He called Ferrie and had him fly Bannister from New Orleans to Dallas to get a first hand evaluation of his attitude and activities.

The three men met in the Carousel, a second-rate strip joint owned by Marcello and Ruby. The music was a bump and grind "Night Train" hot, and the girls were down-market versions of Gypsy Rose Lee without pasties. Ferrie was gay and ignored the talent, Bannister was straight and ogled it. Ruby, rumored to be both, was bored with it.

They sat at a small table and drank no-name whisky, which was all Ruby served. Bannister managed to tear his eyes off a gyrating blonde and addressed Ruby.

"So what's our boy been up to?"

Ruby shrugged. "Movin' around a lot. When he got back from Mexico he checked into the YMCA."

"Why"

"He's got wife problems. They ain't livin' together. A week later he left and got a room on Marsalis street, moved again, and now he's in a rooming house on North Beckley—registered as O. H. Lee."

Bannister chuckled. "Good. He still thinks he's a secret agent. Has he got a job?"

"Yeah—finally. His friend—the Paine broad—told him about something at the Texas School Book Depository and he got it."

"Who's she?

"A Russian immigrant. Part of a bunch that helped Oswald and his wife when they first got to Dallas. The de Mohrenschildt guy's the honcho."

Ferrie asked, "Who's he hanging out with?"

Ruby said, "Mostly with Paine and the Russian bunch. Like I said, he's got wife problems with Marina. But they had another kid a couple of weeks ago. A girl, Audrey."

A stripper sashayed up to the table. She caressed Ruby's balding head and addressed him, but her eyes were locked on Bannister.

"Kahn ah get you anythin' Jack, baby?" Her voice dripped honey.

Ruby took her hand and smiled. "Not right now Tawny. Say 'Hi' to Guy and David."

"Hah Guy—Hah David." Her eyes lingered on Ferrie a moment. She thought his horrid eyebrows looked like greasepaint and quickly looked back to Bannister. "Khan I get y'all anythin'?"

Bannister smiled. "Maybe later, Tawny."

"That'd be fahne." She wiggled her fingers as she started off. "Bah now…"

Ruby said, "Nice broad. Divorced with two kids. Just makin' a livin'."

Ferrie, who could give a shit less about Tawny, got back to the subject. "Anything else we should know?"

"FBI's still trackin' him. Agent by the name of Hosty asked questions in his neighborhood and interviewed Paine and Marina. Oswald got wind of it and was pissed."

Bannister said, "Not a problem. They're probably still trying to see if the CIA is running him."

Ruby asked, "You gonna talk to him while you're here?"

"Yeah. We're going to make a move in Tampa. We'll get both of you there at the last minute. But right now I want to give him a little more inspiration."

"What'll you tell him?"

"More of the same. We're all part of a secret CIA plot that think Kennedy's a threat to Castro, Communism, and the world, and we're committed to taking him out before it's too late. We'll point out Kennedy's wanted Castro out from the minute he took office, which is true and well known, so the kid'll be pretty well primed."

Ruby grinned. "Works for me." He snapped his fingers at a waitress. "Penny—another round and send Tawny back."

CHAPTER 79

TAMPA

On November 16, Roselli and I were having lunch with Trafficante in the dining room adjoining his office. Kennedy's arrival was two days away, and Roselli was still bitching about sitting around with nothing to do. I feigned sympathy—Trafficante was stoic.

A buzzer sounded and Trafficante hit the intercom button. "Yeah?"

The bodyguard in the outer office said, "Mr. Nicoletti's here."

"Send 'im in."

Charles "The Typewriter" Nicoletti was one of the most feared hitmen in Chicago. No one was sure how he got the moniker, and he was mum. He walked into the office impeccably dressed and smiling at three men he knew well.

He stuck his hand out to Trafficante. "Momo says hello."

Trafficante shook it and asked, "Good trip?"

"Great! It was fuckin' freezin' when I left Chicago."

"Grab a drink and sit."

Nicoletti shook hands with Roselli and me. "We set?"

Trafficante said. "You're the last to get here. Charlie Holt and the Frenchman got in last night."

Nicoletti shook his head. "Don't know 'em."

Roselli said, "Charley used to be a CIA contract guy." He laughed and added, "He's also a celebrity portrait artist, and was an accountant who worked for Lansky. The Frenchman's Michel Victor Mertz—a button and kingpin in the French Connection pipeline. Marcello and me do business with them. They're both first class."

"What's the set-up?"

Trafficante said, "Johnny and Dante picked out four areas. They'll take you to scout 'em."

Later that day, while we were was showing Nicoletti, Holt, and Mertz the sniper nests, Trafficante got a call from an informant in the Tampa police department. It was inevitable in light of all the tentacles Trafficante had in the environs of local authorities.

He immediately phoned Marcello, informed him of the news, and when we returned from the scout, Trafficante addressed us in somber tones.

"We have another problem."

Roselli asked, "The Cubans again?"

"No. The Secret Service and every other goddamn government organization in Florida. They know we're gonna hit the motorcade."

Roselli exclaimed, "How?'

"Who the fuck knows. But they've been tipped off, and they put together that it's the same set-up as Chicago. Besides the Secret Service, FBI, and local cops, they've got the National Guard comin' out—over six hundred fuckin' people, and they know we're gonna use sniper nests!"

"It's gotta be the Cubans!" fumed Roselli. "Somehow they found out what we're doin'. They're the only ones who wanna stop us from hittin' Kennedy before December first."

Trafficante threw up his hands. "Whatever the plan, we're fucked. They know it, so there's no way we can pull it off."

I breathed a sigh of relief.

Roselli was completely frustrated. "Twice! Twice we're fucked!"

Trafficante said. "Yeah… We're fucked. But we better get busy. We've got one more shot."

CHAPTER 80

DALLAS

THE NEXT DAY, ROSELLI and I flew out of Tampa on a chartered flight. Nicoletti, Holt, and Mertz left from St. Pete two hours later on a second charter. We landed at Love Field, rented two cargo vans, and rendezvoused at the Adolphus in the heart of the city.

Roselli had an affinity for old world glitz and glamour, and the hotel, begun in 1912 by Missouri beer baron Adolphus Busch, was a flawless example of the baroque. Dallas hotels were already filling up as a result of the president's visit, but when Marcello made your reservations, the mayor himself could be thrown out to make space for the capo's people.

I unpacked and dialed Aldo. It was November 17^t, Elvira's 7th birthday, and I never failed to call and send her something. This year I'd had a specialty shop send iridescent rings for all her fingers, and a dress-up kit. She could be a fairy princess, a pirate queen, Snow White or a dozen other characters.

It was seven o'clock in Chevy Chase, they'd be getting ready for dinner, and Elvira would be answering the phone. She picked up on the second ring.

"Amato residence. Elvira speaking. It's my birthday."

I chuckled. "I know, sweetheart. Happy birthday."

"Uncle Dante! I got your presents! I'm dressed up as Wonder

Woman."

"That's terrific."

"You said you were coming, but didn't."

"I'm sorry Elvira, really. I meant to, but got tied up. What else did you get?"

"Oh, lots of stuff! But the best is we're going to see Granpa and Granma!"

I knew she was referring to Aldo's wife's parents in Texas since the Amato grandparents were referred to as Nona and Nono. Pat's parents were Mr. and Mrs. Farley Harrington—fifth generation WASPs from Fort Worth.

"That's wonderful, Wonder Woman, when are you leaving?"

Elvira giggled. "Tomorrow. Do you want to speak to Daddy?"

"Sure… Happy birthday again…"

"Thank you, Uncle Dante… Daddy! It's Uncle Dante!"

Aldo got on the phone saying, "She really loves the stuff you sent."

"She's a great kid."

"Where are you?"

"Dallas."

Aldo knew nothing about the events in Tampa, but he obviously remembered the Chicago threat because his voice tensed. "But not there for the president's visit…"

"No," I lied.

Aldo's tone relaxed. "Actually we'll see the president. We're headed for Fort Worth tomorrow—staying through next weekend."

"So I've heard. Birthday present?"

"That and the Farringtons' fortieth. As a present, I'm taking them to watch the president's speech at the Trade Mart. I know some of the Secret Service guys, and they're getting us front row seats after we watch the motorcade."

I caught my breath for an instant and said, "That's great. I'm sure they'll enjoy it."

"Right…" He paused and his voice softened. "By the way, I haven't had a chance to thank you for what you tried to do two weeks ago. I can imagine what a tough call it was for you. Whatever your reasons, it was the right move."

"No problem. It worked out for both of us."

He paused again. In light of how he'd felt about me the past twelve years, what he said next must have been difficult. "Umm… Is there any chance you might get down to Fort Worth while you're in the area? Elvira and Lorenzo would love to see you."

I avoided asking, "*What about Pat and her parents?*" Instead I said, "Maybe. I'll try. Give me the Farringtons' number."

Aldo did and we hung up.

We always checked into hotels with aliases, and Nicoletti, Holt, and Mertz did the same in a motel. Nevertheless, Roselli and I were having dinner at a restaurant on the outskirts of the city because mainstream places were off limits. Johnny had a recognizable face—mine less so, but it had appeared in the papers.

I picked him up, but as we were about to leave, the phone rang. Like Trafficante, whenever he changed locations, Roselli let his office know where he was. His secretary at Columbia Studios told him there was a message from Mr. Morales, and he immediately dialed the JM/WAVE number. There'd been a continuous flow of information coming from Morales in the past weeks, and he listened intently to what Morales told him, then said, "Thanks, David. When you retire, there's gonna be a golden parachute waitin' for you that'll include points in a Las Vegas casino."

He hung up. "Artime flew in from Nicaragua for meetings in Washington. Morales says he's gonna get final invasion instructions from Bobby before the December 1 coup. He stopped in Miami to drop off your squeeze because he wants her close when they take Cuba. So there's also no doubt that the goddamn coup's going forward, and the only way to stop it is to make sure we get Kennedy in Dallas." His tone changed and there was a smile in his voice. "Go ahead. Call her, then come back and pick me up when you're done."

I nodded, said thanks as I started out so I wouldn't have to face him, then went back to my suite and dialed.

Marissa called out, "I've got it, Adelaida…"

I asked, "Have a nice trip?"

"Dante!" She laughed. "Somoza again?"

"Not this time. Are you back for good?"

"Hopefully—one way or the other."

"I'm in Dallas. I have to stay here a few days. Care to join me?"

There was only a moment's pause. "Yes… I have to meet Artime when he gets back from Washington tomorrow, but then there's nothing for me to do until after the first. I'll be on the first plane Tuesday morning."

"Call me at the Adolphus with a flight number. I'll pick you up at the airport."

CHAPTER 81

TRAFFICANTE HAD CALLED Marcello as soon as he knew the Tampa attempt was blown. The New Orleans godfather responded to the news by dispatching Bannister and Ferrie to Dallas to ferret out the president's motorcade route.

They met Roselli, Nicoletti, Holt, Mertz, and me at the Adolphus the morning of the 18th. Bannister's contact at the *Dallas Morning News* had informed him the motorcade would go from Love Field to Mockingbird Lane, to Lemmon, to Turtle Creek, to Cedar Springs, to Harwood to Main, then under the triple underpass to the Stemmons Expressway and on to the Trade Mart.

Roselli wrote it down and told Bannister and Ferrie to bird dog Oswald but not make contact. He wanted make absolutely sure their patsy didn't have any brilliant last minute ideas. Dallas was their last shot before December 1· and they had to be sure nothing fucked it up.

The rest of us then began going over the route with me driving the white cargo van. Roselli was in the passenger seat, but Nicoletti, Holt, and Mertz were unseen in the rear, sitting on folding chairs. We were using vans because we figured five men in a car cruising back and forth along the president's motorcade route might be suspicious—especially after the reports that had to have come in from Tampa. When we got to Dealey

Plaza, Roselli told me slow down. He wanted a good look at the Texas Schoolbook Depository where Oswald was working. If it were possible to set up a nest in the Depository we wouldn't have to move Oswald—just put one of the three shooters in there with him.

I turned right on Houston Street, left on Elm. Roselli looked around, and after taking in the entire area, said, "No good. It's broadside shot from the schoolbook building, across the plaza to Main Street and the cars won't be slowin' down. They'll be goin' straight ahead through that triple under-pass."

Nicoletti said, "I could set up on top of the underpass. Get a shot at him comin' right at me."

Roselli shook his head. "Too exposed. Let's see if there's anything further up."

I reversed our course to Main Street, went through the triple underpass, but found we couldn't get on the Stemmons Freeway because of the center divider. But it was the route Bannister had said the motorcade would take, so Roselli accepted it.

"They'll probably block traffic and set up a ramp over the divider. Anyway it don't matter—there's nothin' good from here on. Go back to the top."

I drove back to Love Field, and it was again obvious the first part of the route was worthless for an ambush. There were mostly small, one- and two-story buildings in the area. But when we entered downtown on Harwood Street, the tall buildings began and Roselli studied what seemed to be an ideal spot for an ambush. It was where the motorcade would have to slow down on Harwood for the right turn onto Main Street.

Roselli turned to Nicoletti, and pointed. "Whadaya think?"

Nicoletti checked the intersection and said. "It's good. A straight-on shot from the building on the southwest corner when they slow to make the turn onto Main. And we can put shooters in the other two sides."

Holt said, "Yeah, it works.

Mertz nodded, and Roselli said, "Okay, this is what we go with."

Since he didn't want any of our faces remembered scouting inside the buildings, Roselli added, "I'll have Bannister and Ferrie select firin' positions above the third floor in all the buildings. In a worst case scenario, we go from the roofs."

Nicoletti asked, "Where're you gonna be?'

"I'll make sure the cop on Marcello's payroll is in position to whack Oswald while he's tryin' to escape. If the cop blows it, I'll make sure Ruby's in a good spot to finish the job. After that, I'll set up where I can watch everyone." He looked at me. "You want a piece of this, Dante?"

I shook my head, "I've already fucked up two hits in Cuba. If 'three's a charm,' you don't want me anywhere near this."

Roselli laughed "Okay... Just hang around in case somethin' comes up."

"No problem. My brother's going to be in Fort Worth to see his in-laws and Marissa's flying in. I'll be a half hour away."

Roselli kissed the tips of his fingers and thrust them upwards. "L'amour, toujours l'amour..."

That afternoon, before I was again to meet Roselli for dinner, I slipped out of my room and walked to a phone booth three blocks away. I dialed the Dallas FBI office and got the same transfers I'd gotten in Tampa until I finally reached the ASAC. The agent had obviously heard of the anonymous calls about prior threats in Chicago and Tampa but didn't question me about who or how I'd gotten the information. Knowing he'd be trying to trace the call, I got directly to the facts.

"The assassins will be in three buildings on the corner of Harwood and Main. In upper floors or on roofs of those on the northwest and southwest side of the intersection and the one on the southeast corner. They'll begin shooting when the car carrying the president slows down to make the right turn from Harwood onto Main."

I hung up before the call could be traced and returned to the Adolphus.

CHAPTER 82

"WHY THE HELL DID YOU have to stand up in the car?"

Kennedy chuckled. "For industrial strength waving. The Tampa crowd was fantastic and it sounded like a good idea at the time."

Bobby exclaimed, "A good idea to make yourself an easier target?"

"There were no tall buildings around."

"Fine, but you damn near gave us a heart attack."

"Sorry about that, but all in all the trip was a success."

The president and his brother were in the Oval Office prior to Bobby's meeting with "Harry" Ruiz-Williams and Manuel Artime. They were discussing the final countdown for Almeida's December 1 coup, which was eleven days away, and reviewing everything they'd recently done to show Almeida the strength and resolve of U.S. support.

Bobby said, "I saw the press coverage of your speech at Cape Canaveral after the Polaris launch and it was outstanding. They quoted you talking about 'control of the seas,' and having 'the most modern weapons systems in the world.' That won't go unnoticed by Khrushchev if he toys with the idea of starting a war after Almeida's coup."

"I agree—and there were large spreads covering my meeting with General Adams at McDill. He assured me privately that Strike Force Command has Army, Navy, Marine, and Air Force units on standby and ready to go."

Bobby opened a copy of the *Dallas Times Herald*. "This just came in." The front-page banner headline read: *Kennedy Virtually Invites Cuban Coup*. "It's a reference to the speech you made in Miami with code words for Almeida. They only thing they got wrong was their use of the word 'Virtually.'"

Kennedy smiled. "I don't know if Almeida will see that, but I'm sure he got the message over the air. Any word on the Lisa Howard front?"

Kennedy had disregarded CIA objections and kept abreast of Howard's negotiating effort. He couldn't publicly approve or stop her from talking, but he felt there was nothing to lose by letting her try.

"Only that they're not going well. But Jean Daniel, the French journalist, thinks he might have some success as soon as Castro agrees to see him."

The president asked, "What are his chances?"

"Only fair. But Daniel is a smart, second, back door effort. If either of their negotiations is successful it'll prove to the world that we did everything possible to reach rapprochement. It'll save a lot of Cuban and American lives. But if not, we're fine as long as our knowledge and involvement in Almeida's coup remains unknown."

Kennedy nodded. "We'd best pray it does. If word gets out we were aware of what was happening on two diametrically conflicting fronts we'll be cannon fodder in the world press."

The situation was even more explosive than they knew. Without their knowledge, and while they were trying to negotiate a peaceful rapprochement with Castro—in Paris, the CIA was preparing to deliver Rolando Cubela a poison syringe-pen to assassinate him. If the duplicity were exposed, the Kennedys would be crucified.

Bobby asked, "When do you want to set up a meeting for Rusk and McNamara to let them know what's going on?"

"When I get back from Dallas."

Artime and "Harry" were waiting in Bobby's office when he returned from the White House, and as usual, there were warm embraces and pleasantries between the friends. Coffee was served and Bobby addressed Artime.

"Are you sure you'll be ready to go on the first?"

Resigned to his mandate, Artime spread his hands. "If it were up to me I'd like another month. Somoza has been unfocused because of the Sandinistas, and some of my recently arrived volunteers are still green, but we'll go and be first-rate when we get there."

"Excellent. You and the exiles from Fort Benning will be first in after the coup. I was there last week for an inspection. They're ready. It's important that you both hold the fort until Almeida calls for our help. Then, we send in Strike Force Command."

Artime smiled. "Do not fear, my friend. We will 'hold the fort' for however long it takes."

Bobby turned to Harry. "We want you to go into Cuba through Guantánamo on the twenty-second. Contact Almeida and meet him. We need someone we trust very close when he makes his move. We have to be sure that Almeida's actually killed Castro and it's not just staged in a double-cross of you and us. His death is the trigger that launches Manuel and his troops from Nicaragua and exiles out of Benning. We have to be sure."

CHAPTER 83

I RENTED A CHEVY, drove to the Hilton, and checked in. Suites were non-existent, and I was lucky to get a tiny room because of a cancellation. All the hotels were booked because of the president's impending visit.

I dropped off my bags and immediately left for the DFW airport. I'd spent the entire morning calling hotels and was late. I double-parked the Chevy in front of American's terminal and got to the gate as Marissa walked off the plane. She was wearing dark glasses that probably made gawkers think she was a film star in town for the president's visit.

She saw me, smiled and rushed into my arms.

I kissed her and said, "Welcome to the 'beginning of the West.'"

She hooked my arm and we headed for baggage claim. "Is that what they call it?

"It is. Good flight?"

"On my way to you? Always."

"Your flattery is flawless."

"I have an easy target."

Two hours later, we sat up in the single-bed in the ridiculously small room and eyed the bathroom—which was in scale with the rest of the accommodation.

She pursed her lips and smiled at me, clearly contemplating another round in the shower. It was no more than 4x4 wide.

I said, "Don't even think about it."

"Avoiding a challenge?"

"A chiropractor. You first."

She pecked me on the cheek, bounced out of bed and took the two short steps into the bathroom.

I dialed the Harrington house and a distinctively English female voice answered. "Harrington residence…"

"Good afternoon. My name is Dante Amato. My brother Aldo is staying with the Harringtons. He's expecting my call."

"One moment please."

I was put on hold—there was a second set of rings and Aldo picked up. "Yes…"

"It's me. I just got into town."

"Ah—glad you called. I told the Harringtons you'd be here, and the kids would love to see you. They've invited you and Marissa to dinner. Cocktails at five. Can you make it?"

"Sure."

"They're very proper so please act like a gentleman, and watch your language."

At 5:05 we pulled the Chevy up to an impressive Baronial home adjoining the Colonial Country Club, not far from Texas Christian University— clearly the residence of a wealthy man. The butler must have been lurking behind the entryway's double doors because they opened immediately, and he stepped out to greet us.

"Good evening Mr. Amato and Miss del Valle…" he said in another very English accent, "Your brother, his wife, the children and the Harringtons are waiting in the drawing room."

"*Really*," I thought.

He led us down a chandeliered hallway and into a large formal living room decorated in the style of the house. Seeing this, it was obvious why Pat was not happy living in a middle class Chevy Chase neighborhood, on a CIA agent's salary. Her parents were rich, the whole family was TCU graduates, and they probably told her she'd married down.

A double set of shrieks pierced the air the second we entered. Lorenzo and Elvira tore across the room and threw themselves at me—their voices overlapping in a jumble.

"Uncle Dante—you came—can you stay—I missed you—I love my presents…"

"Children! Children!" Pat swooped in and disentangles the kids. "Calm down! Behave yourselves…"

I bent down and kissed them both. "I'm fine Pat. I'm glad to see them too." I got up and indicated Marissa. "And this is Marissa del Valle." We'd agreed to forgo fiancée and the questioning that invariably went with it.

Aldo stepped forward with his hand extended. "I'm sorry we missed each other in Washington."

Marissa smiled. "We were only there a day."

I noticed how she stared at Aldo. Most people did when they saw us together. We were both tall and olive skinned and could have been twins except my older brother's frame was a bit rounder.

Pat came forward and said, "Nice to meet you."

Marissa replied, "And I you."

I again saw Marissa staring. Pat was Aldo's polar opposite—very fair, with a lovely, fine-featured face, and a petite figure.

The Harringtons approached. She—a very attractive, sixtyish, grande dame. He—roughly the same age, with a full head of white hair and a pencil mustache—a distinguished "Chairman of the Board" type.

Mrs. Harrington introduced herself to Marissa, saying, "Regina—pleased to meet you…" She had a pure Texas drawl. Elegant, but pure Texas. "And you Dante… My goodness, your resemblance to Aldo is remarkable."

Mr. Harrington kissed Marissa's hand. "Farley—a pleasure." He glanced at me, and added, "And may I say sir, your taste is exquisite."

I smiled. The old boy was a bit of a roué.

Harrington clapped his hands together. "Anthony—drink orders please…" Taking Marissa's arm he said, "Come… be seated."

Orders were taken amid idle chitchat, and when we were served Harrington raised his glass to Marissa and me.

"Welcome to Fort Worth—the beginning of the West!"

Regina and Pat murmured, "Here—here," and we all drank.

Harrington said, "Aldo tells me you're in real estate, Dante. Is that what brought you to Dallas?"

I glanced at Aldo. It was partially true. The Chicago mob owned the land under our hotel-casinos in Las Vegas. I nodded and said, "Yes. My firm has me investigating ranch land north of Dallas. They're looking to diversify."

I caught the wide-eyed look on Pat's face out of the corner of my eye and almost broke out laughing.

Harrington said, "Well by all means let me know if I can be of service. My firm has handled some of the largest land transactions in this part of the country."

"A very kind offer. I may take you up on it."

"We have an office in Dallas in the Old Red Courthouse. As a matter of fact, I'm taking all of us there to watch the president's motorcade. We'll have an unparalleled view from a third floor perch. Care to join us?"

I said, "Thank you, no. Unfortunately, we have to leave Friday morning."

Regina turned to Marissa. "Farley thought you might have difficulty finding accommodations at this late date. Did you?

"We did. But have a room at the Hilton." She laughed. "It's almost big enough for two people."

Harrington barked, "What? We can't have that. It's an insult to Texas hospitality." He turned to me. "Our guest house is obviously occupied by your brother, but I have a charming cabin on Lake Worth. And the cabin cruiser docked behind it is truly a joy. You're welcome to use both."

I was a bit taken aback. "Well, that's very generous of you, but…"

"No buts! It's done. You can enjoy boating, swimming, and take the children there fishing."

I smiled and shrugged. "You give me no choice."

Throughout dinner the Harringtons were formal—Pat aloof—Aldo wary—Marissa—friendly, and the kids ecstatic at fishing with Uncle Dante.

CHAPTER 84

THE FINAL DAYS
DALLAS
WEDNESDAY NOVEMBER 20

ROSELLI POURED COFFEE from a carafe and began breakfast after an enjoyable night with an exceptional call girl sent by Marcello. Jack Ruby had offered to send over a few of the Carousel strippers, but Roselli had seen them and declined. The call girl, a striking redhead who could have rivaled Dee, came out of the bedroom fully dressed and ready to depart. Her name—or the one she went by—was Blossom, and she had a drawl to go with it.

She smiled coyly and pecked his cheek. "Thank you, Mr. Roselli, Ah had a truly enjoyable time."

Roselli protested. "After last night—Johnny, please."

She laughed. "Johnny…"

"My offer stands. Come to Las Vegas, and you'll double your income in a month."

"Ah'll talk to Mr. Marcello, and think about it—promise."

She wiggled her fingers, sashayed out, and Roselli resumed breakfast. A few minutes later the door chimes sounded and he admitted Nicoletti. He'd brought two newspapers with him.

"Morning Johnny—I think we been workin' with bum dope."

"Yeah? What?" Roselli headed back to the breakfast cart to resume eating.

"I just got a call a from Bannister. He got a call from his contact on the *Dallas Morning News*—the guy who tipped him on the motorcade route. He and Ferrie spent all yesterday double-checkin'. And now they're sure what they first told us was wrong…" He held out the newspapers. "And the info in these papers is right."

"About what?"

Nicoletti opened the papers. "The route. These are yesterday's *Dallas Morning News* and *Times Herald*. It's in both of them. They got a different route from what Bannister originally found out—not much, but actually a helluva lot better for us."

Roselli stopped eating. "The hell are you talkin' about?"

Nicoletti pointed to a small front-page map. "The first part of the route—up until Main Street—is the same. But when they get to Houston, they don't go straight—through the triple underpass. They take a right, go down to Elm and take a left before they get on the access road to the Stemmons Freeway!"

"So why's that better for us?"

"Because it takes them right past the Texas Schoolbook Depository! That's where Oswald is. We don't have to move him. The patsy's already there and he's been there for a month. We couldn't've planned it better. It's perfect!"

Roselli wiped his mouth, threw down his napkin and got up. "Get hold of Mertz and Holt. I gotta see this again."

Not wanting to have the white van seen cruising the area twice in as many days, the four men took the black van. They cruised into Dealey Plaza via Main Street and turned right on Houston toward Elm. Nicoletti was driving, Roselli was riding shotgun, with Mertz and Holt on chairs in back.

When they passed the Texas Schoolbook Depository on Elm, Roselli again scanned the area. He stared at a gentle rise to his right that adjoined the triple underpass. It was more of a knoll covered with grass and had a fence at the top.

Roselli said, "Drive around behind that little hill. I wanna see what's on the other side of that fence."

They drove down Elm and bore right onto the access road that led to the Stemmons Freeway. As they passed behind the fence on the knoll, they took note of the railroad yard and parking lot across from it—then looped back to Elm.

Roselli grinned at Nicoletti. "You're right in more ways than one. The patsy bein' in that book depository building is perfect… But what's really perfect is that little hill with fence on it." He turned in his seat and pointed to the corner of Houston and Elm. "That's damn near a hundred-twenty degree turn. Kennedy's car has gotta be comin' around that corner doin' around ten miles an hour. We'll put Holt in the book building and Mertz in that Dal-Tex building. They'll have clean shots from above at a slow target, but it'll be movin' up in their sights—not ideal." He turned back to Nicoletti. "But you I want behind the fence on that little hill. "You'll have 'im in your crosshairs comin' straight at you. Perfect. You can't miss."

Nicoletti smiled. "I won't."

CHAPTER 85

FORT WORTH
THURSDAY NOVEMBER 21

HARRINGTON WAS RIGHT. The four-bedroom, four-bath A-frame was "charming." A large loft was suspended under a soaring twenty-five-foot peaked roof, and a floor to ceiling picture widow allowed a sweeping view of the lake. And *Regina* was indeed, "truly a joy." The classic forty-two-foot varnished mahogany Chris-Craft looked like it had just motored out of the boatyard where it'd been built in 1939. A sprawling teak patio behind the house led to a short pier where it was moored.

Marissa and I were finishing a Texas lunch of steak and chili on the patio when Aldo drove up with Lorenzo and Elvira. We were taking them fishing a second time because we'd been skunked the day before and I'd promised to make up for it with a bonanza.

They jumped out of the car, dashed off to the dock, and Aldo chuckled.

Marissa said, "I'll get them settled on the boat. You bring the cooler."

Aldo watched her go and said, "She's beautiful *and* delightful. You're a lucky guy."

"Thanks. I know it."

He laughed. "Even Pat and her parents like her. You two serious?"

"Yeah, we are."

"And she knows what you do?"

"She does."

"It's hard to think of you settling down."

I shook my head. "Tell me about it."

Later that afternoon, I drove an exuberant Lorenzo and Elvira back to the Harringtons with a cooler containing two small-mouth bass, one large-mouth bass, three white crappies, and one catfish. It had been a helluva day for them, but I knew Pat would scream if they trounced through the entryway with fish in a sweating cooler. So I drove around back to the kitchen entrance and deposited them and the fish into the cook's appreciative hands.

That evening Marissa and I went on a twilight cruise and anchored the boat on the eastern shore of a small island. I made Marissa a Mojito, myself a Jack-rocks and we settled into chairs on the afterdeck to watch the sunset.

Marissa sipped her drink and sighed happily.

I said, "Penny."

"Children."

"What about them."

"I realize I want them."

I smiled. "Fine. No problem."

"I'm glad… But have you thought about raising them?"

I considered a second and shrugged. "Like everyone else."

"Everyone else doesn't have a 'family' like yours."

I turned toward her. "Roselli?"

"Among others."

"They're my business associates."

"Very violent associates, Dante."

"Violence concerns you? This from a woman who tried to assassinate Castro and was at the Bay of Pigs?"

"I'm not afraid for me."

"I can protect them."

"How? Where? Los Angeles, Las Vegas? And what would you be

doing?"

"I'm not in a business you walk away from."

"You've made my point."

I took a long pull on my drink and downplayed the issue. "Roselli and I've been primarily involved with unions and casinos."

She was incredulous. "He's trying to assassinate the president!"

"And I'm trying to stop him."

"Which could get you killed. Again you've made my point."

I took a deep breath, let out a long sigh, and lit a Marlboro. "Look. Tomorrow's their last shot at Kennedy before December first and I'm sure it'll fail. We'll see what happens with the coup—but whether it succeeds or fails, Roselli and the Bosses will be done with Cuba and concentrating on Vegas. It's exploding. New and bigger hotels will be built. Their casinos will have to be managed. I'll tell Roselli I want to handle that end for the family. I'll say we're getting married and that's where we want to settle. The violent days are over out there, Marissa. The town's going corporate. There's even a rumor that Howard Hughes is interested in buying properties on The Strip. We can make it work."

She suddenly sounded a bit hopeful. "Do you think your 'family' will agree?"

"Why not?" I answered exuberantly, "Somebody has to handle things in Vegas, and I know as much or more about that town than anyone other than Roselli. It'll be win-win for everyone."

She nestled her head against my neck and whispered, "I love you, Dante Amato."

CHAPTER 86

DALLAS
FRIDAY NOVEMBER 22, 1963

THE PRESIDENT AND JACKIE rose early for a Chamber of Commerce break-fast and speech at the Texas Hotel in Fort Worth. The evening before they had retired to Suite 850 made regal by the Monet, Picasso, and Van Gogh on honorary loan from local museums and patrons of the arts. Jack used the large master, but inexplicably, Jackie decided to sleep in a small separate bedroom.

After the Chamber of Commerce speech, the president and his entourage boarded Air Force One at Carswell. The Fort Worth morning had been misty but was clearing when the plane took off for the thirteen-minute flight to Dallas. When they landed at Love Field at 11:40 a.m., the motorcade was already lined up.

The lead car was an unmarked white Ford driven by Dallas Police Chief Jesse Curry—with Secret Service Agent Winston Lawson, Sherriff Bill Decker, and Agent Forest Sorrels as passengers. The second car was the president's open limousine—a modified Lincoln Continental driven by Agent Bill Greer. It carried Agent Roy Kellerman, Texas Governor John Connally, his wife Nellie, President Kennedy, and Jackie.

As soon as everyone had settled, they began making their way through an estimated 200,000 Dallas residents waiting to greet the president as he passed through downtown on the way to a sold-out luncheon for 2,600 more at the Dallas Trade Mart. The President was hatless, handsome, tanned, and smiling as he waved to the adoring throngs. They were young and old, white, brown and black, children waving flags and toddlers held aloft by parents. Jackie, stunning in her strawberry pink suit and matching pillbox hat, joined him in acknowledging the cheering crowds. The outpouring of emotion swelled as the limousine passed, and Agent Bill Greer heard Jackie remark, "There's no question of how Dallas feels about you."

Roselli had gotten up at nine o'clock, had breakfast with Nicoletti, and sent him to a pancake house to meet Jack Ruby. The place reeked of stale smoke and griddle grease, and Nicoletti found Ruby in a booth, He was eating a super-stack swimming in maple syrup, and he looked up as Nicoletti slid in opposite him.

His mouth full and chewing, Ruby asked, "You want anything?"

Nicoletti shook his head. "I ate. You bring it?"

Ruby nodded and reached into his jacket pocket. He pulled out an envelope and handed it over. Nicoletti removed a forged Secret Service I.D. with his photo. Roselli had ordered it as a precaution in case Nicoletti was questioned when getting into position behind the fence on the hill.

Nicoletti pointed at the stack of pancakes and said, "When you finish with that mess, go to the Adolphus and hook up with Roselli. I gotta grab Holt and Mertz."

Nicoletti drove to the Cabana Motel where the other two shooters had spent last night after taking delivery of three high-power riles. He knocked on Room 15 and was let in by Mertz.

The rifles, fitted with scopes, were on the bed, and Nicoletti asked, "They been sighted-in?"

Holt nodded. "Yesterday, as soon as we got 'em. They're good to go."

CHAPTER 87

As the president's motorcade began in Dallas, Marissa and I sat down on the A-frame's patio for a seafood brunch. We'd slept late, taken a long swim, and were famished. In what was a surprising departure from the past, I caught a whiff of perfume. She'd never worn perfume before and I wondered if her sudden nod to femininity was a glimpse at a more family-oriented future.

"Nice perfume," I commented.

"Thank you. It was my mother's favorite. I haven't worn it since she disappeared."

I'd inadvertently hit a sore subject. "I'm sorry."

She smiled. "No need. I'm done pretending she isn't gone. I want her aura around me. Her things, her smells, this perfume and," she lifted the coffee pot, "the smell of fresh coffee in the morning. My mother loved it... For you?"

"Please,"

As she reached for the carafe, my eye caught the *Dallas Times Herald* lying next to it. It was the previous evening's newspaper, and the front page had a map of Kennedy's motorcade. It showed a jog off Main Street at Houston with another turn at Elm.

I blurted out, "My God..."

"What's wrong?"

"This map… The motorcade route."

"The president's?"

I nodded rapidly and remembered Roselli wanting to check out the Texas Schoolbook Depository to see if a sniper nest could be set up in the building. Oswald was already there—in place. He'd vetoed the idea because of the broadside shot across the plaza from the Depository to Main Street where the cars wouldn't be slowing down. But the depicted route would have the cars turning off Main onto Houston and then slowing for a 120-degree turn onto Elm directly in front of the Depository! I remembered Nicoletti saying he could "get a shot of him comin' right at me" from atop the triple underpass. Also vetoed because it was too exposed. But there was a grassy knoll to the right of the underpass. I remembered seeing a fence on top of it.

"Good God! It's perfect!"

Marissa recoiled. "What?"

I leapt up and grabbed her hand. "We've got to get to Aldo!"

I pulled her after me and we dashed for the Chevy. She gasped, lost a thong in the driveway and yelled, "Dante, wait!"

I paused a second and swept it up before hurling open the passenger door, and yelling, "Get in!"

I didn't wait for her to climb aboard. I ran around the front of the car, threw myself into the driver's seat and started the engine. Marissa was staring at me but still too stunned to say anything.

Tires spinning, I screeched away from the A-frame and headed for the Dallas-Fort Worth Turnpike.

Marissa cried out, "Where are we going?"

"To find Aldo. The Secret Service has the wrong place staked out. They're going to hit Kennedy in Dealey Plaza."

"We should call the police!"

"Too late for an anonymous call! But Aldo knows the Secret Service agents. He'll tell them and they'll listen."

She suddenly understood. "We're going to the Old Red Courthouse."

I nodded. "Harrington said he was taking Aldo and the family there to watch the motorcade from his office. Just pray we're not too late."

CHAPTER 88

ROSELLI AND HIS CREW met for a final briefing in his Adolphus suite. When it ended, Nicoletti, Holt, and Mertz went to their motel, disassembled the three rifles, and put them in large shopping bags.

Ferrie had returned to New Orleans, but Bannister remained and was assigned to drop off Nicoletti behind the fence on the knoll bordering Dealey Plaza.

Roselli was to confirm Oswald was in place, return to pick up Holt and Mertz, then bring them to the sniper nests in the Schoolbook Depository and Dal-Tex buildings.

Ruby would go to the *Dallas Morning News* offices—four blocks from Dealey Plaza, to establish his presence. He would then sneak out and get into position to back up the cop assigned to kill Oswald making his escape.

Roselli's final position would be on Main Street across the plaza from the Schoolbook Depository where he could observe all three nests.

In Washington, as the motorcade approached downtown Dallas, Bobby was having a celebratory lunch at his Hickory Hill estate. The guest of honor was Robert Morgenthau, U.S. Attorney from New York who'd handled the prosecutions resulting from the arrest of Joe Valachi. Televised hearings of the events had electrified the nation by dragging Mob secrets out of the shadows and into American living rooms. Bobby raised a champagne glass to toast his outstanding work, and Morgenthau returned the toast, wishing him many happy returns. Two days earlier Bobby had celebrated his thirty-eighth birthday.

In Havana, Fidel Castro was having lunch at his Varadero Beach residence with Jean Daniel, who'd arrived with another round of peace feelers from Kennedy. A flurry of calls on the 11th, 18th, and 19th, had made Castro fairly certain Kennedy was seeking an accommodation with Cuba.

In Moscow, Khrushchev worked late in the Kremlin. He had grown to respect Kennedy, and was convinced he wanted détente. He looked forward to their second summit meeting, which would be quite different from their first in Vienna. This time he would join with Kennedy to seek a course away from nuclear brinksmanship and toward a new world harmony. His only concerns were militaristic forces in Washington he knew were determined to stop their efforts.

Ruby entered the offices of the *Dallas Morning News* as the motorcade entered downtown Dallas. He established his presence and slipped out.

Roselli pulled up behind the Dal-Tex building with Holt and Mertz where they got out and walked around the corner to take up their positions.

Bannister drove behind the fence on the Dealey Plaza knoll with Nicoletti. He scanned the area and observed a few bums and locals in the adjacent railroad yard. None of them was paying any attention, and he said, "Clear."

Nicoletti began re-assembling his rifle.

In Chicago, Sam Giancana was at home when the motorcade turned from Harwood onto Main Street. He'd just finished reading a copy of *The Green Felt Jungle*. Enraged, he cursed and threw it across the room. It'd been released earlier that week and exposed Roselli's lead role in the

Chicago Mob's skimming of their Vegas casinos. Since everyone in law enforcement knew who Roselli's boss was, Momo dreaded the new barrage of indictments he knew were headed his way.

In Tampa, Santo Trafficante was apprehensive as he put down his office phone. An informant had just told him a carload of heroin seized at the Texas-Mexico border had been linked to him. A year earlier, twenty-two pounds of seized heroin had also been connected to him. The case was still pending, but he knew the pressure was about to get a lot worse.

In New Orleans, Carlos Marcello was relaxed, even though he was sitting in a Federal courtroom awaiting a verdict that could lead to permanent deportation. He knew a key juror had been bribed, and he was looking forward to a victory celebration that evening.

In Miami, Jimmy Hoffa feared his seven-year dominance of the Teamsters would soon come to an end. He ruled a union with 1.4 million members, two hundred and fifty-nine million dollars in pension funds, and a billion in assets. But his jury tampering trial was due to begin in Chattanooga in two months, and an informant told him that a former union official had made a deal and was going to testify against him. Bobby's "Get Hoffa" squad had all the key evidence plus an informer. He knew he's go to jail.

Roselli had had to loop around several streets before finding a parking place two blocks from Dealey Plaza. Walking back to Main Street, Roselli saw throngs of people flanking Houston and Elm. He took up a position where he could see the fence on the grassy knoll to his left and the sniper nest windows in the Depository and Dal-Tex buildings dead ahead. He then lit a cigarette and waited.

CHAPTER 89

I TURNED OFF THE Dallas-Fort Worth Turnpike at South Lamar and sped toward Main Street with my fist on the horn. Traffic was light, and I tore by everything on the road. Marissa found a Dallas map in the glove compartment and called out directions.

"When we get to Commerce, turn left," she shouted over the blaring horn, "we can parallel Main Street and park behind the courthouse."

A motorcycle shot out of a side street on my left and I swerved hard to pass behind it. The move threw Marissa against the door and she cried out.

I yelled, "You okay?"

"Fine," she gasped.

I screeched around the corner onto Commerce and yelled, "How far?"

"Two blocks."

I checked my watch—12:25.

Marissa pointed. "There!"

I saw the back of The Old Red Courthouse and scanned ahead for a parking place. There were none. I barreled into what was little more than an alley called South Record Street and we abandoned the car, I grabbed Marissa's hand and sprinted toward Main and the front of The Old Red Courthouse.

CHAPTER 90

AS THE PRESIDENT'S MOTORCADE turned into Dealey Plaza, Roselli heard a roar from the crowd. From a window at the corner of the sixth floor of the Schoolbook Depository, he saw Holt's muzzle. A few seconds later, and three windows to the left, he saw Oswald's.

He cut his eyes to the Dal-Tex building, saw Mertz's rifle appear in a window on the fifth floor, then looked at the fence on the knoll. Two men were standing there, but no rifle was in sight. *Good,* he thought. Nicoletti was waiting until the last moment.

Seconds later, another roar went up from the Elm Street spectators as the president's limousine headed for the 120-degree turn in front of the Schoolbook Depository. He again glanced at the fence on the knoll and his heart beat faster. Nicoletti's rifle had appeared.

Marissa and I were breathing hard as we fought our way through tightly-packed, five-deep crowds blocking the front of the Courthouse. Marissa lost her thong a second time, but the congestion made it impossible to bend down and pick it up.

She shouted, "Keep going!" and we pushed on.

I didn't know exactly where the motorcade was and prayed there was still time to reach Harrington's office, have Aldo contact the Secret Service, and stop the president's limousine before it hit Dealey Plaza. Spectators who had been in high spirits angrily swore at us as we frantically elbowed our way through, but we ignored them.

We finally made it to the courthouse entrance. I reached for the door and yanked down the brass bar.

Shots rang out and we froze.

The crowd's exuberance hushed.

The momentary lull was followed by horrified screams.

And finally the wail of sirens.

I released the brass bar.

We were too late.

AFTERWORD

THE POLITICAL LEADERS

BOBBY KENNEDY heard the news while still at lunch with Robert Morgenthau. It came via phone call from his archenemy, J. Edgar Hoover. In their *Time* piece, David Talbot and Vincent Bugliosi wrote, "For the rest of the day and night he wrestled with his howling grief using whatever power was left him to figure out what really happened in Dallas. He talked to people who had been in the presidential motorcade and conferred with a succession of government officials—at one point confronting CIA Director John McCone. Bobby asked him point-blank whether the Agency had killed his brother. McCone denied it."

From that moment on Bobby was obsessed with finding out who was responsible for this brother's assassination and became the nation's first conspiracy theorist. The Mob's prediction regarding Johnson's behavior proved correct. In September 1964, Bobby was forced to resign as Attorney General. Two months later however, he was elected senator from New York, and in 1968 he ran for president. Regarding Hoover's call he later said, "I think he told me with pleasure." On July 5, 1968, after winning the California primary during his race for the presidency, he was assassinated while moving through the kitchen of Los Angeles's Ambassador Hotel.

FIDEL CASTRO was still discussing Kennedy's offer of "accommodation" with Jean Daniel when a phone call informed him that Kennedy had been shot and wounded. Obviously disturbed, he said, "This is bad news." He then shook his head and he muttered the statement two more times. Shortly thereafter, at two o'clock, the president was pronounced dead, and he said, "Everything is changed... Everything is going to change." Later that day, he released the following dispatch. "In spite of the antagonism existing between the Government of the United States and the Cuban Revolution, we have received the news of the tragic death of President Kennedy with deep sorrow. All civilized men grieve about such events as this. Our delegation to the Organization of the United Nations wishes to state that this is the feeling of the people and of the Government of Cuba." In 2008, he turned over the reins of government to his brother Raúl after 49 years in power. Although ailing at 82, he'd survived over three dozen known assassination attempts.

NIKITA KHRUSHCHEV heard the news, and sobbed. He was in the Kremlin, and for days he was unable to perform his duties. He believed Kennedy, despite his youth, was a real statesman. He also believed that, if Kennedy had lived, they could have brought peace to the world.

THE CIA AND THE PRINCIPAL EXILES

MANUEL ARTIME was in a staff meting at his Nicaraguan base when a sergeant rushed into the room and told him Kennedy had been shot. Shocked and saddened, he knew that if the president died, so would Almeida's coup. He immediately broke up the meeting and sat by the radio awaiting further word. An hour and a half later, his worst fears were confirmed. In early 1964, President Johnson cancelled the U.S. support for his, or any other, invasion of Cuba. Artime participated in another failed assassination attempt against Castro in 1965, and in the 1970s organized the Miami Watergate Defense Relief Fund for the burglars, a number of whom were American or Cuban veterans of the Bay of Pigs— one of them being E. Howard Hunt. On November 18, 1977, prior to a scheduled appearance before the House Select Committee on Assassinations, Artime suddenly died of cancer under circumstances considered very unusual.

ROLANDO MASFERRER was in Miami when he received the news and had mixed emotions. He hated Kennedy's past betrayals but was aware of his support for Almeida's planned coup. He'd met the President in 1961, but Kennedy disliked Masferrer's radical and fanatical personality, and the two never established a rapport. Throughout the 1960s Masferrer plotted and accumulated weapons to invade Haiti. He wanted a base free of U.S. law to attack Cuba, but his attempts to land were defeated. Because of his activities both before and after Cuban revolution, pro, as well as anti-Castro Cubans widely regarded him as a terrorist. Masferrer was killed by a car bomb in 1975.

DAVID MORALES considered the assassination a job well done and remained in the CIA for many years. He was reputed to be involved in the capture of Che Guevara in 1965 and in 1966 was ordered to take charge of a black operations base at Paske in Laos, where he focused on political paramilitary action. In 1969 he was moved to Vietnam and in 1970 to Chile to undermine left wing forces in the country. He told friends that he had personally eliminated several political figures and was involved in helping Augusto Pinochet overthrow Salvador Allende in September 1973. But Morales was aware that he knew too much and began to worry about his own vulnerability while being questioned by the House Select Committee on Assassinations. He had to make several trips to Washington, and after his last, in May 1978, he became mysteriously ill and was put on life support. The next morning, a friend went to visit him in the hospital and found that no one was allowed into his room. It was being guarded by sheriff's deputies. Later that day, on May 8, the decision was taken to remove life support. Inexplicably, Morales's wife requested that there should be no autopsy.

ROLANDO CUBELA was in Paris with Desmond Fitzgerald, and he was in shock. Fitzgerald had just told him that Bobby Kennedy had approved the latest plan to assassinate Castro—and it was his brother who'd been assassinated. Fitzgerald was lying. Bobby knew nothing about the latest attempt on Castro. It was CIA plot. A year later, in Madrid on December 27, 1964, he met Artime and asked for a Belgian FAL rifle with a silencer to kill Castro. A CIA memo suggests that he received it in February 1965. In 1966, the Cuban security police arrested Cubela after uncovering evidence proving Cubela's attempts to assassinate Castro. Cubela was tried and sentenced to death, but the sentence was never carried out. Incredibly, it was reported that Castro not only sent books to Cubela while he was in prison but eventually allowed him to leave Cuba. Rolando Cubela remains one of the very few players to survive the era.

WILLIAM KING HARVEY was a hard drinker and probably celebrated the president's assassination by getting drunk. He'd hated the Kennedys with a passion since being removed as Commander of Operation ZR/RIFLE in 1962, and knew the Kennedys were responsible for his demotion. Furious over his actions during the Cuban Missile Crisis, the brothers had him exiled to Rome where he became Chief of Station. He remained in contact with Johnny Roselli after his exile and continued his hard drinking ways. By 1975, when he appeared before the Senate Committee on Intelligence to testify about ZR/RIFLE, he was dying of alcoholism.

THE MOB

SAM GIANCANA was elated. He was in his luxurious Chicago home and told his brother: "On November 22, 1963, the U. S. had a coup; it's that simple. The government of this country was overthrown by a handful of guys who did their jobs damned well." But Giancana's joy was soon marred and by troubles that extended far beyond the FBI's lockstepping. He had aroused the ire of Tony "The Big Tuna" Accardo, who was still in overall charge of the Chicago Mob. Not only was he attracting far too much federal scrutiny—his private life with Pyllis McGuire had gotten too high profile for Mob tastes. He was forced into exile, and fled to Cuernavaca, Mexico. But after seven quiet years he was suddenly arrested by Mexican authorities, and deported. Upon arriving in the United States. he was ordered to appear before the Senate Select Committee on Intelligence. Led by Senator Frank Church, it was investigating CIA and Mafia collusion in plots to assassinate John F. Kennedy, Robert F. Kennedy, and Martin Luther King, Jr. He never appeared. Two days before his scheduled appearance, on June 19, 1975—while frying Italian sausage in the handsomely finished basement of his home—Giancana was shot in the back of the head. After falling he was shot six more times in a circle around his mouth.

SANTO TRAFFICANTE, in anticipation of Kennedy's successful assassination, had made dinner plans with his lawyer, Frank Ragano, and Ragano's girlfriend. He was taking them to Tampa's International Inn where Kennedy had made a speech just four days earlier. It was a delicious irony that delighted him. Because of the assassination, the normally crowded restaurant was almost empty that Friday night and Trafficante greeted Ragano saying, "Isn't that something? They killed the son of a bitch. The son of a bitch is dead." For most of the next two decades, Trafficante was under government surveillance and was frequently called to testify before investigatory panels. In 1986, racketeering and conspiracy were charges brought against him, and although the case ended in a mistrial, the government quickly indicted him again for taking kickbacks from the International Laborers' Union. On his deathbed, according to Ragano, Trafficante confessed that he and Marcello plotted the assassination of Kennedy. He died March 17, 1987, three hours after undergoing a triple-bypass.

CARLOS MARCELLO had just heard the judge deliver his charge to the jury in the New Orleans Federal courtroom. He stifled a smile, knowing what the verdict would be. Suddenly a bailiff handed the judge a note. Very quietly, the judge announced to the room that the president had been shot and might not survive. Calling an hour's recess, he dismissed the jury. Court resumed at 3:00, and fifteen minutes later the jury returned the verdict. Not guilty. Marcello left the celebration early that evening and went to his office as if as there was something bothering him that had to be taken care of. There most certainly was. Oswald had not been killed as planned. He was in and out of jail between 1971 and 1989 when he suffered a series of strokes that left him severely disabled, and by the end of March, he was showing signs of Alzheimer's. In October, after having served six years and six months of his sentence, he was released and returned to his family's care in Metairie. He died on March 3, 1993.

JIMMY HOFFA heard the news in his Miami Beach hotel suite and called Frank Ragano. Ragano was his, as well as Trafficante's, lawyer. "Have you heard the good news? They killed the son of a bitch! This means Bobby is out. Lyndon will definitely ax him!" Less than four months later, on March 4, 1964, a Chattanooga Federal jury convicted him of conspiracy, jury tampering, mail and wire fraud. After exhausting his appeals, he spent nearly five years behind bars. President Richard Nixon granted Hoffa clemency in 1971, but things had changed significantly in the years he was gone. The Mob, who had worked hand in hand with him for years, found Hoffa's handpicked successor, Frank Fitzsimmons, more pliable, and they loved that. Believing he was on his way to discuss another run for the Teamsters' presidency, Hoffa met with Detroit mobster Jack "Tony Jack" Giacalone and New Jersey labor leader Anthony "Tony Pro" Provenzano—a made member of the Genovese crime family. The meeting was scheduled to take place July 30, 1975, the day Hoffa disappeared and was never seen again.

CHARLES "THE TYPEWRITER" NICOLETTI was allegedly involved in as many as twenty mob hits during his career as a hitman. But on March 29, 1977, it was his turn. He received three .38 slugs to the back of his head. Nicoletti was waiting for someone in his Oldsmobile in a Northlake, Illinois, restaurant parking lot. The engine was never turned off, and consequently it overheated and the car burned. Many thought that The Outfit's day-to-day boss, Joseph "Joey Doves" Aiuppa, ordered the hit because he believed Nicoletti had become an informant. At the time of his death, Nicoletti was due to appear before the House Select Committee on Assassinations.

CHAUNCEY "CHARLIE" HOLT worked for the CIA for nearly twenty-five years in some of their most important "black ops" in Guatemala, the Dominican Republic, Cuba, Brazil, Laos, and Chile. His skills as a pilot, munitions expert, and accounting whiz made him invaluable to both the Mob and the CIA. During his tenure running front companies for The Agency, Holt worked closely with many legendary CIA "spooks" and fellow "cowboys" (contract agents who carried out field operations away from CIA headquarters). Holt died of cancer on June 28, 1997, at the age of 75, eight days after completing a documentary about his life, *Spooks, Hoods and the Hidden Elite*. In it, he confesses to his involvement in the assassination of John Fitzgerald Kennedy.

JOHNNY ROSELLI had left Dealey Plaza the minute he saw Nicoletti make the shot that took out the back of Kennedy's head. He calmly walked back to his car and drove to Houston where he boarded a plane for New Orleans, anticipating a celebration with Marcello. But the cause for celebration was short lived. Giancana's murder caused Roselli's power base to disappear and forced him into early retirement. He permanently left both Los Angeles and Vegas and settled in Miami. On June 24, 1975, and again on September 22, Roselli was called to testify before the Senate Select Committee on Intelligence regarding CIA plans to kill Castro and Operation Mongoose. Then, in April 1976, Roselli was again called before the committee. But this time it wasn't about Castro and Mongoose. They wanted his testimony about a conspiracy to kill President John F. Kennedy. Trafficante and Marcello were not happy that he appeared and was answering questions. They then became alarmed when the committee again recalled him in July. On August 9, Roselli's decomposing body was found in a 55-gallon steel drum floating in Dumfounding Bay near Miami. He'd been strangled, shot, and his legs had been sawn off.

THE OTHERS who played part in the events: Guy Bannister, David Ferrie, E. Howard Hunt, Charles Nicoletti, Charles Holt, Juan Orta, José Miró Cardona, Allen Dulles, Richard Bissell, James Angleton, McGeorge Bundy, Dean Rusk, Chester Bowles, Arthur Schlesinger, Maxwell Taylor, and Edward Lansdale, are all dead.

As of this writing, five men remain alive.

Rolando Cubela, who lives in Spain.

Jim O'Connell, whereabouts unknown.

Michel Victor Mertz, who was last heard of as director of a French casino.

Robert Maheu, who is reportedly having a film made of his life.

Commander Juan Almeida, second in power to Premier Raúl Castro, was recently seen sitting next to him at an official function.

IN THE FORTY-SEVEN YEARS since the assassination of John F. Kennedy, there has been a flood of investigations into who perpetrated the crime and how it was accomplished. Among them were: the Warren Commission, the House Select Committee on Assassinations, the Senate Select Committee on Intelligence, the Rockefeller Commission, the Ramsey Clark Panel, ABC News, and countless other non-official inquiries, which have resulted in a deluge of books on the subject. New Orleans District Attorney Jim Garrison's investigation alone resulted in a trial, a book, and a controversial film.

Theories implicate everyone from Fidel Castro to Lyndon Johnson, and include the anti-Castro Cuban's, the FBI, the CIA, the Mafia, and the Eastern Bloc—or some combination of the above. The only thing they all agree on is that they don't agree about anything.

While there is no question that controversy still surrounds the assassination of President John F. Kennedy, there is now little doubt that there was a conspiracy, and that it was the result of the president, and his brother's obsession with bringing down Castro, Hoffa, and the Mob.

SOURCES

The invaluable resources without which this novel could not have been written are: *The Warren Commission Report*, Frank Church's Senate Select Committee on Intelligence, the House Select Committee on Assassinations, Wikipedia, *Spartacus Educational* by John Simkin, *Education Forum* by Wim Dankbaar, *Cuba and the United States: A Chronological History* by Jane Franklin, *The Road To Dallas* by David Kaiser, *Brothers* by David Talbot, *The Man who Knew Too Much* and *On The Trail of Thee JFK Assassins* by Dick Russell, *Timeline of the Life of Lee Harvey Oswald* by W. Tracy Parnell, *Let Justice Be Done* by Bill Davy, *The JFK Assassination Chronology* by Ira David Wood III, *On the Trail Of The Assassins* by Jim Garrison, *Sightings* by Timothy S. Cooper, *JFK Murder "Confession" Video* by Edward Bell, as well as newspaper stories by Nicholas Pileggi, David Edwards, Don Fulsom, Bill Warner, and Sam McClung, but with special thanks to *Legacy of Secrecy* and *Ultimate Sacrifice* by Lamar Waldron and Thom Hartman.

ACKNOWLEDGMENTS

MY HEARTFELT THANKS go to four unique gentlemen whose efforts were irreplaceable in bringing this novel to fruition: Ed Victor, my legendary literary agent, Fred Altman, my intrepid business manager, Peter Mayer, renowned President and Publisher of The Overlook Press, and Herb Simon, dear friend, and brilliant co-founder of Simon Property Group…

As well as…

Two incredibly talented ladies whose insight, suggestions, and encouragement were indispensible: Lindsey Sagnette, my editor, and Tracy Carns, Publisher of Derby Publishing…

And finally…

My loving and supportive wife, Pamela Hensley Vincent, without whom everything else would be meaningless.

FIC
Vincent

Vincent, E. Duke.

The Camelot
   conspiracy.

WITHDRAWN

$24.95

DATE			